T0162821

# THEY WERE
# EXTRAORDINARY

# THEY WERE
# EXTRAORDINARY

A NOVEL BY

# RICHARD F. MANGES

iUniverse, Inc.
Bloomington

# THEY WERE EXTRAORDINARY

iUniverse books may be ordered through booksellers or by contacting:

iUniverse
1663 Liberty Drive
Bloomington, IN 47403
www.iuniverse.com
1-800-Authors (1-800-288-4677)

ISBN: 978-1-4759-1246-3 (sc)
ISBN: 978-1-4759-1248-7 (hc)
ISBN: 978-1-4759-1247-0 (ebk)

Printed in the United States of America

iUniverse rev. date: 05/24/2012

I sincerely thank my lovely wife Barbara, my wonderful daughter Vanessa, her husband Gene, and my astute grandson Dylan for their encouragement, patience and advice to me as I endeavored to create this novel. I gained strength and confidence from your support and assistance. My lovely granddaughter Genevieve helped me keep my humor over the months of labor.

Instantaneously they were masked and brandishing pistols. The burly man shouted, "All of you down on the floor, face first." One took rope from inside his coat and tied them together. Keith held onto Barbara for dear life with his mouth and eyes wide open. She hugged him tightly, shuddering herself and aghast as to what was happening.

*Just hold onto me honey. All they want is money*, to herself she thought and prayed that to be the case. They went to their knees and lay prone on the hard wood floor. She continued to hold Keith tightly with her right arm, holding her purse with the left, feverishly trying to squeeze it under her body. The other two customers were near them. The woman was crying, "Please don't hurt me. You can take all my money but please don't hurt me."

Keith was sobbing, appropriate for a nine year old, at the horror of it all. Barbara was trying to shield him but was only partially successful.

There was a pounding at the bank door. Barbara was praying that someone outside noticed that the bank door was locked and the shade drawn. The leader heard the pounding and became very agitated. "Hurry up, we haven't got all day!" he shouted as the other two were in the safe, stuffing cash in whatever they could find.

"O.K. boss we can't find anything to put more in," one robber answered.

"We're outta here then," came the response. "O.K., lady. You and the kid are going with us for insurance. We'll keep you for a while just in case." The leader and another thug grabbed Barbara and Keith, blindfolding them and half pulling and half dragging them out the back door where they had parked in advance once they got the all clear from their driver who had the getaway car ready to go. She and Keith were both sobbing uncontrollably as they were shoved face down on the rear floor. One of the thieves sat in the back and held them down with his feet.

It seemed forever to Barbara as she kept praying for her and Keith's safety, trying to comfort him in her grief. She wasn't sure he could even hear her with the engine racing and the leader shouting instructions;

"Don't attract attention by speeding. They probably don't have any idea yet and they don't recognize the car."

It seemed like forever as the getaway car kept pulling them further from home. She just could not believe that this would ever happen, fearful of what would become of them. She silently asked God to intervene somehow. Her heart was beating so fast she thought it would break. Her thoughts then focused on her young son. He was just nine. She tried to dispel thoughts of them dying, but realized this terrible calamity could affect him for a lifetime. She was certain it would stay with her. Keith kept sobbing, not fully understanding all that happened to him.

Richard arrived home, like normal, around 6, to an empty house with no notes or phone messages. He thought, *this is strange and unusual. Barbara has always left some message if she expected to be out when I arrived from work.* He checked with the neighbors, one of whom told him she noticed the car leaving around noon. He also called some friends to see if they had heard from her. When he knew that was a dead end, he was really beside himself and dialed the police, giving his wife and son's descriptions and the description of her car.

He received a call back around an hour later. "Mr. Fredericks, this is Officer Calloway. We found your wife's car. It's in the parking lot at the town bank. The bank was robbed today. We are still investigating the robbery. One of our detectives interviewed the employees and another bank customer who were tied up. They told him that the thieves took a younger woman and her son with them when they fled late this morning."

Richard felt the tears flow as his mind raced, thinking what might have happened to them.

## Chapter 3

# GENEVIEVE CARTER AT 12

"Hurry up, Genevieve. I have to get you to school early today. The bus will be leaving the school at 7:30," Vanessa shouted to her precocious almost 12 year old.

"O.K." Genevieve answered. Vanessa and her dad, Gene, enrolled her at the University School. She was truly blossoming since the transition. Vanessa looked in amazement at her dynamo as she shot past her swinging her book bag in one hand and munching on a bagel with cream cheese, which she called a cheese doughnut, in the other.

"Did you bring the camera, Mom?" asked Genevieve as they pulled out of the driveway.

"Yes honey. I have it right here. I'll pass it back. Please be careful with it and take lots of nice pictures in New York. I wish I could be with you today but I have a doctor appointment I need to keep."

They saw the busses parked next to the school as they arrived. Vanessa maneuvered the van to get in line and walked Genevieve to her classroom, where her teacher would explain the trip. Ann Rickert, Genevieve's teacher, motioned to Vanessa to speak to her. "Genevieve is making great progress. Even more than the last time we spoke," she advised her.

"She really loves it here. She has advanced even more than we could have hoped for," Vanessa responded.

"The staff is planning a play for the school. We are enlisting the help of the University's Drama Department and several of the drama students are interested in tutoring and working with the kids," Mrs. Rickert continued. "Many of the staff think, as I do, that Genevieve would be a natural for a lead role." She stopped and waited for Vanessa, who was momentarily speechless, to respond.

"Wow," Vanessa murmured, holding her hand to her cheek. "That's quite a compliment, but I don't have the time."

Mrs. Rickert smiled. "I'll see to it that you won't be more involved than you want. I promise that she will receive all the tutoring and effort needed from us. All you need to do is continue to encourage her and make sure she rehearses and gets to rehearsals." Vanessa breathed deeply. Mrs. Rickert continued, "Let's just introduce the idea of the play in class and see who is interested in actively participating. We cannot give many of the students speaking parts but we will have prominent roles for some and have the rest be part of the greater public. By adding music, all of the children will provide a contribution and it will be a splendid complement to the project. By the way, Mr. Brandon, our music teacher, tells me that Genevieve has a lovely voice and she carries a tune naturally."

Genevieve's mom nodded. "We see that in church. Our director also told us she was impressed with her voice. We have thought about singing lessons but need to find dollars in the budget."

"I hope you do, because she may be one in a thousand or maybe ten thousand and the earlier she gets training the better it will be," the teacher emphatically suggested.

"I hear you loud and clear," Mom agreed.

"O.K. that's great that Genevieve will be in our production. We'll be introducing the plan to the students. We'll be sending home scripts as part of their homework. It will be a few weeks until we decide on who plays what role, so it's important that they practice and memorize at home as well as in school.

We'll also use part of the reading period maybe twice a week for additional practice and rehearsal as it gets closer to show time. The faculty is really excited about it."

"Can I dare ask if you have a play in mind?" Vanessa asked pensively.

"*My Fair Lady*," smiled the teacher.

"Wow, that's ambitious. What about the costumes?" asked Vanessa.

"We'll keep it simple. Both girls and boys can, for the most part, wear their own clothes, except in a couple of scenes we'll have special dresses sewn. The masses and chorus can wear their own Sunday best, if you will. The play itself is the most important thing. Teaching the kids to study their parts and acting them out will teach organization and concentration. Maybe we can enlist the help of some sewing moms for the elaborate stuff."

Vanessa thought a moment or two, and said, "I can help with that if she has a costumed role."

Mrs. Rickert nodded, "I'm SURE she will." Vanessa noticed the emphasis on the word "sure" and it pleased her.

"All right, boys and girls. Let's get ready to board the busses," announced another teacher. "Be sure to take your notebooks because we will talk about New York on the bus. It's a fun trip and it's also a trip where you can learn a whole lot." The students dutifully followed suit. Genevieve found her mom and gave her a big hug and kiss and disappeared onto the bus with her class.

Vanessa drove home with a great feeling and a good deal of satisfaction with the school and Genevieve's future. What a marvelous improvement in Genevieve's learning and overall attitude and personality since she left the public school system. Vanessa was really thrilled at the teacher's praise of Genevieve and her assessment of her personality and abilities. Imagine if, at age 12, she could assume a lead role in a rendition of *My Fair Lady*. Reality set in also. She would need to keep Genevieve's feet on the ground and make certain she remained a 12 year old. But oh, the possibilities and the confidence her child would achieve.

Genevieve remained extremely attentive to the performance, absorbing the message and particularly the performance of the female lead. Her mind pictured herself, as an adult, on the Broadway stage. During the intermission, she approached Mrs. Rickert.

"Mrs. Rickert, I was wondering if you could find me a copy of the words and music to *My Fair Lady*? I would like to practice it at home."

"I can ask Mr. Brandon. I am sure he will be able to help you," said Mrs. Rickert, astonished that Genevieve had asked. She felt certain that she had a special—make that a very special—student. The word "prodigy" came to mind. She put her arm around her. "Genevieve you can be certain that Mr. Brandon and I will help you," she said emphatically.

"Thank you, Mrs. Rickert," she said with a smile.

## Chapter 4

# DAVID KELSEY IN MIDDLE SCHOOL

David couldn't resist looking out the classroom window every time Mrs. Ohlander, his mathematics teacher, turned to illustrate a problem on the board. It was early June, and he just couldn't wait until summer vacation to play baseball with his friends, a structured tournament arrangement of regular games all summer. He ate, slept, and dreamed baseball, somewhat to the dismay of his parents, Helen and Fred. While they welcomed the social and health benefits of such activities they tried to emphasize the importance of excelling in school. Occasionally David rewarded them with concentrated effort and received more B's and an occasional A instead of a plethora of C's and an awful D or even the occasional F. Spring, however, was his downfall. It never failed and at age 13 his diversion seemed to increase and intensify.

"David Kelsey. Are you here or elsewhere?" He heard his name in the distance like a dream. He was looking at the school's baseball diamond, envisioning himself stepping up to the plate. "Eyes front—NOW!" Mrs. Ohlander screamed a shrill command. David and several other classmates nearly jumped out of their seats. With her hands on her hips she ordered, "I want you to explain how to approach this problem I have on the board. Come up here and show us—NOW."

David could see a couple of friends with big smiles wondering how he would survive this test. He organized his brain in a matter of seconds as he slowly arose from his chair, wondering that himself. At first the sound didn't register with him as his brain tried, as it might, to focus on the problem at hand and on the board. Then he realized he was saved by the bell. The period was over—Hallelujah!

Mrs. Ohlander took a deep breath, then shook her head announcing, "Class write your assignment for tomorrow in your notebooks. Oh, Mr. Kelsey, you WILL open tomorrow's class by explaining how to solve the problem on the board." She smiled, knowing she would make her point another day.

The friends hurried to their lockers to grab their lunches and get drinks in the cafeteria to gulp down their lunch so they could get about a half hour on the field before their next class. "Wow, that was a close one Dave," laughed George Greenly.

"What were you going to do?" asked Wally Proka.

"I was going to slowly repeat what was on the board. I knew the bell would ring, only it was faster than I thought. Lucky me."

"What about tomorrow?" George asked.

"I guess I'll have to open the book tonight and learn it. Let's hurry so we can get a game started." The boys rushed through lunch, not exactly what their moms preached, and ran outside to play under the brilliant midday sun like probably many thousands of other American boys were doing in every time zone. They met Gene Urman, Jack Panne, and some others they regularly played with. They were all fired up for a short game. They had about twenty-five minutes or before their next class. Fortunately, some of the teachers were becoming attuned to this welcome spring diversion and several actually gulped down their lunches as quickly as the students to see this spirited event unfold on a beautiful day. Some of the women actually brought umbrellas and folding chairs to the game. Needless to say, the first of the classes after lunch could be delayed. Although the principal and assistant principal, the school disciplinarian, normally were not part of the fan audience, they did not watch the clock as the school year was winding down.

The guys usually had predetermined teams, with the exception of absences. On those days, they would loan a player or two to the other side to balance the teams. Today they had almost two full squads of 7 players each. A teacher, Mr. Felton, was the "steady catcher" and would often joke that he should be allowed to come to bat for both sides. With 7 players, one outfielder was missing so righties were called out if they hit the ball to right field and leftys were out if they hit the ball into left field. Balls and strikes were ignored but the batter had to swing by the third pitch or the batter would be called out, as time was of the essence.

David's team won the coin toss, so they were up first. George Greenly, a good hitter with speed, was up first. George let the first pitch go by. He swung at the second and lined it just fair over third base. Wally Proka, in left, cut it off but George made it easily to second for a double. His English teacher, Allyson Wirth, yelled, "Good hit, George." Jack Panne was up next and popped out to second. David, hitting left handed, waited for the outfield to shift. "No hitter," Mr. Felton joked as David took a couple of practice swings and stepped up to the plate, smiling at his teacher, who knew darn well that David was a superb hitter. The first pitch was tempting but on the outside which, if David connected, would have sailed into left for an automatic out. Ray North was always trying to tempt him with a sucker pitch, but David usually recognized that. The second pitch was a bit short, so David held off. Hoping Ray would give him a decent third pitch to drive, he took a half step up at the plate and his wish was granted. He uncoiled the bat quickly, slamming the ball high and far over the head of the right fielder. Score 2-0 in favor of the Mets over the Yanks. Mr. Felton cheered and shook David's hand. The final score after 20 minutes or so was 6-3 Mets.

Mr. Felton walked back toward the school building with David and encouraged him to try out for the high school freshman team next year. "I sure will Mr. F., I sure will."

"I hope so, David. You sure have the makings of a very good hitter. You look like a natural."

"Gee, Mr. Felton, you really think so?" he asked his teacher.

"Yes, I do. I haven't mentioned it to you before, but I played high school and college baseball and tried out for a Mohican's minor league team, but couldn't quite hit professional pitching the way I hit in college," he said somewhat dejectedly.

David noticed his disappointment "Gee, sorry about that Mr. F."

"That's O.K. David. It was a long time ago. If you do well, I can follow you and I will be one of your biggest fans—I promise," and he held out his hand and David shook it with a strong grip."

"Thanks, Mr. F. I will take your advice."

His teacher also knew of David's dreaming in class. "Do try and concentrate on your classwork too, David. You are smart. You just need to separate the game from the classroom. It's important for your development. If your marks are good you could receive a scholarship at a university with a great baseball tradition and an opportunity to play for them."

He noticed David's eyes light up. "Do you think so, Mr. F.?" David had never thought much about it, certainly not that far ahead.

"I do, David. I really do. It won't be easy. You will have to work hard, but I think you are made of the right stuff," he answered with sincerity.

"Wow," David exhaled, feeling mighty good. Reality then crept back into his thoughts as he remembered what Mrs. Ohlander said as the bell rang. He would need to apply Mr. Felton's advice tonight and tomorrow on that math problem.

"O.K., David. See you later in class. Remember what I said now,"

Mr. Felton called to him as they separated in the hall.

"You bet Mr. F." He was still dreaming about baseball, but now he put things in proper order.

In effect, with this advice from a respected teacher, he began to put priorities in prospective without actually realizing he was. One good teacher was the catalyst.

## Chapter 5

# VICTORIA MAGNUSON IN MIDDLE SCHOOL

The firstborn in any family has a unique position. They can set the example for and be a leader and guiding light to their siblings who follow, or they can harbor a dislike toward them for "horning in" where they, the firstborn, often owned 100% of their parents' affection and attention.

Victoria Magnuson was born in that unique position. It was quite evident that once she reached about 10 she was developing into that guiding light. She had a beautiful head of curly blonde hair until she was just beyond two when an unthinking hairdresser cut the curls off. Fortunately, unlike the mythical Samson, she didn't have to rely on her hair. She had a very inquisitive and well-organized mind as she approached her teens. Her propensity for leadership began around age 12 as she was entering middle school. Her parents, Kathy and Ken, were expecting her to excel.

It was early October and the incoming 7th grade class of Middletown Junior High was beginning to settle in. The cafeteria was buzzing with chatter of kids hurrying to eat and run out to the playground to stretch their legs and catch the still warm early October sun. Laurie Fassert, Victoria's good friend, was talking to her non-stop. "Vicky, I think you should run for class president. I'll vote for you and talk to all of our friends and classmates and ask them to talk to the other kids. What do you say?" she asked.

"Why are you asking me to do it Laurie?"

"Well, I think you always know what to do, what to say, and you kind of take over when we are together with our friends and the other day in class when Miss Abrams asked that really hard question about the government in Washington."

Vicky smiled and recalled that incident when the teacher asked someone to explain the make up of the United States Government in Washington, D.C., and she was the only student who raised her hand.

"You answered her question so good that she gave you a gold star in her book," Laurie excitedly exclaimed.

"Well, when I am sure of something I think it is important to explain everything, otherwise someone else trying to learn may not learn everything there is to learn about whatever it is," replied Vicky, shrugging her shoulders as a simple matter of fact.

"That is exactly what I mean, Vicky. I know I wouldn't be able to do that and probably no one else in our class or the school can explain things like you can."

Victoria just smiled, wondering if she should act on Laurie's suggestion. She took a deep breath, then suggested, "We should go outside on this sunny day before lunch period is over."

"All right, but can I get the word out?" Laurie persisted with an impish grin.

Vicky took a deep breath. "I wish you wouldn't. I need to think about it some more. I have some pretty hard subjects that will take up a lot of extra time," and she sort of twisted her nose. Laurie just laughed as they half walked and half skipped, as twelve year olds will do.

"Hi," said Ann Herman, another friend as she joined them. "What were you two talking about? You looked so serious."

Victoria wanted to remain quiet about the class president conversation she had with Laurie until she resolved it in her mind but Laurie just blurted it out. "I told Vicky she should run for class president. She would be the best. Don't you think so too?"

"That's a great idea," Ann agreed. "Will you, Vicky? You would be terrific."

Victoria took a deep breath. These were two good friends and she didn't want to disappoint or offend them. It was amazing, how at 12, she had these instincts. "I really need to think on it, Ann. I'll let you two know first but you have to promise me NOT to talk about this to anyone else—PROMISE ME!" she emphasized, and raised her hand. "Scout's honor, too," as they were all Girl Scouts.

"Scout's honor," they all said with raised hands, then skipped arm-in-arm out to the playground.

This was the inaugural year of the class president program. The brainchild of Peter Wright, the principal, it was occurring around the time of the U.S. presidential election. This timing greatly increased the interest of the students, faculty and parents. The candidates for class president would be chosen in each of the four 7th grade classes by the last Friday in October. Some classes had but one candidate, as in Victoria's class, where she was the unanimous nominee. Other classes had as many as three candidates who had to campaign before their own class for a runoff. The next step would be the election of one of the four by a combined "convention" of the four classes to be held on the second Friday in November. The candidates would have two weeks to prepare a ten-minute speech. A secret ballot vote would elect the officers with the first runner up becoming the Vice President, the second runner up the Secretary and the fourth runner up the Treasurer. In effect, there would be no losers, as all four officers would comprise the "Board of Officers" for the 7th grade students and the four 7th grade teachers rotating as advisors. Victoria was a bit nervous, which was no different than the other three candidates. They watched as the classes filed in and settled down. She would be the third to speak, so she had about 20 minutes in which to compose herself. She thought to take some notes of the first two candidate speeches should she learn something or utilize what she heard to some advantage and to avoid unnecessary duplication. She duly noted the duplication in the first two speeches. One idea she had included she changed to go beyond the previous candidates' limited proposal. She also noted the uneven delivery of the two previous candidates and made a mental note to ensure her speech would be powerful and uplifting. She stepped up to the podium and was surprised and gratified that the butterflies all but disappeared. "Good afternoon. It's an honor to be here before all my 7th grade classmates," she announced in a crystal clear voice, devoid of any nervousness. She paused and momentarily looked out over the auditorium seeing her class smiling. It was as silent as a morgue as everyone sat, waiting for her speech. She took a deep breath and then delivered her monumental proclamation. "When I am elected," she began, differently from the previous candidates who had both opened with, "If I am elected." "I will form a council of the four officers and one additional student from each class as a legislative body to agree on the most desirable suggestions from our total number of classmates," she continued.

The other candidates sort of blinked when she said, "When I am elected." The teachers and Mr. Wright blinked when she suggested increasing the student involvement into a legislative body. Mrs. Carter, her teacher, only grinned. She wasn't surprised, and wondered what other new ideas her prize student had in mind. Mr. Wright initially thought she should have cleared the idea of an expanded legislative body with him, but decided that he appreciated the soundness of the idea. Although limited, his goal was to bring to life how the democratic process works.

Victoria continued, "Naturally everything to be recommended has to be within the boundaries of the official school process. We can, however, work within that framework." Mr. Wright, the school's administrative staff, and the teachers were, at this point, intensely concentrating. "We can recommend innovative changes that challenge ourselves, our teachers and our administration to exceed our expectations and most importantly put a charge into our time here at Middletown to prepare us on an even greater level for the last few years of our education," said Victoria. A few hoorahs were heard from the student audience, and some students applauded. Victoria wasn't sure but thought it might have came from her friends and she never thought to ask them to be demonstrative. Mrs. Carter maintained that pleased grin. Victoria was on a roll now. She quickly glanced at the auditorium clock. She had only two minutes left. Mr. Wright, very impressed with her speech, looked at his watch kind of nervously. He preferred to have the candidates finish voluntarily rather than to pull the plug on them. He leaned forward at the ready.

Realizing she had everyone's undivided attention and that her time was dwindling, Victoria gripped the podium tightly and revealed her stunning proposal. "I propose, with my council and, of course, administrative approval, that a classroom rotation be adopted so that we all receive the benefit of each teacher's strength and teaching methodology. In my opinion, this will also increase our knowledge level and make our years here infinitely more interesting."

Mr. Wright was truly taken by surprise yet enthralled by Victoria's original thinking and creativity. He leaned over to his assistant and whispered, "She's a little dynamo. Listening to her suggestions made me think I was listening to the United States Congress." His assistant nodded. Before he could stand, thank Victoria, and announce the next candidate, it seemed the entire seventh grade stood and clapped loudly as she walked back to her seat, still flushed with her last proposal and now the exuberant response from her peers. Mrs. Carter had an even larger smile than before. Victoria didn't expect such a response. She won the election in a landslide.

# Chapter 6
# KEITH FREDERICKS
# GRADUATES HIGH SCHOOL

It was Memorial Day weekend just prior to High School graduation. Keith, Nick and Nelson remained friends through their teens even though the Fredericks family moved from Pennsylvania to Delaware. The boys still communicated by phone and enjoyed infrequent visits to each other's home. They decided on a fishing trip to celebrate graduation. Keith's parents had a mobile home on the water in Southern Delaware and a boat the boys could use.

"I hooked a big one guys. Look at my rod," yelled Keith as they trolled the 21 footer in and out of the inlet at Indian River Bay in search of Blues and Stripers.

"Hold onto him," answered Nelson. "I'm heading back in under the bridge and there are boats both port and starboard coming out."

"It's crowded today. Everyone had the same idea," shouted Nick, as he recast his rod. The boat heaved and yawed from the force of the tide and the waves created by the surrounding boats.

"He's tough—probably a big Blue or a Striper," shouted Keith.

"I just had something on my lure, and it feels big," Nick chimed in. Nelson maneuvered the boat back thru the inlet and into the bay.

"I see mine jumping," yelled Keith as a big Blue broke water and tried to free itself from the line.

Nick followed suit "Wow, mine looks bigger than yours, Keith."

"O.K., Nick, let's wager a five spot on that," Keith answered. It would be close. They both slid their fingers into the gills of each fish and held them up next to each other. Nick's fish was one inch longer but Keith's was the fatter of the two.

"Let me be the judge," laughed Nelson. He took a good look and decided it was a tie. "One is longer but one is fatter so they're the same, as far as I am concerned," he judged. Then they all laughed and headed out through the inlet for another try before dark. The ocean was getting rougher, so Keith took over the controls.

As they passed the rocks they spotted a Coast Guard Cutter heading south by southeast at a good clip. They also noticed that the wind had picked up; the spray from the bow covered the windshield and, at times, spilled over the gunwales. "Wonder where he's going," motioned Keith toward the cutter.

"Well, they don't just go joyriding. It's very expensive," Nick responded. "Turn on the ship to shore emergency channel and see what's happening," added Nelson.

They heard voices through the static: "We are taking on water. We have our jackets on. Our pump is not working. We are bailing by hand but it's a losing battle."

Another voice came on. "This is Lt. Gardner. What is your twenty?"

"We are near Buoy 16 moving about 10 knots" the first voice answered.

"I will kick it up. Hang on we will let you know when you are in our sights."

"Wow, a real Coast Guard rescue! That is exciting," Nick shouted.

"I wish I was on that Cutter," said Keith with enthusiasm. Just then, a large wave lifted their boat's bow several feet.

The boat came down with a thud and a significant amount of water came over the bow and down the gunwales and aft.

"Switch on the pump," shouted Nelson.

"I just did," Keith answered. "I'm turning us around."

"Make it between waves, old buddy, or we will be calling the Guard ourselves," Nelson joked, laughing despite the situation.

"O.K., Captain Keith. Show us how to do it," Nick shouted.

"You bet," Keith exuded confidence even as he gripped the wheel so hard that his knuckles turned white. The boat responded. He reduced the power as the incoming waves lifted and propelled them back through the inlet.

"Wow, that's all the excitement I want today, and maybe even tomorrow," blurted Nick. "Good job, Keith" he added.

"Yeah, Keith, that was great," added Nelson "Let's go back and cook these fresh fish. I'm hungry."

"Amen to that," added Keith as he leaned on the throttle and the 225 horsepower motor pushed them along nicely through the choppy bay back to the docks.

The fish were cleaned, gutted, trimmed and put on the fire after oiling, along with three large sweet potatoes. They were enjoying Mr. Fredericks' non-alcoholic beer. Keith's dad had a long talk with him about not drinking alcohol and felt if he could not be there, it was best they not be tempted, so the non-alcoholic beer was the suitable choice. The boys moved inside to eat their feast and escape the insects.

"What is the forecast for tomorrow?" Nick asked.

"Let's turn the radio on," Nelson suggested, as he got up to do just that. It was almost 7:30, time for news. "Today at around 5 p.m., the Coast Guard out of Lewes rescued three crew and nine fishermen on the 42-foot Marlin, which suffered heavy seas and a faulty water pump several miles from the inlet. There were no injuries. They managed to tow the Marlin back to dockside. Apparently, the heavy seas were not expected but a strong storm kicked up suddenly, reported Captain Banks of the Marlin, and their water pump became inoperable. Salute our Coast Guard," added the news reporter.

"Salute Keith, too," exclaimed Nelson as they knocked their non-alcoholic beer cans together and all laughed as only teenage boys can and do. "That Coast Guard rescue really got me thinking," Keith said thoughtfully.

"What about, Keith?" asked Nick.

"Well, I am graduating this year and I want to do something exciting with my life. The Coast Guard can be exciting. Just look at what happened today. My dad was in the Navy and did some time on a Destroyer Escort and has great memories of it. Anyhow, I was just thinking."

"You are right, Keith," added Nelson. "If you stay in, I think 20 years, you can get paid the rest of your life and you can travel, wear neat uniforms and meet lots of girls," he added, laughing.

Nick laughed also and added, "You forgot following orders, hard work, and marching."

"Heck, you work hard as a carpenter or a cement guy," he said, looking around for a better description.

"Mason," contributed Nelson.

"Right a mason."

"But you have to buy health insurance and you can wear out your body, and then what?" asked Keith.

"How come you know all about these things?" asked Nick, wide-eyed.

"Because I talked to my Dad about it," Keith answered.

"But," interjected Nelson, "In the service you can get REALLY hurt, like DEAD." They all laughed, not at what he said, but how he said it.

Keith sat back and rather thoughtfully threw out a question to the guys. "Just say we go into the service—which would we choose?"

"We? why we?" asked Nick with a smile. They all laughed.

"Well, I was thinking Navy, or even the Secret Service," Keith continued.

"I remember a few years ago, I think, you said you might like the Secret Service," Nick commented.

"I remember that too," Nelson agreed.

"I will need to get a college degree first," Keith added.

"Wow, that can be tough," Nelson shook his head.

"I'll say," Nick agreed.

"Nick and me have talked about the Air Force, right, Nick?" Nelson turned to his brother.

"Right," Nick agreed.

'Wow—do you think you can be pilots?" Keith asked, astonished.

They both shook their heads a bit. "We wish. We were thinking mechanics or something else," Nelson responded.

"If you do go into the Secret Service, you have to promise us one thing," Nick requested.

"What is that?" asked Keith, looked puzzled.

"You have to introduce Nelson and me to the president." They all laughed.

"Guys, I promise," said Keith, raising his hand like an oath. "Well, that's it. It is all decided," he exclaimed and put out his hand. Nick and Nelson added their hands to Keith's. They sealed the promise with hearty laughs.

Nick turned to Nelson. "We probably have to tell Mom what we are thinking."

"Well, you have one year to graduate, and I have two, so she will have time to think about it."

"Even though I said I want to join the Secret Service, I will still speak to Mom and Dad about it anyway—it is the right thing to do. They can give me more advice or find out where I can get advice."

"We have a plan," added Nelson, as he looked at the clock. "Wow—time flies. It is almost 10. When is high tide?"

"6:04," Keith answered. They settled into their sleeping bags with thoughts of tomorrow and big fish swimming in their heads.

Keith's June graduation day was sunny, hot, and sticky. He invited Nick and Nelson, who came and sat with his parents, Barbara and Richard, and other relatives. There would be a small party back at the Fredericks' home in Newark. Keith did not win any awards for his four high school years, but he was a better than average student with an exemplary record. He had applied to several colleges, and had decided to apply to some requiring air travel when returning home for visits. This was something he had not discussed with his buddies, deciding to break the news at his graduation get together. They were surprised and a bit hurt that he hadn't told them earlier but understood.

"If we had the chance, we would go to college and see the country too," Nelson told him.

Nick agreed. "You're lucky Keith. We hope you do great and have a good time too. We will always be friends."

"Yeah, and we should write to each other," Nelson added.

"I will," Keith promised, and meant it. He did not, however, mention that upon or near college graduation he would apply for a Secret Service commission. Anyway, that was years away and might not occur after all.

The brothers were still weighing joining the Air Force: one year away for Nick and two for Nelson.

**Chapter 7**

# GENEVIEVE IN COLLEGE
# AND ON BROADWAY

At age 18, Genevieve Carter was a beautiful young lady with dark blond hair, hazel eyes, and a lithe figure. Precocious at 12, as a pre-teen, as a teen she became very perceptive with an extremely engaging personality, with a superlative voice worthy of a solo or choir lead. Her acting ability was truly marvelous. She was praised for her high school performances.

"Honey, I suggest you begin choosing your clothes for our trip. It is only two weeks away. This way, if we need to add to your wardrobe we will still have time to shop and catch some great sales," Vanessa called up the stairs. "Who knows? We may even buy something in New York," her mom added, knowing that they would have a great time shopping in the Big Apple.

"Okay, Mom, I will get right on it. I just need to decide on what to bring. Do I need a different outfit for each day?"

"One for traveling to and fro and I would take one party dress in case, and four different separates. Vary the colors so you have a totally different look each day while you rehearse and meet different people," suggested Vanessa.

Genevieve saw herself lugging multiple suitcases. Perhaps Mom was a bit excessive, she thought. "Did I hear you say we could buy clothes in New York?" she called down.

"Yes, I did sweetheart, but we may not have time," She laughed. "I thought you might not have heard that."

"Maybe I should leave one suitcase pretty empty," Genevieve laughed back.

"Not to worry, honey. If necessary, we can rent a car or a truck so I can add to my wardrobe as well," Vanessa responded in a merry tone. They were both deliriously happy. Genevieve was about to begin the rest of her marvelous life.

To understand how this June New York trip came about, we have to go back to the previous fall at State University where a decision was made, or even farther back in Genevieve's senior year at Central High. Ron Barrister, a Broadway producer, originally a Long Islander whose sister still resides there, visited and attended local events with her and her family. It had been almost two years since the last visit, so she invited him to see the Central High student production of *Magic Man*, and especially to see Genevieve Carter. Genevieve had the lead role of Maryanne.

On the way to the school his sister, Eve Truitt, filled him in. "You know the play, Ron but wait until you see the beautiful girl playing Maryanne. She is absolutely marvelous. Johnny knows her personally. She is in his homeroom and other classes. She's a gorgeous thing and has such a sweet personality and can she act."

"So you have seen her in other productions?" he asked.

"Yes. Twice actually, once last year in *Fabulous Girl* and this past spring in *Olivia*. As a matter of fact, Johnny told me some other students are miffed because she wins out, hands down, when auditioning. They don't have a prayer, as he puts it."

"Talent, duly recognized, always comes to the top and wins out. That's showbiz, someone said. This is very interesting indeed. I was looking forward to being with you tonight, Eve, and this will be an added treat." He put his arm around his sister as they walked into the school and the auditorium. Eve waved to her son, Johnny, sitting with friends, and she and Ron settled in their seats, studying the program about twenty minutes prior to curtain time. "Did you remember your opera glasses so I can get a super close up of this Genevieve" he asked.

"I did." She fished them from her purse.

"Splendid," he retorted.

The auditorium was filling quickly as the orchestra warmed up. Ron trained the glasses on the students and smiled. It was a really nice scene. The whole undertaking, as he thought of the future, assured professional show business with all these marvelous youngsters and their devoted teachers involved. He, briefly, conjured the potential effect nationwide but decided to rest his head for the show rather than do such complexities in his brain when he was supposed to relax. He was, after all, here to be entertained. The lights flickered, prompting a hush from the audience and the orchestra. The Performing Arts Department Head came before the drawn curtain. "Welcome, everyone, to Central High's spring Spectacular, *Magic Man*. Our students, orchestra, and instructors have been working long and hard to make this a memorable evening. We promise that you will not be disappointed." He pointed to the orchestra.

"All right, maestro, hit it."

The orchestra came to life. The curtain parted to show a colorful main street and about twenty characters in various costumes marching twice around to the opening music. They left the stage when the male lead Harvey Feld entered, dressed to the nines with a neat straw hat and a medium size suitcase, looking rather puzzled. The music stopped and another actor entered. "Hello, I am Harvey Feld and I just arrived on the train. Can you please show me the direction to a hotel?"

"Over yonder," the person pointed.

"Thanks Mister, much obliged. This is a real nice town."

"Sure is," said the man, walking off the stage. He disappeared and the curtain closed for scene two.

In the next scene, the hotel lobby, he met several of the townspeople and introduced himself as a music professor on vacation. He said that he had heard this town, Branford, was real nice, so he decided to stop for a few days before continuing on to Chicago. In reality, he was a first class con man looking for a high stakes poker game, craps or whatever. He was a master of them all.

Genevieve entered the stage in the sweet shop scene. Eve whispered to Ron, "What do you think?"

"You called it Sis. She is beautiful."

Harvey takes a long glance at her and begins to sing, "Hello, I am Harvey Feld. How do you do?" and extends his hand. He has a passable voice. She hesitates, then gives him a half smile and timidly extends her hand. Then the words flow and come richly to life and her voice is strong.

"Hello, how do you do. I am Maria. It is so nice to make your acquaintance, Mr. Feld." Ron continually stared at her through the binoculars. Eve was anxious to hear his thoughts.

On stage, Harvey answers with a big smile, "Oh just call me Harvey. It sounds friendly."

She smiles back and beautifully retorts in song "We haven't been properly introduced and a lady must be properly introduced, you see, or she cannot do that, no, she cannot do that." Her voice rose in a crescendo.

Ron turned to Eve and smiled. "She is marvelous. What a beauty with a voice to boot."

"I told you" she responded with a huge smile.

"O.K., big sister, you told me and I am glad that you did. Really glad, as a matter of fact." They settled back to watch the rest of the play and he continued to be astonished at Genevieve's poise. She really lit up the stage with her presence.

With approximately fifteen minutes to the play's conclusion he asked Eve, "I would like to introduce myself to Genevieve and congratulate her on a marvelous performance."

"I am sure she'll be thrilled," she responded.

"Does she know that I was in the audience?"

"No," Eve responded. "It might have made her nervous."

The applause was deafening. Central High had a marvelous hit that would be impossible to equal, as Genevieve Carter was just a month from graduating and moving on to State University.

It took them a while to maneuver through the crowd down to the rear of the stage and the dressing area. A teacher recognized Eve. "Hello Eve—can I help you?"

"Yes, I want to introduce my brother Ron to Genevieve Carter. He's a Broadway producer and he would like to meet her."

The teacher's eyes opened wide and her mouth followed suit. She gathered her thoughts. "It is certainly a pleasure to meet you."

"Ron Bannister."

"My pleasure likewise" he smiled and extended his hand.

She smiled "Please follow me. I will be glad to take you to her, Mr. Bannister."

"Thank you," he responded, smiling and taking Evelyn's arm in his and following the teacher. Genevieve was still flush and excited after the closing act and stood talking to some of the cast. She spotted Eve and Ron with the teacher. Eve gave Genevieve a huge hug and big kiss. "You were marvelous, sweetie," she almost screamed.

"Thank you, Mrs. Truitt," Genevieve gushed. "Genevieve, I want to introduce you to my brother, Johnny's uncle, Ron Bannister."

"Hello, Genevieve. You were marvelous. I thoroughly enjoyed your performance," Ron exclaimed, catching the gleam in her beautiful blue eyes. He was captivated by her looks and charm at 18.

"Thank you very much, Mr. Bannister, I appreciate that."

"Hello Eve, you got backstage to congratulate our daughter before we did." Vanessa Carter surprised them as she and Gene entered the dressing area and hugged their daughter.

"Vanessa and Gene, I want to introduce you to my brother, Ron Bannister."

Ron held out his hand. "Vanessa and Gene, it's a pleasure indeed to meet the parents of such a lovely and talented daughter." They both thanked him with the distinct feeling that this was no ordinary man or occurrence.

Eve spoke, "Vanessa and Gene, Ron is a Broadway producer. I may not have mentioned him either of you." They both swallowed hard, as did Genevieve, whose eyes opened real wide.

"No," Vanessa managed, "I don't believe you have."

"Wow," Gene responded.

Ron, not wishing to make them ill at ease, started slowly. He turned to them and graciously began "You obviously know that you have a very special daughter here."

"We certainly think that," Gene quipped, trying to reduce the excitement he and Vanessa were feeling. They all smiled.

"Well, Gene, let me say you suspected quite correctly," Ron answered, understanding the importance of humor. Mom and Dad seemed to relax a little, but Genevieve was squeezing her hands until her knuckles were white. Ron looked directly at both her mom and dad. "What are Genevieve's plans beyond graduation?"

"She's going to State U. and plans to major in drama. We understand they have a great program. Her drama teacher recommended her," they responded.

"That's marvelous," Ron exclaimed. He turned to Genevieve "I will make it my business to ask my sister," he said, turning to Eve, "to make arrangements to see you at the University."

Eve smiled and nodded. "Thanks to Genevieve, here, we may see more of each other," she said, and everyone laughed.

Genevieve reached out for Ron's hand and looked him straight in the eyes. "I am really pleased to have met you and look forward to talking with you again, real soon. Perhaps you can give me some advice," she said,

Ron returned her look as intensely as he received hers. "Genevieve, I'd be happy to. Right now I would say you are miles ahead of probably any high school actress and singer. You can always learn more from your teachers and more experience will certainly hone your skills. I'll be sure to receive updates from my sister here." He nudged Eve in the ribs and she nudged back.

"O.K., Genevieve, you can look for me dead center in the front row of every show you do," said Eve. They all laughed. When Ron and Eve left, Vanessa and Gene hugged their daughter and told her how proud they were.

"Do you guys," she started, turning to her parents, "think I have what it takes to be on Broadway?"

"I sure do, honey," Gene answered and gently squeezed both her hands.

Vanessa hugged and kissed her. "You sure do. You sure do, sweetie."

Dad then gave some fatherly advice. "Let's stay grounded and have you get more education and experience as Mr. Bannister suggested. Learn as much as you can at State U. It's possible he can get you roles in summer stock productions before you graduate." The gleam in Genevieve's eyes sparkled like diamonds and Vanessa hugged her again.

Ron Bannister and Eve came to see her perform, a second time, at State U. the next spring. Again, to prevent any nervousness on Genevieve's part, she was not told ahead of time. He and Eve came backstage after the show, showing proper credentials. The faculty was impressed, and Genevieve was surprised. This time Vanessa and Gene saw Eve and Ron coming down the hall.

"Eve you did not tell us that you and Ron were coming."

Ron came to Eve's rescue. "You can blame it all on me, Mrs. Carter. I am sorry, but I thought it might affect Genevieve's performance. I didn't want to take that chance. Will you please forgive me?"

Vanessa smiled. "I suppose that was best. I probably could not keep it a secret and that would probably have unnerved her."

"That's how I felt. I saw both of you twice since I knew Ron was going to make it," Eve added. "I am glad I did. I have a surprise for Genevieve."

Ron held out a folder and handed it to Gene. Vanessa and he opened it together. "Oh my God, it is the script for *The Swinging Fifties*. Oh my God," Vanessa screamed again. Gene was astonished, as well.

"Just think, my dear friends. I knew about this for a month and I had to keep this a secret. Just think!" Eve was practically shouting so that several cast members and faculty in the hall stopped to listen.

"Shall we see Genevieve now?" Ron suggested.

"We had better or she will be worried about where I have gone," Vanessa said, and squeezed the script as she led them to Genevieve. Ron noticed a medium size star on her door He made a mental note to make sure the NYC dressing room door had a much larger one with some other adornment. Vanessa knocked on the door and Genevieve opened the peephole. She let her mom and dad in.

Vanessa broke the news. "Honey, you have some special company; Mrs. Truitt and her brother saw the play and loved it." Ron Bannister and Eve entered after Genevieve's parents. Genevieve's mouth fell open. She had to sit; her mom helped her to the large armed easy chair fit for a star.

"My apologies, Genevieve, but I thought it best to avoid possibly affecting your performance tonight," Ron said, looking at her for an "It's O.K.," answer as did Eve, who added "I am sorry also Gen—but wait till you see what your mom has to show you."

Genevieve's eyes shifted to the folder with the blank cover. She opened it and tears flowed. Vanessa was close to tears herself. Ron just stood with a very large smile, patiently waiting for the ladies to come back to Earth. "Genevieve and Vanessa, please sit." Vanessa knew why. Genevieve opened her eyes widely. Gene tightly held one of Genevieve's hands in a fatherly way. Ron Bannister then gave her the reason.

"Genevieve, I feel very strongly that you have the makings of a true star. From my observation, all that you need to improve would be training your voice and your lungs to hold your breath a little longer on the really high notes, and to slow down your delivery a little on lengthy dialogue." He stopped to see her reaction. He received from her what he had hoped he would: acceptance of his expert well-meant criticisms, which in effect, was a critique.

"Thank you, Mr. Bannister, I really appreciate that," she smiled and meant it.

Ron Bannister thought to himself *My God what an objective young woman. I hope, as success will do, she never changes.* He quickly replied, "I suggest from now through the end of June you work with your professors on those areas. The last week of June I want you and your mom," he turned to Vanessa and nodded with a smile, which she returned, "to come to New York and start rehearsing Glenda Bishop's role, in, as you can see, *The Swinging Fifties.*"

Genevieve's eyes opened larger than she thought possible. Finally, a happy gasp left her throat and reached her lips the same time that happy tears flowed. Vanessa and Gene gave her loving hugs like only parents could give. Their happy tears matched Genevieve's one for one.

"Congratulations! Broadway here you come, and Broadway will never be the same," Eve shouted.

Ron had a feeling that Genevieve would never be the same either but he felt that to be a positive development. He felt obliged to add that it would be as a summer replacement and not interfere with her college schedule.

He filled them in on the traveling and lodging details and the approximate schedule he envisioned for rehearsals. He doubted Genevieve and her parents heard half of what he told them, so he promised to send them a letter with all the details, and advised them to call or e-mail him with any questions, also that he would also quickly advise of any schedule changes. He and Eve hugged them all.

"Thank you, Mr. Bannister. Thank you very much," Gene shook Ron's hand.

"Thank you, Gene, for Vanessa and yourself raising such a beautiful and talented young woman."

"Pinch me Mom," Genevieve said, joyfully turning to Vanessa as the limo rolled into the Big Apple, "Is this for real or am I dreaming?"

"This is for real sweetie," Vanessa answered and added "Dad and I are so proud of you." Genevieve hugged her as hard as she could.

"I wonder how I will feel on a real Broadway stage. I hope I won't mess up," she added.

"Just immerse yourself in the role as you always do, Sweetie, and you will be great, I am sure," Mom answered. Ron Bannister had arranged for them to stay in a luxury condominium overlooking Central Park. It would be Genevieve's for the summer with accommodations satisfactory for family visits.

"Wow, just look at this view!" Genevieve gushed. She had been to New York City several times but only on day trips to theatres or when Dad wanted to see a baseball game. He was a New York Marauders fan as he and Mom were originally New Yorkers after all. He hails from Brooklyn and she from Queens.

Vanessa was busy checking out the condo, which had two good size bedrooms, two and a half baths, a large living room with office furniture in one corner and a picture window with a breathtaking view of Central Park, a modern eat-in kitchen, and a dining room. The furniture was practically new and very modern. "Mom, come and look at this view!" Genevieve gushed again.

"Sorry honey, I was absorbed with the rooms and furniture."

"I figured as much," Genevieve laughed. Vanessa just smiled and looked out over Central Park.

"Wow—you are right. What a view indeed." She too, was bedazzled. Genevieve left the view and walked into the kitchen and noticed a note that Vanessa had not, since she was into studying the decor. It was from Ron, saying that he hoped they would like the "digs." It went on to say that he had the fridge stocked and advised where they could find convenient mini markets and phone numbers or ask for deliveries all to be charged to his account. He ended with "See you both soon—I will call to see how everything is."

"Hey Mom, Mr. Bannister left a note and a full fridge and pantry and where we can call or shop when we need to."

"Wow," Vanessa gushed, "We are being treated like royalty." "Come here sweetie and sit by me."

Genevieve plopped on the sleek sofa. "Oh Mom, this is just unbelievable."

"It is all for you sweetie. You are the one and I am just so happy and proud to be part of it," she hugged her daughter.

"Mom, you and Dad made me who and what I am," she said. Then she snuggled up to Vanessa and gave her a dazzling smile.

They relaxed the rest of the day, munching and watching TV and sitting on their patio staring out at Central Park, wishing they had binoculars. On Sunday, they called Gene, found a nearby church to attend services, and strolled the park until mid day. They then took a cab to Bleming's Department Store to do a little shopping. Although there were fine stores at home, this was a real treat, as mom and daughter tried on an uncounted number of outfits, hats, shoes, and you name it. Vanessa reminded her, "Dad and I discussed it and we established a budget of four outfits—hopefully two each."

Genevieve laughed. "Maybe we can find a two-for-one sale and we can have four each."

"Honey, I am afraid Blemings doesn't have those type of sales, and Dad will be coming with more of our clothes since we'll be here till late August."

"Shucks, a girl can dream, can't I?" She sang beautifully and Vanessa gave her a broad smile. They both found two outfits that suited them and grabbed a cab back to the apartment.

Dinner was nice with the stock provided by Ron Bannister's staff. They thought that they would be eating on the fly a lot and, on this, their first Sunday, they could relax and enjoy their digs. While they were eating, Mom noticed that Genevieve appeared somewhat sad.

"Are you O.K.?" she asked. "You're very quiet all of a sudden."

"It is just that I thought I will be leaving all of this in less than two months. I wonder if I will be able to adjust to my 'real life'," she said, using her fingers to make quotes around the phrase.

Mom left her seat and put her arm around her daughter. "I know honey. It may be hard at first but it's not the end, but just the beginning for you. Mr. Bannister will wait for you to finish college. You are honing your skills and each summer you will be a Broadway star if only for a little while. Eventually that will be you for the rest of your life. How many young women can say that, sweetie?" They hugged with tears of joy streaming down both their faces.

The limousine arrived at 8:25 a.m. the next morning. They had been looking out over Central Park watching the walkers and the runners and the cabs go by since before 7. Genevieve had trouble falling asleep even with sleep aids that Mom had suggested and woke up early. She let Vanessa sleep in a little since they had talked late into the night. The trip with midtown traffic took over half an hour to get to the theatre. Both Vanessa and Genevieve were in a sort of dreamland as the limo pulled up to the theatre's rear door.

A woman waiting for them came out when she saw the limo pull up. '"Hello, I am Dana Biggs, Ron's assistant. It is great to meet you. Ron has told me all about you, Genevieve. We are excited to have you here and really looking forward to working with you." She had on a navy blue suit and white blouse and medium flowing blonde hair, about 5'11", rather attractive and very efficient.

"Thank you, Ms. Biggs, I am truly thrilled to be here," Genevieve responded.

"Please call me Dana," she answered, trying to put them at ease.

She personified business and was very friendly at the same time. "How did you like the script," she asked Genevieve.

"Oh, I just loved it. It was familiar. Mr. Bannister told me about it the last time we talked." Dana smiled at her for calling Ron "Mister Bannister." Then she remembered that Genevieve was barely nineteen. She held out her hand to Vanessa. "I just love the music too—it is so bouncy and vivacious," Genevieve added. Dana obviously enjoyed her response.

"Great, I think from what he has told me, from meeting you," she emphasized. "He has picked a winner. I think you will do fine."

Vanessa put her arm around Genevieve's waist and squeezed a little to show her approval and how proud she was. Dana led them to the dressing room. Genevieve's eyes popped open. Vanessa was also surprised; the dressing room was huge. "Fit for a star!" Mom exclaimed. Dana smiled. It had a private bath, convertible sofa, easy chairs, fridge, small dining table, four chairs, micro and the largest mirror and bureau they ever saw, covered with scads of makeup. The entire main area was richly carpeted except for under the table. Genevieve stood in front of the three-way mirror for a full look at herself. *One could easily get accustomed to this*, she thought.

"Wow!" Mom blurted out.

Dana interrupted their daydream "How about this for wardrobe choices?" she exclaimed, opening four large doors of a wardrobe closet measuring about fourteen feet wide with pull out clothes poles. A selection of gowns, dresses, skirts, slacks, blouses, hats, shoes, coats, and accessories appeared like magic. "Wow," said Vanessa. "I have to convince your father to put one of those in our house," and the women all laughed.

Genevieve soaked it all in with her mind and eyes. "I thought this room would be special but I had no idea. It surely beats my high school and college accommodations," she added.

"Glad you like it," Dana continued. "As a suggestion perhaps you should start rehearsing with one of these everyday-type dresses for the opening scene out in front of the high school. That way you will get the real feeling of the play—a dress rehearsal."

"All right," Genevieve responded, and excitedly started to choose something. "I will leave you two for a while and have Sadie Wissman, our makeup specialist, prepare you. Sort of a dress rehearsal you might say. So the next time I see you, you will *be* Sally," she emphasized. "I can't wait to see how you look, but I *know* you will look great. Any questions right now?"

Both Genevieve and Vanessa just shook their heads. "Thank you, Dana," Vanessa responded as Genevieve became immersed in her preparation. Dana hugged her and left to find Sadie. Mom silently hugged her also, like she never hugged her before. Genevieve plopped on the sofa put her head back and let out the biggest sigh of her life as if she had held it in for all of her 18 plus years. Mom plopped down next to her and did a close facsimile. A knock on the door brought them back to earth and Sadie Wissman entered.

"All right, young lady, let's get you ready," she cheerfully announced with a smile. Genevieve and Vanessa, although still excited, were put at ease by this very personable woman.

Dana returned and was pleased with Genevieve's appearance. She then led them through the backstage corridors to the edge of the stage. Genevieve looked out into the semi-dark theatre. There were five people: three men and two women in the first two rows. She thought they might be directors, choreographers, and the like. Several people were on stage, men and women dressed in 50s clothing, and more came in behind her, laughing, smiling, and bidding her good morning. The pianist was warming up. Then she saw Bobby Nelson, her co-star playing Denny, the lead. He started warming up by singing "Hip hop is here to stay." She was thrilled to be here and realized how nervous she was. She had never been this close to an accomplished star. She was mesmerized—to say the least—and momentarily overwhelmed as she just stared at him.

Dana took notice and kindly put her arm around her. "I can imagine it is all rather overwhelming at first, Genevieve. I know you will be fine once you get out there and let yourself go. You will be fine," she repeated. "Go out there and show everyone a new star is born." She squeezed her hand and gave her a little nudge. Vanessa threw her a kiss and sat with Dana and the others, who introduced themselves.

Genevieve did a sort of half skip and strolled toward Bobby. He was resplendent in his black suit and pink shirt and greased black hair leading to a perfect ducktail. He saw her coming out of the off stage shadows and did a double take. She was absolutely a beautiful Sally in her white dress. It was the Sewanhaka High School dance scene. Bobby, as Denny, smiles broadly and puts out his hand. Genevieve, as Sally, takes it and they start dancing to the pianist's rendition of Beautiful Moon. They looked perfect together. Genevieve was in seventh heaven. She wanted to stay transfixed in this position forever. Vanessa's eyes were tearful, as only a mother's can be, as she tapped her feet and clapped her hands to the music. It took her a while to realize that Ron Bannister had quietly joined them. "Oh, Mr. Bannister, I did not hear you," she whispered.

"Sorry to surprise you. I just could not bring myself to interfere with your very special moment. After all it is rare, indeed, that a mom gets to see, firsthand and up-close, her daughter rehearse the lead in a Broadway play" he smiled broadly.

"I will say, it is just—well, just unbelievable. I cannot express to you how much Genevieve, myself, and Gene appreciate the opportunity you have given her." She grasped his hand in gratitude.

"Vanessa, believe me, I am thankful myself. It is not every day or even every year a talent such as Genevieve is discovered. New talent is needed to keep show business vibrant, especially, to keep patrons returning to the theatre," he said with conviction.

Ron and Dana sat with Vanessa as they watched the choreographer coach and explain changes and adjustments to the performers. Genevieve adapted well. The lawn scene brought the best of Genevieve to the forefront. Her voice sparkled as she sang to Bobby Nelson, "My eyes are red crying over you. Why do I wait? I am crazy over you. Why am I crazy for you? Why oh why. I cannot let you go—it is hopeless you see."

Ron turned to Vanessa. "She is marvelous. She will be great, I am sure. See you later—enjoy the condo." He left the theatre once he was sure the summer production was in good hands. In a week or so Genevieve would be a new star on Broadway. Dana sat with Vanessa and squeezed her hand for support as the rehearsal continued from scene to scene. Genevieve needed only minor prompting as she had, with Vanessa's assistance, rehearsed the script well. Her voice and stage presence, however, was unmistakably brilliant. Mom took some notes to play the script out at the condo so Genevieve would be 100% perfect tomorrow. In a week this would be for real.

Both women were still flush with excitement as the limo took them back to the condo. "Driver, please stop a few blocks early so we can walk. Is that O.K. with you, Mom?"

"Sure honey. It is a gorgeous day—in more ways than one," Vanessa agreed. The driver let them off at 60th and

Lexington with Bloomingdale's on the corner. They gushed at the beautiful clothes on the window manikins but decided to peruse the store on an off day, as Genevieve just wanted to take a nice stroll back to the condo. They walked down 59th to Fifth and to the Condo across from Central Park's entrance. "We should stroll the park occasionally," Mom suggested. "It will be much larger and busier than the parks at home."

"I would like that," Genevieve agreed.

"But we still need to rehearse and polish your lines and delivery. Maybe in two weeks or so we can plan some walks in the park," Mom added and she put her arm inside Genevieve's as they made the turn to the condo's entrance.

"O.K., slave driver. I get it. You are my coach and my honest and best critic too," said Genevieve, snuggling up to her.

When they entered the unit, Vanessa noticed the answering machine flashing. "It's your father," she said, dialing home.

"Hello there," he answered cheerfully. "How did today go and what did you do? I want to hear everything. My night is clear, so fire away," Gene said excitedly in one breath.

She filled him in as completely as she could. It must have taken her a good half hour. He listened intently, almost without interruption. "Wow what a day. I wish I was there to see all that," he added.

"Well—you will, you will," she added emphatically.

"That is what I was going to tell you," he responded. "I have wrangled a week's vacation starting next week so you and I can hold hands while we watch our star perform."

"Wonderful," she gushed. "I will get Genevieve and you can tell her yourself. She will be so happy."

Genevieve quickly walked to the phone, wrapped in robe after her quick shower and shampoo. "Hi, Dad," she said in her perkiest of tones. She told him firsthand about her excitement and nervousness when she came face to face with Bobby Nelson and began the duet.

"He was probably more nervous to meet you than you him," said Gene. "With all that, you still did well. That's my girl—my bright star. I knew you would knock them dead, as they say on Broadway."

She laughed and added, "Well, I did flub some lines but Mom will work with me and it will be even better tomorrow."

He laughed, "I am sure you will fix that sweetheart."

She bid him good evening so she could dry her hair and gave the phone back to Mom.

"Hi, Gene. When do you think you can get here?"

"I will try for Thursday, if I can arrange it. That way maybe I can see two rehearsals and we can do the town, so to speak, together before she needs her sleep for the real thing."

"You and I can also do the town together as she sleeps," Vanessa responded.

He laughed, "Of course, you bet. Just like the old days," and they both laughed.

"Great. I can hardly wait to give you a big hug and show you our digs here."

"I want to see the digs but I sure want some hugs. It is a bit lonely without you."

She planted a big kiss over the phone. "Oh, Gene it is so exciting here. Everything and anything. It's like a make believe world and we are in it."

"Well keep your feet and Genevieve's feet on the ground till I get there so I can fly with you to wherever we want to go. I certainly do not want to chase you somewhere in outer space," he said, and they both laughed.

"Thanks. You will keep us grounded. We need that." They gave goodbye phone kisses.

The rest of the week flew by and Genevieve became very accomplished and comfortable in the role. Having both Mom and then Dad with her was a big assist. They all had a marvelous several days together. Quickly, Genevieve's Saturday night opening performance was only hours away. Arm in arm with Genevieve, they walked beautiful Central Park. Gene and Vanessa felt like shouting to all they saw,

"This is Genevieve Carter, the beautiful budding Broadway star—our daughter."

Genevieve held on to them tightly, warning them not to. They stopped at the zoo and became immersed in the animals and children frolicking, laughing and shouting with joy.

Gene became very reflective "It all went so fast. It feels like yesterday."

"What does?" Vanessa asked.

"Looking at these little kids," he said, turning to Genevieve. "I remember you at that age. Now look at you."

"Oh Daddy." She buried her head alternately in both their shoulders.

"You said 'Daddy,' not Dad. Was that on purpose?" He smiled.

"No—it was automatic. It just came out that way. With you guys I can't act." They laughed and hugged each other.

The flower bouquet was arguably the most beautiful they had ever seen, and definitely the largest. The doorman brought it up to the condo after their return from the park.

"Wow, what is this?" Dad asked.

"A bouquet," Vanessa answered.

"I know. But from who? I guess I should check the card, or maybe not." He started to reach for it, but stopped and said, "It is obviously for you kiddo—so check it out." She had already started to open the envelope. It read: "Here's to you, Genevieve. Break a leg. Barry."

"That is nice—Barry Nelson, an accomplished star, thought enough to send you flowers," Vanessa said as she put her arm around her daughter.

"He has really been great, giving me suggestions, and he is so easy to work with," she said, wiping a tear from her eye. "Mom and Dad, I think I will take a short nap. Can you wake me in an hour or so? Mom, a light dinner around 4:30 would be good. Dana told me the limo will pick us up around 6:00."

"O.K., Sweetie, rest up" they almost responded together. As

Genevieve headed to her bedroom, the couple hugged and then plopped onto the couch themselves for a short nap, both thinking about their wonderful daughter and still wondering if this was real or just a dream.

The limo came at 5:55. It was no dream. They settled into the specially equipped Lincoln, and Genevieve closed her eyes to try and relax, but it was a losing battle. She managed to get only about fifteen minutes of sleep. The trip took a while in Saturday evening traffic. The driver called Dana about fifteen minutes before their estimated time of arrival and she met them at the business entrance. They noticed quite a line forming on 48th street next to the theatre. The crowd was trying for box office tickets, but only a few were probably available. The crowd spotted the limo pulling up. Seeing Genevieve, some shouted, "She must be in the play. She's a beauty." Genevieve and Vanessa smiled.

"They sure are perceptive," Gene agreed.

In the dressing room, there was another large flower bouquet. The card read, "To Genevieve. Just be you and you will be great. R.B."

"Wow," Vanessa gushed.

"He must have spent a fortune on these" Gene added.

"Absolutely gorgeous." Genevieve shook her head in amazement.

Dana knocked and came in. "Hi. Well, Genevieve, how are you on this eventful evening?"

Genevieve took a deep breath. "I have to admit I have some goose bumps."

"We will make sure to have Sadie use extra makeup to cover them."

They laughed, which somewhat relieved Genevieve.

Dana gave Vanessa and Gene special guest tickets for front row center and handed them vouchers for refreshments. She then put her arm around Genevieve's waist to encourage her "You will be fine—I've got lots of money on you," she kibitzed.

"I will help Genevieve get started," Dana added.

"Good idea," Vanessa said, and motioned to Gene to leave just as they heard a knock at the door. He opened it for Ron Bannister.

"Hello, there. The gang's all here, I see," he quipped. "I arrived here just in time. The best of wishes, Genevieve. You won't need luck—you have the talent. Just think of it as rehearsal and concentrate on your fellow performers on stage. Forget about the rest of the theater. Make believe it is empty and you are playing to your colleagues on stage."

"Very good advice," Dad said, nodding his head. They kissed her again and gave big hugs. Genevieve blew them kisses as they left and started to get ready for the rest of her life.

What would be a capacity audience began to arrive in force after 7. The orchestra began tuning up their instruments. Gene and Vanessa decided on champagne cocktails to celebrate and calm their nerves if that were possible. They decided not to go for two as it might put them in overdrive and they didn't want to risk that. So what better than to tightly hold each other's hand and squeeze the seat handle with their other hand until it begged for mercy or their hands gave out? At around 7:45 Ron and Dana joined them. "She's fine—she will be great," he assured them, and they all settled in.

The music started, the curtain rose, and the first scene unfolds before them. Genevieve and her actress friends came onto the stage walking to the small group of students milling around. The audience claps. Barry Nelson enters from stage right as the audience claps loudly, recognizing him. The two actors eyes locked. She excuses herself from her friends and they walk toward each other. They link arms and begin a slow dance. Genevieve begins the song, "Where have you been? I have missed you terribly. Where oh where have you been" and a career is launched.

## Chapter 8

# DAVID KELSEY DISCOVERED

The Long Island, New York summer began hot and humid. School had ended two weeks before, and to keep busy, David, had in advance contacted neighbors as well as acquaintances of his parents to mow lawns, weed gardens, paint, babysit, or whatever he could do to keep busy and earn some money. It helped that he had a major goal in mind. In late summer, the New York Marauders were holding a baseball camp for teens in Clear Beach, Florida. His parents wanted him to have this marvelous opportunity. They realized he had what appeared to be a very special talent. They felt that his working constructively this summer to earn even a small portion of the cost to go to the camp would help him appreciate the opportunity even more.

For diversion, relaxation, and to keep his skills sharp he practiced when he could with a group of friends at county ball fields, as well as played in an organized YMCA league twice a week.

It was the Red Wings versus the Blue Devils. The Red Wings were in first place after a 4-0 start, thanks in major part to David's torrid batting. The Blue Devils, at 3-1, were tied for second place in the eight team league. This would be their first meeting of the summer. David's friends, George Greenly and Wally Proka, were with the Blue Devils. All in all, 15 games were scheduled, then the playoffs. Eric Greenwaite, a former professional ballplayer, had developed the very ambitious schedule. He had a couple of short visits to the "big show" and played over ten years as a Triple A major league wannabe. He had taken a real liking to David immediately, recognizing David's talent as well as seeing a bit of himself as a boy, which he readily admitted.

David's mom, Helen, drove David, Stan Mars, and Gene Urman to the game scheduled to start at 4. They were due at the field by 2:30 for batting and fielding practice. "I have to pick up your sister around 3:30. I'll try to be back by the start of the game," she said, half turning to the guys as she entered the park.

"O.K., Mom. You and Lauren can be our cheering section, so yell loud," responded David.

"Yeah," added Stan. "I guess we won't have standing room only," and they all laughed as 16 year old boys can. So did Helen, marveling in their joy and spirited personalities.

"Coach is here already," noticed Stan.

"He is always early so that he has everything ready for us," added David.

"You boys are fortunate to have Mr. Greenwaite as your coach. He is a fine man, and very interested in you," added Mom. She stopped the car and let them out, waving to the coach, who waved back. Other cars were coming in and a few boys who lived close to the park were arriving on bicycles.

"Hi, guys we have a tough one today," said Coach Greenwaite. "The Blue Devils have won their last two by 8 and 9 runs. They were really smacking the ball around and getting good pitching."

"Don't worry, Coach, we will teach them a lesson today," Gene wisecracked back.

"Yeah, they will finally play a *real* team," blurted out Stan.

David laughed, and then offered, "I think we have a better team but George and Wally are good bats. We have to pitch them real smart or they will make us pay."

"David's right, guys. They will be very aggressive early to get a lead, so we need to be on our toes right from the start," added the coach.

Tony Cirano, the Red Wings #2 pitcher, was scheduled this day and he started his warm up under the coach's watchful eye. Coach was very careful concerning his young pitchers, allowing them to throw only five or six innings, depending on the pitch count, in order to protect their arms. As a further precaution, no curve balls or screwballs were allowed in the league.

By now, players from both teams were almost all on the field or putting on their spikes to take batting and fielding practice. Coach Greenwaite and Coach Brown of the Devils shook hands and engaged in conversation while their pitchers warmed up and the guys assumed their respective positions next to each other in practice. The game would start within the next half hour. David assumed his first base position alongside his school friend, George Greenly. They alternated fielding batting practice grounders and throwing to their respective shortstops, second and third basemen, and catchers.

Mr. Carver, an assistant coach, was hitting the ball.

"How's it going, Dave," George asked.

"Great! How's it going with you, George?" Dave responded

"Real good. We're playing super now. I think your undefeated season will be over tonight, old buddy," George chided, laughing.

"We will see about that, Georgie. We will see about that," replied Dave, and both boys laughed good-naturedly. As competitive as they were, they were good friends to the core.

Game time. Let the balls fly and the fun begin. After four innings, the Devils led 5-0 as a couple of key hits, three bases on balls, and two Red Wing errors opened the gates. Coach Greenwaite was not pleased, and encouraged the boys to settle down and not be anxious at bat. He urged them to take more pitches to make their opponent's pitcher work harder. David, in his first two at bats, was impatient, trying to tie the game on one swing. He struck out, then popped out with two on base, shaking his head all the way back to the bench. The Wings, as the visitors, were up at the top of the 6th. Stan Mars led off with a double. The Wings right fielder singled him home. Then David, batting fourth, strode to the plate. After the last at bat Coach Eric suggested he be more patient: that he wait for the right pitch and just try to meet, not kill, the ball, as it is how you make contact with the pitch that will provide the result and not over swinging. David of course, knew that in his head, but he let his emotions get the better of him. He heard his mom and now his dad, Fred, yelling for him to get a hit, and he looked up to the stands and smiled at them. He took what he thought was a high pitch but the umpire called it a strike. He breathed deeply, took some practice swings and watched two balls wide of the plate. One was darn close to a strike as the umpire briefly hesitated. David figured that squared him with the umpire and now it was up to him. He stepped out and took a couple of practice swings. The umpire swept off the plate and the catcher called time and ran out to his pitcher to talk things over.

David stepped back in. The pitch was knee-high, right down the middle. Certainly not where the pitcher and catcher wanted it. It never made the mitt as it sailed well over the 300-foot right field fence. Devils 5, Wings 3. The score remained 5-3 until the last of the 7th when the Devils scored twice. In the top of the 8th David was slated to hit fourth. A talented lefty, Chad Robbins, also heading for Florida summer baseball camp with David, was in relief for the Devils. He had held the Wings scoreless for the last two innings. Up first for the Wings, Stan Mars flied to left and went dejectedly back to the bench. The Wings were down to their last four outs, losing 7-3. Gene Urman got his second single. Al Hastings smacked it to left, on the line. Wally Proka, also going to baseball camp in Florida, was playing left. He made a spectacular backhand grab in the corner and an excellent throw to third, preventing Gene from scoring. David stepped in for his fourth at bat. At

RICHARD F. MANGES

this point the Wings had been held to only six hits and hit into two double plays.

The Devils manager called a conference at the mound. The ump walked toward the mound to hurry things up as David stood limbering up at the plate. In addition to the team and some other Red Wing parents, Mom and Dad were loudly cheering him on. He wondered if this was a small sample of what the big leagues, if he ever got there, would be like. He quickly came back to reality. He remembered Coach Eric's advice to just meet the ball, not to try and overpower it. Just make good contact. Robbins was tough on lefties with the natural talent to produce a very live fastball. The previous batters were right-handed. David was fooled by two quick strikes, as there was a lot of movement on his pitches. David then fouled off three straight, only one of which he was sure was a strike. He could not take any chances. He stepped out as Chad walked to the rear of the mound and rubbed up the ball. David asked the ump to use a new ball. Even though there was no chance, in this league, of doctoring up the ball in use, he would feel more comfortable with a new one: an intelligent decision by a sixteen year old as a new ball is less controllable by the pitcher. Chad Robbins pumped three times, kicked high, and fired. The ball went out to left center like a cannon shot, slammed off the wall about one foot short of going over, bouncing beyond the left fielder's reach. Devils 7, Wings 5, as David cruised into second. Chad just stared, shaking his head wondering how David could hit that ball so hard. That's how the game ended.

Ultimately, the Wings were summer champions, finishing 11-4, and the Devils were third with a 9-6 record. Next stop for David and friends—New York Marauders summer camp in Clear Beach, Florida.

The boys gathered with their parents at LaGuardia Airport, their excitement at a fever pitch. Chad, David, Stan and Wally hugged their folks and entered the 727's passageway. David was the only experienced flyer, and he had been trying to explain how the take off and landing felt. The guys were nervous about it all.

"I wonder who we'll meet at camp and who our coaches will be," David said at liftoff. Chad, Stan's and Wally's knuckles turned white from squeezing the armrests, then they all said "Wow" as the plane went airborne. David, smiling at their amazement, had the aisle seat across from the three. Their parents had coordinated so they would sit together. It helped the first time fliers.

"I guess they are all retired," Wally managed to blurt out after the powerful thrust of the 727's takeoff passed.

"Naturally," Chad added, "It is summer and active players are still with their teams. Duh," he added.

They all laughed good-naturedly.

"Blame it on the blood rushing through his noggin at take off," David remarked, and they laughed again. "Coach Eric said they would work us hard but feed us, good and the minute we hit the sack we will be out like a light."

"I like the food part and the sack part," laughed Stan. After a while they all settled down to watch a movie, then had lunch and caught some shuteye. They would arrive at Clear Beach well before dinner.

Al Redford, the head coach of the practice facility and a retired Marauder outfielder of 15 years, met them at the airport with an excellent career record including 302 homers and a .309 batting average. He enjoyed working with young players hoping, someday, to coach a star.

"Wow, Al Redford," they whispered when they saw him. They all shook his strong right hand vigorously.

"Hi guys—you are all from Long Island—right?" he asked.

"Right. Home of the Marauders," Stan answered. "It sure is great to see Marauder fans among you guys. Follow me and I'll get you set up at the barracks. Dinner is at 5:30. Is anyone hungry now?" he asked.

"We are starved," they kind of answered in unison.

"O.K. Let's stop at a Big Burger for you guys, since it will be about two or so hours until dinner at the camp."

"Great!" responded David, who was feeling very comfortable with the ex major-leaguer.

He could hardly believe all this was happening. Wally, Stan, and Chad were just starry-eyed with big grins and let David do most of the talking. Al asked them a lot of questions about their playing and what their ambitions were. They all expressed their wish to play in the big leagues and hoped their summer experiences here in Florida would help them.

Al was realistic. "Myself and my coaches will help you all we can, give you pointers, and try to correct what needs to be corrected. Each person, though, has to be endowed with natural talent that can be sharpened enough to meet that certain standard which will allow them to compete on a professional level. Hopefully all of you will have that natural talent so that we can help you achieve your goals."

"Wow—nobody ever explained it like that before," Stan exclaimed. Wally sat there transfixed. Chad almost swallowed his big bite from the burger whole trying to say something. David gave him two hard slaps on the back so he wouldn't choke.

"I hope I didn't upset you, Chad," Al apologized. David just motioned a no with his hand as Chad's choking subsided.

"I guess he thought it would be all fun and games," David offered.

Chad managed to say, "I just figured we would go out and play, then rest and whatever happens, happens. I just want to have fun—that's all."

"Don't misunderstand," Al responded. "I want you to have fun. Just be serious about your performance if you want us to evaluate your results. If you do have sufficient talent for us to evaluate and help you achieve a higher standard, it will be to your benefit as well as the Marauder's benefit. But, try to have fun, in any event."

"Thanks Coach. That was a great explanation," David responded, and all the guys agreed, gulping the rest of their food like the normal teenagers they were—future major leaguers or not.

The morning drill started at 7, so wake up was 5:30 and chow started at 6:00. "I hope I can handle these hours," Chad groaned.

"Me too," Wally stretched and yawned.

Chad and Stan just sat there while David rubbed his eyes, yawned and blurted out "Get used to it. We will be here two weeks." They all just sat at the edge of their bunks, stretched, did some exercises and slowly got dressed. David laughed, "We must look like we are in slow motion. Some group of athletes we are."

"I guess we'll improve," Wally contributed.

"Yeah, but we had better knock off watching TV until midnight or we will look like zombies on the field," Chad added.

"Amen to that," emphasized Stan, yawning twice more and they finally, in slow motion, left for the dining hall with their spikes and mitts in tow. They intermingled with other boys from various locations around the U.S. A few came from Alaska, Hawaii and the Islands as baseball was extremely popular in the Western hemisphere, and the Marauders had scouts following high school baseball wherever prospects played.

Al, Harry Grant, and Ernie Harvel, also retired Marauders, were the head coaches with several assistants who put all the participants through their paces. Calisthenics was the first order of business, to limber up the bodies, then running, then batting and fielding practice. They were each assigned teams designated by color. Actual games would start around 9 and they would try to finish by 1, at the latest, for lunch, and to avoid the hottest part of the Florida day. Evening practice would include instruction specific to what each player wanted, or what the coaches recommended after viewing the abilities, strengths, and weaknesses of each boy. Evening games would begin later in the week when the boys were in a more advanced condition and was, of course, optional, depending on the boy.

Every week throughout the summer a new group of boys would arrive to replace those that left. They were starry-eyed to be working with and getting instruction from former major leaguers and in a very short time begin practicing and actually playing games on fields used by former as well as active minor and major leaguers during spring training.

To avoid taxing the young arms of the would-be pitchers, the coaches limited the throwing of curves and screwballs, as well as limiting the number of pitches thrown. Coaches pitched batting practice themselves. Early on, Al noticed David during batting practice. When he was busy elsewhere he had Harry and or Ernie watch him closely and take notes. Two days into workouts and batting practice, they compared notes over lunch. "He sure looks like a natural," offered Ernie, a former infielder.

"I agree," added Harry, who played part of three years with the Marauders and had additional major league service elsewhere. "He can read pitches and has very quick hands."

"You are both thinking like me," Al nodded. "He looks like a gamer. He needs some work; he is only sixteen, after all—but he is better than most I have seen at his age."

"What's next?" asked Ernie.

"Well, we must not ignore everyone else for the Marauders' sake—that is our job. But, and I mean but, let's keep a very, and I mean *very*, close eye on David Kelsey. When I spell one of the kids on the mound, I will put a little heat on my serves and add some curves in the mix. If he hits me, I can call Ron. If he continues to mash our pitches, let's see how he hits Ron. What do you guys think?"

They agreed, and Al picked up the phone to call Ron Millman, a former major league pitcher with a 209-126 record and a 3.77 career earned run average. Al asked him to assist in pitching batting practice this evening and beyond, if necessary.

Ernie added a profound observation: "It will not be the first time a phenom has been discovered and signed. Remember that 16 year old Iowa farm boy," he chuckled.

"Yeah, but that was over 70 years ago, I believe," added Harry.

"So what? Talent is talent. That hasn't changed in 70 years," chimed in Ernie, and they all agreed.

Ron Millman answered the phone. "Hi, Al—what's up, old buddy?"

"Ron, we may have a prodigy in camp now. His name is David Kelsey, and would you believe he's from Long Island, the Marauder's backyard. He will be the first baseman on Team C."

"How about that," Ron responded. "How can I help?"

"This will be a test of sorts. I want to see how he does with REAL (emphasis on the real) pitching rather than our batting practice variety. Mix up your pitches. No need to exceed 90 mph."

Ron laughed, "I don't think I can anymore. I wouldn't want to chance throwing out my arm. Who knows, I may try for a comeback." They both had a good laugh over that.

"Can you make it," Al was hoping.

"Sure."

"Great, see you at eight or so tomorrow morning so you can warm up a bit."

"I may need more than a bit," he laughed.

Al turned to Ernie and Harry. "He'll be here. He wouldn't miss it for the world—he's a real trooper."

"That's great" they said nearly in unison, excited to perhaps witness a prodigy in the making. They decided together to have Ron appear without any fanfare, which could make the boys nervous and affect their experiment with David.

It was a beautiful Tuesday evening in Clear Beach. The temperature hovered around 83 degrees as the sun began to disappear and the lights were turned on. The guys noticed a different coach warming up in the bullpen. "Who's that?" they asked each other and they all shrugged their shoulders. Ron was now almost 44. He retired about 7 years ago when most of them were 9 or 10.

Someone asked Al. "Why, that's Ron Millman. He's going to do some pitching for both sides to give your pitchers a rest. He retired when you guys were still in diapers," Al exaggerated. They laughed and asked who he played for. "The Browns who are now the Orioles, the Senators who are now the Twins, and the Braves who are now the . . ." he hesitated. "the Braves." The boys looked at each other, more than a trifle confused, and walked away shaking their heads. Al laughed, as did Ernie, who had heard most of the conversation.

Several minutes, later after Ron finished warming up, Al walked past Wally and David. "Coach, the guys told us the pitcher warming up was in the majors. How will he pitch to us? We want to hit the ball," said Wally. Al hesitated at first, then responded, "Don't worry, Wally, he will go easy on you guys." Al put a very slight emphasis on the word "you" so not to give the plan away.

The teams were named one and two. George and Wally were on team one and David on team two. Chad would be pitching for team one after Ron Millman did his thing. David batted fourth in the first inning, a decision that Al made after three days of observation. Ron started throwing much like Al, Harry, and Ernie did in practice: in the 70mph range with an occasional 80mph and all straight balls, the equivalent to a major league changeup. They went down 1-2-3 as did team two. Team one came up again in the second inning and managed a single and that runner was stranded. Ron was surprised he allowed a hit—but he remembered he was supposed to, except when pitching to David Kelsey.

David led off the second for team 2. Ron was prepared to mix up his pitches—no plain soft straight balls for this guy. Let's see what he was made of. Ron looked him over carefully. He was almost 6 foot and looked to be about 175 lbs and still growing. David felt nervous after learning that Ron was a very good former major league pitcher. He forced himself to concentrate. Ron threw a dandy curve that David let go by. It was a ball, just off the plate. *Good eye*, Ron thought. The young catcher was surprised at the curve and it went to the backstop. Ron called to him and told him he would flick his glove a certain way for a curve, another for a change, and another for a slider. The poor kid was confused. As a high school catcher, he never had so many pitches to handle. Ron thought that was a weakness with this masquerade. He would probably be found out after this at bat, so he decided to throw some curves to other hitters once in a while also—just slower.

David had been carefully observing Ron's pitching since the first inning. Ron had not expected David's keen baseball intellect, just his talent. David's intellect allowed him to notice the difference in speed between the next pitch, a fastball around 90 for a strike, and the curve and, more importantly, the slower speed Ron was pitching, so far, to the previous hitters. He made a mental note to react more quickly.

Ron then showed him a real major league move—a slow nickel curve on the outside corner that created a breeze in the warm Florida night as David overswung, expecting another 90mph plus fastball. He almost lost his balance on the over swing and called a timeout to regain his composure. Ron had delivered that pitch with a 45-degree arm angle and had David completely fooled as it nipped the corner. Welcome to big league pitching. He stepped out again and took a deep breath. He was trying now to interrupt Ron's rhythm, which didn't, after all the hundreds of major leaguers that tried the same thing. Pitch number four was an 88 mph fastball right down the middle, and David could not catch up. He sat down feeling humiliated. He learned something however—with a *real* pitcher, don't sit on a certain pitch. Ron finished the second inning getting six straight outs, then he sat down so that the young pitchers could do their thing.

Al had Ron come back in the top of the fifth. David would be hitting in the last of the fifth. With one out, David came to bat determined to battle this guy. His previous at bat produced a major league double off the right center wall about 390 feet. Pitch one was an inside fastball and David was able to check his swing. Pitch two was a 70 mph changeup and David lined it foul to right. Ron had him swinging early. Pitch 3 was a curve in on his hands. David adjusted his swing. to Ron's surprise, and lined it just foul, again to right. *This boy does have some acumen and coordination*, he thought. Pitch 4 was a 90 mph fastball and David fouled it back. Al was watching intently. Pitch 5 was a diving sinker which David topped foul at the plate. It was probably ball 1 but he reacted quickly to it. Ron was amazed at his adjusting from the first at bat. This kid has something special all right. That's what Al and Co. were thinking about this time in their respective dugouts. Ron threw two fastballs just off the plate and was amazed that David didn't offer at them. He decided with the 3-2 count to blaze it right down the middle. David rocketed it to dead center. It was caught but it traveled over 400 feet. Al and staff saw what they wanted to see—a real talent. Still raw, but very, very trainable.

When he picked up his glove, David winked at Al and smiled. "I really enjoyed that battle coach."

Al sort of saluted him with a laugh and answered, "I thought you might Dave. For your information, so did I. So did I." To run this camp year after year it was surely satisfying to have at least one special player that could make the big show, and he felt he saw that in David. His coaches had been taking notice of all the boys and saw some really strong players in the mix, but none had impressed like David. Ron took a bit of a rest and let the student pitchers do their thing.

Ron took the mound for the fourth time, and David was up second with bases empty. David's keen eye earned him a 3-0 count advantage. This really impressed both Al and Ron, as they had spoken about David's patience and ball and strike recognition. Ron had purposely kept two of those pitches out of the strike zone. Then Ron zeroed in on pouring on the mustard, so to speak, and David fouled off five pitches. Ron walked to the back of the mound and rubbed up a new ball. Stan, Wally and Chad were all eyes as they saw their buddy battle a former major league pitcher. So did Al Redford. It did his heart good to see this battle. Ron pumped three times and fired his last fastball which, with the crack of the ash bat, flew out to deepest center over the head of the center fielder, or about 415 feet to the wall. David settled for a double—only the second hit off Ron. Stan, Wally, and Chad cheered, as did Al, Harry and Ernie. They had a prodigy to be sure. Ron walked off the mound having pitched more today than in several years. He wondered if the boy would have hit him nearly as well several years earlier. Still, he thought, he is quite the prospect; quite the prospect indeed.

Al continued the experiment, without Ron, for several days with he and his coaches pitching their hearts out to David and getting soundly knocked around, as David did not disappoint. Al decided to contact the Marauders Assistant General Manager, Harold Baker.

"Harold, we have a 16 year old in camp, David Kelsey, who is knocking the cover off the ball. I experimented and had Ron Millman pitch to him for several at bats and he held his own. He's pulverizing our pitches, to be sure. He may be the best prospect I have seen here at summer camp in the six years I have been here."

"O.K., Al, he sounds like a winner. I will be down late tonight and spend some time with you." Harold Baker was not disappointed as he observed David over the course of three days just before David's stint at summer camp was coming to a close. David and the guys noticed this new person with the broad brimmed straw hat taking notes in the first row of seats, talking on and off to Al and the other coaches. "Who do you think he is?" Wally wondered.

"Could be a big wig of some sort," added Stan.

"Maybe he is a reporter for the newspaper," David offered.

"They use laptops, I think," Chad contributed.

"Anyway, whoever he is he sure likes being here. It has been three days, I think," David scratched his head.

"Yup," Wally added, and they went back to practicing, absorbed in the game.

At dinner, Al and Harold Baker conferred. "I agree, Al, he looks like a special prospect. I will let the boss know and we will go from there."

"Should we say anything to the kid?" Al asked.

"No, not until we talk to his parents. Give me their names and phone number. I tell you what; I will call Randy first, and we will go from there." He dialed his boss, General Manager Randy Cameron. "Randy, Al spotted what looks like a winner, David Kelsey, down here in camp. He's 16 and from Suffolk County, Long Island, would you believe? A lefty first baseman who tears covers off the ball and a better-than-average first baseman. A really mature kid. I have watched him the better part of three days now. I think we should contact his folks, Helen and Fred, to talk bonus, etc."

"O.K., Harold, I trust your and Al's judgment. When you come back we'll discuss an offer to his folks." Harold hung up and gave Al a thumbs up.

"Great." Al smiled. "Maybe we should speak to the boy. I think we should tell him something."

"Sure, I agree. Just tell him we were very pleased with his performance. Randy needs to call Mr. and Mrs. Kelsey first before we say anything else to David. He's only sixteen and they must agree to whatever we do."

Al responded, "You're correct—I guess I let my emotion get the better of me"

Al answered. "No problem. I can understand your enthusiasm. It's exciting. How often do we discover a prospect like this young fellow?"

"I haven't since being in charge down here," Al answered.

"Be ready for my call. I hope it will be what we all hope it will be," Harold responded, and they shook hands confirming their agreement.

Helen arrived home late in the afternoon after a day of socializing and lunch with her ladies' group. She checked her crock-pot to see how dinner was progressing. Fred would be home in about an hour plus, depending on traffic. She took her shoes off, eased into her slippers and walked into the bedroom to change into more comfortable clothes. She saw the answer machine blinking. "I wonder who that could be," she said to herself nonchalantly. She pressed the button to play the message.

"Hello, Mr. and Mrs. Kelsey. This is General Manager Randy Cameron of the New York Marauders major league baseball club. I would like to meet with you concerning your son, David. As you know he just spent some time with our summer camp for youth in Florida. Our staff there evaluates the youth to determine the possibility of talent to be considered worthy of consideration. David is definitely worthy of consideration. My staff, whom I consider excellent, as well as my assistant, who flew down to observe him, consider David *very* worthy. Please call me at my New York office, 212-999-8888, as soon as you are able. I am looking forward to meeting with you and meeting David.

Thank you."

She was thrilled and listened again to make sure she heard what she heard. She turned the crock-pot off when she heard Fred pull into the garage. He came into the house. "Sit down honey, I have some special news to tell you but I'll let Mr. Cameron do it. He can explain it much better than I, much, much better in fact."

"Mr. Cameron?" Who is Mr. Cameron?" he asked with a puzzled expression. She pulled up a desk chair and pressed the magic button. Their lives and David's would never be the same after that.

The flight seemed long. All four boys were sorry to see their time fly by and for the summer to be over. Their Florida experience was something to treasure for the rest of their lives. After a while, they tried to doze off and eventually succeeded. David thought about some of his great at bats against Ron Millman. His imagination had him in a New York Marauders' uniform, at bat in a crucial situation, and then he dozed off. The next thing he felt was Stan shaking him. "Wake up, Dave. We are about to land."

"Fasten seat belts," came over the loudspeaker. David yawned, sat up and followed the announcement. Wally laughed, "Boy you must have had some dream. You had a big smile on that mug of yours since the Carolinas. Care to clue us in on what you were dreaming, Davey?"

David gave them a big smile. "It was a grand slam, guys." They looked at each other and just shrugged their shoulders.

Fred and Helen met David as he came through the tunnel. They exchanged greetings with Wally, Stan, and George, then led David to a chair and began talking to him very excitedly. In a matter of only a few minutes, David smiled as wide as a home plate. In a matter of seconds the three Kelseys were hugging and kissing and being observed by his friends and their parents who greeted them, although a good deal more conservatively, as well as the rest of the departing passengers and their greeters. From that moment on the Kelseys were in a different universe.

# Chapter 9

# VICTORIA MAGNUSON IN HIGH SCHOOL

The lazy hazy days of summer were fading fast. Victoria and her friends, Laurie and Anne, planned a full day at Henlopen Beach. Victoria drove her bright yellow Pontiac convertible that her Dad bought and had restored for her seventeenth birthday as a reward for having the third highest grade point average in NuWalk High. They lugged the beach cart, umbrella, cooler, and various other beach accessories to where they would be close to a lifeguard stand to chatter and flirt. Laurie was an excellent swimmer, so she would use that as a pretext for flirting, and ask why there weren't any female lifeguards at the stand, and how could she become a lifeguard. Of course, it always worked on the guys.

"There's an open spot right next to the stand," Anne observed.

"The tide's going out so we should be in great shape for blanket laying most of the day" added Vicky. "Let's ask the guards to help us plant the umbrella. That ought to get things started," she grinned. Of course that would give them a great entree to start a conversation and make it easier, if not obvious, to the guards.

"Can one of you guys help us sink this umbrella?" Laurie asked with a smile that could have blinded.

"Sure, be glad to help," the blondish guard answered, jumping off the stand in record time.

"Hurry up," the other guard called after him. "This beach is too busy for one pair of eyes to cover."

Laurie deduced he might have been jealous. She began gushing with small talk as he was pounding the umbrella stand into the sand.

"There, that should do it," he said grinning.

"Gee, thanks ever so much," she responded with a large grin.

"What's the water temp now?" she asked.

"Around 70 and it's only 10," he glanced at his watch.

"When's high tide?" She kept asking questions as his buddy on the bench kept looking over.

The guard appeared a bit spellbound by her, finally answering, "Around 2:30. I'm going off at 3. Can I buy you a soda or ice cream then?" he said in one breath.

"That's great. It will give us lots of time to sun and swim, and sure, I would like an ice cream about then," she added much to his pleasure, and flashing her pearly whites again.

"Super. It will give me lots of time to watch over you." He hesitated for a moment. "I mean, in the water," and he blushed a bit.

"Oh, I knew what you meant," and she turned to Anne and Vicky, both of whom were all eyes and ears, taking the flirtation in.

"My name is Doug. What's yours?"

"I'm Laurie," and she held out her hand. He took it gently and blushed again—visible under his tan. His buddy called him and he jogged back, turning and waving as he jogged back to the stand.

"He is cute," Vicky said. "Are you trying to get him to ask you for a date?"

"Why not?" Laurie asked. "We'll see how things progress. He sure seems like a clean cut guy and I don't have a steady right now."

"Go for it," Anne chimed in.

They spent the morning with Victoria and Anne mostly on the blanket and only briefly in the water. Laurie spent her time mostly gabbing with Doug, who ignored his chair partner unless Laurie was on her stomach trying to tan her back. After snacking on their lunch, they decided to go up to the boards for an ice cream and bathroom break. They each came out with small cones in deference to watching their figures. Laurie bought one for Doug and his partner, Adam, as sort of a peace offering since she had taken up so much of Doug's time. They told her this might be against the lifeguard rules, but she really didn't care. The girls gave her a tsk, tsk with their fingers but she just laughed and merrily skipped back onto the sand and to the lifeguard stand. Instead of going back themselves Vicky and Anne decided to walk the boards a bit while slowly munching on their cones.

As they walked further, Vicky thought she recognized a man, sitting on a bench with a woman and children. Then she figured it out: it was U.S. Representative Howard Woodson and his family. She turned to Anne. "Anne, If you don't mind I'll see you later. I want to talk to someone."

"Who?" Anne asked.

"I see Congressman Woodson up ahead. I want to ask him about being a page or having an internship next summer in Washington. I sure hope I can get one," she turned and said.

"Good luck," Anne nodded, heading back to the beach and Laurie's budding romance.

Vicky quickly moved in the Congressman's direction, thinking about how she would approach him. She took a deep breath, shook her head, fluffed her hair, and put on her best smile. Taking the direct approach that had always worked well for her, she used her sweetest voice and held out her hand. "Hello Congressman." Woodson and his wife looked both a bit surprised.

He stood up, smiled, and shook her hand. "Hello, young lady. I take it you're one of my constituents?" he responded and returned her smile. He was an attorney in his mid-forties, immensely popular, now serving his third term, and exceptionally popular with younger voters. He was a moderate politician.

"Well, I will be in October, just in time to vote for you," she smiled broadly.

"Well, thank you," he smiled back and turned to his wife. "This is my wife, Shelley."

"Hello, nice to meet you. Sorry, I forgot to introduce myself. I'm Victoria."

Mrs. Woodson smiled. "These are our children, Tommy and Jenna.

"Hello," Victoria smiled at the teens. Tommy had been staring at her since she walked up. Jenna nodded hello. She was more interested in getting down to the water where they were headed after organizing their things.

Vicky wisely decided to get to her point rather than risk being more of an annoyance she already was. "Congressman, I am very—and I mean *very*—interested in government," she emphasized. "To get to the point, I would like to work with the congress in some manner next year during vacations, as well as after I graduate from high school." He just stood there, not indicating any special emotion. Then Victoria took a deep breath and gave him the full treatment, realizing she had to make an exceptionally strong first impression. "I have been my class president through Junior and Senior High School for five straight years, and I have every intention of making it six straight this October. I also plan to major in Political Science at U of N.D."

She took a deep breath and waited. He stood staring at her for what seemed an eternity. Finally, he smiled broadly and shook his head. "That's a marvelous achievement young lady." He turned to his wife.

"I'll say, that's extraordinary," she corroborated.

"Do you realize you have held office as long as I have?" the Congressman exclaimed. "That's truly marvelous. You have a great head start on your career plans, that's for sure."

"I'll tell you what. I'll try and help you," he said, taking a card from his wallet. "Send me a letter and write a summary of what you have achieved through your school years, courses you've taken, and just a general autobiography. I may have a position for you myself. If not, I can possibly have one of my colleagues consider you. In any event I am very impressed, and will do my very best to give you that experience you seek. It's been a pleasure to meet you," he said, holding out his hand.

"Thank you, Congressman and Mrs. Woodson," she smiled. "I will do that. Thank you again and good luck in November. You will get my very first vote."

"Thanks," he smiled, and patted her on the shoulder. He and Mrs. Woodson bid her good day and had to hurry to catch their impatient teens, who were already fast walking to the beach.

Vicky took a deep breath, pleased with the outcome from this chance meeting on the beach. As she walked back to Ann and Laurie, her mind flew ahead, imagining what she would experience in the United States Congress. But for now, she was curious to see how Laurie's budding romance with Doug the lifeguard was progressing.

The rest of the summer flew by faster than usual, or so it seemed to Victoria. In her senior year she had several major goals in mind, just as she did every year. However, this year she had even more fervor to achieve. She wanted to be chosen Class Valedictorian. In order to do that, she would need to bring up her 3.88 class point average, as there were two students with slightly higher averages. The final choice of a college was a major reason to maintain her excellent point average. She was, even without raising her GPA, a shoo-in for the University of Northern Delaware. Her other goals were obtaining a page position in Congress—her big dream. And, of course, being class president for the sixth straight year, unheard of in her school, district, and state. Her eleventh grade government teacher, John Snyder, went the extra mile to research that for her. She spent much of her remaining vacation time composing her letter to Congressman Woodson. She would include letters of recommendation and testimonials from several of her teachers and her principal. She had Mr. Snyder's home address and phone number, so she contacted him.

"Vicky, I'll be pleased to help you out. I'll give my colleagues a heads up. I'm sure they will agree. Also, if you wish, I will gladly critique your letter, and it can't hurt to have another opinion also. So I will elicit at least a signed endorsement from my colleagues, even if they don't provide a letter, but I'm sure most will, as they all respect you."

"Thanks Mr. S. I'll see you in September."

It wasn't a slam dunk, but she won her sixth consecutive class president nomination by 237 votes, or about 18% of the 1309 votes cast, which was her lowest plurality of the six elections. She mainly attributed that to her reduced campaign effort. She was so intent on elevating her grade point average that she didn't put as much time into her campaign as she usually did. Raising her GPA would prove very difficult, since mathematically even a perfect 4.0 in her senior year would elevate her to 3.93. She would need both her rivals to falter a bit from 3.93 and 3.94 respectively, and that was very unlikely.

"Have you heard from Representative Woodson yet?" Mr. Snyder asked her as she entered class on October 30th.

"No, I haven't. It's only been a couple of weeks since he received my information. I'm sure he's very busy. I don't believe for one minute that he would not respond," she replied.

"I saw last week that he went on a special Asian trip. He's on the foreign affairs committee. I suppose that and his other responsibilities keep him hopping" Mr. Snyder offered.

"Would he delegate my request to an aide," she wondered.

"That's possible, of course. But having met you and talked to you about it—it's not like he just got your letter in the mail as something out of the blue. Besides, having met you he should realize you are a special person," he smiled.

She blushed a little showing she had humility despite much success. He thought that was a very good as well as mature trait.

Victoria decided not to remain idle waiting for a response from Congressman Woodson. As this would be her final class presidency she wanted to do something really special for her graduating class and she decided to get started on it early so it would come to fruition by June. She wanted to hold an event they would always remember. Of course there would always be the Senior Ball and a special production by the drama and music departments, but she was searching for that something really special that would be a knockout event. She asked for a special meeting with Mr. Snyder, Mrs. Phillips, the Assistant Chair of the Civics Department, and her Vice President, Stephan Coska.

They all thought it was a great idea, but were unsure what the event would actually be. "Let's just throw out ideas as they come to us," Mrs. Phillips suggested.

"O.K., that's a good idea," agreed Mr. Snyder.

Stephan started off. "How about an extra play in addition to the one planned for May?" he suggested.

Victoria assumed the role of scribe at the board. "O.K. an extra play is idea number 1."

"Perhaps an extra concert by the orchestra might go over well," Mrs. Phillips added.

"O.K.," Victoria said, adding that.

"I like both ideas," said Mr. Snyder, "but they will add considerable work for drama and music. They will have to agree. The drama department would have the most concern, rehearsing for another play."

Victoria scratched her head. "That's right. I would hate to put that burden on them."

"How about a special speaker, then," Mrs. Phillips suggested.

Victoria added Speaker on the board. Then she automatically blurted out, "Congressman Woodson or Senators Gable or

Ryan. We'll have a better chance at their availability if we ask them now rather than later!"

Mr. Snyder shook his head. "I don't know, Vicky. Elected politicians may not generate much excitement except bipartisan criticism, especially from the adult guests, and that's certainly not our goal. We want excellent attendance and enjoyment. In fact, politicians may create an election type of atmosphere, especially with parents and adult relatives in attendance."

"I agree," added Mrs. Phillips.

"What about some other famous person, like an athlete or an actor or actress?" suggested Stephan.

Victoria lit up like a Christmas tree. "Great idea, Stephan! Now how do we get someone like that? Who do we contact?"

Stephan shrugged his shoulders.

"Perhaps we can contact a major television or motion picture studio to help," said Mrs. Phillips. "It would probably a more successful endeavor if we were to target, so to speak, someone from our own state."

"Does anyone know who that might be?" Vicky asked.

"I think Larry Givens was born and raised here," Mr. Snyder advised.

"He hasn't exactly been a role model in real life though," Vicky said, kind of screwing up her nose.

"You are right on that, Vicky," Mr. Snyder agreed.

"Well, I need to get to my after school job," Stephan interrupted, looking at his watch.

"O.K. Let's all think about this some more and set another meeting date and time," suggested Mrs. Phillips.

"O.K. How's next Tuesday after school?" Mr. Snyder offered. They all nodded. Victoria took a deep breath, resolving to herself that she would reach a workable solution and conclusion next week. She felt time was of the essence. She was more than determined not to let this idea disappear or fall on the cutting room floor, so to speak.

Over the next few days, Vicky became almost obsessed with reaching a solution by next week. An assignment from Mr. Snyder triggered an idea. She was reading the NY *Times* and came across an interesting article on the U.S. Secretary of State Carla Reese, and was especially impressed.

After class she showed the article to Mr. Snyder.

"Well, she is liked by people of both parties, and she is exceptionally articulate, bright, and attractive, as well as very, very busy. How do you propose getting her to accept a speaking role at a high school?"

But Vicky wouldn't back down on her idea. "I'll think of something if we can all agree. The committee I mean. Maybe Congressman Woodson can help."

"Maybe, Vicky, but he needs to answer your letter first. If he doesn't—" he hesitated. She lowered her eyes. He then wished he hadn't said anything about the Congressman's silence. The last thing he wanted to do was to discourage her, probably the brightest and most articulate student he had the opportunity to teach in his career. He put his hand lightly on her shoulder. "Sorry, Vicky. I'm certain he will in time. He must be very busy."

Next Tuesday arrived, and the Committee of four readily agreed to try and somehow entice Carla Reese, U.S. Secretary of State, to come to NuWalk High. Victoria took full responsibility to make it a reality. John Snyder was always there to bounce ideas off of and give sound advice. They agreed to give Congressman Woodson two more weeks to respond. If not, Mr. Snyder would personally contact his office on Vicky's behalf.

Howard Woodson's phone rang above the drone of the C-5 engines on his return trip from Korea to London via a stopover in Germany.

"Hello, Representative Woodson, I hope I am not interrupting something important," his secretary, Lucy, said.

"No, Lucy, I finished my report on Korea and was about to start on my London agenda." He smiled to himself, still a bit groggy from his little nap. "What's up?"

"Well, you wanted me to keep you posted on mail and calls, so here goes. Are you ready?"

He grabbed his notebook "I'm ready go ahead."

She read off some twenty plus messages from members of Congress, the president's office, several constituents, and staffers from various departments.

"That's all? I'm disappointed," he said, tongue in cheek.

"I'll bet you are," she laughed. "I had one more inquiry which can probably wait, but she sounded so sweet so I treated it as special."

"Go ahead," he said, grabbing a clean piece of paper.

"You received a beautifully composed letter from a young lady. Her name is Victoria Magnuson."

"Oh," he involuntarily answered.

"It can probably wait," Lucy continued.

"No Lucy, I want to hear it. I promised her something and I've been neglectful."

"Well the crux of it is that she wants to do a summer internship as a legislative assistant or a page. Also, she asked, almost pleaded in a very sweet way, might you be able to talk to Carla Reese about giving the commencement address to her graduating class? Apparently she met and talked to you at the beach last August."

"Yes, she did; I'm glad she reminded me. Please send her a letter. Call her first, then send the letter to confirm I will contact her when I return home. Make sure you tell her I have been somewhat out of touch with home," he added.

"I will," Lucy answered. "I see her phone number in the letter. I'll take care of it right away."

"Now, let's have some data on the other messages, starting with the president's office. I gather none will be as sweet as the first" he kidded.

Vanessa Magnuson came through the door carrying two large grocery bags and saw the phone blinking away. She hit the button.

"Hello, this is Lucy Anders calling Victoria from Representative Woodson's office. The congressman apologizes for not having answered your letter, but he has been out of the country. He wants you to know that he was very pleased to receive your lovely letter, and promises to be in touch with you later next week. I will confirm this with a letter. Thank you again."

"Well, how nice, how very nice," Vanessa said aloud to herself. "Vicky will be so relieved and happy."

Howard Woodson had about two hours at the airbase in Remagen, so he closed his notebook, grabbed his briefcase, and strolled to the Air Force canteen to see what kind of lunch he could muster up. Being a Navy vet he remembered he could always count on some chow in the ship's mess hall fridge even if it deserved to be long gone rather than in his sailor's stomach. He asked a non com, who directed him to the canteen. On his way he spotted an administrative office and walked in.

"Lieutenant, I'm Congressman Woodson from Delaware and I need to make a call to our London Embassy. Can you help me with that?"

The young Lieutenant looked at his credentials. "Certainly Congressman, I'll patch you through."

The young officer went about calling certain numbers to be connected to an air base in England who connected Remagen to the London Embassy. It took a few minutes, and Representative Woodson peered out the window behind the Lieutenant's desk where the roar of engines revealed a fighter jet preparing for take off on what was probably a practice mission. He smiled and thought of the U.S.A. protecting freedom around the world and realized it wasn't really that long ago when in 1945—but his thoughts were interrupted.

"Here sir," the Lieutenant said, bringing him back to the present and handing him the phone.

"Hello, Mr. Ambassador, how are you? I'm fine, sir. Just a bit tired from flying all day from Korea. I'm calling to see if Secretary of State Reese has arrived."

Graduation Day was less than a week away, and Victoria was taking more deep breaths than she could remember. Everything was coming together. Rain or shine, this would be the most exciting graduation in the history of NuWalk High, and most of the credit was rightfully bestowed on the dynamo Senior Class President, Victoria Magnuson. First, Congressman Woodson would say a few words and introduce Secretary of State Reese. He also used his influence to have a section of the U.S Third Naval District Band perform before and after the commencement address from Secretary Reese. The timing was perfect—Memorial Day weekend, then Flag Day on graduation day.

"Vicky, I am immensely proud of you," said John Snyder, taking her hand in his. "You have accomplished something I have never before seen in a student and probably never will again. It's really been a great, great pleasure to have known you. I can only imagine what you will accomplish in college and beyond for the rest of your life. I see much greatness in your future." He couldn't help it but a tear or two formed in his eyes. On impulse she stepped forward and gave him a big hug and tears ran down her cheeks.

"Thank you Mr. Snyder. I will never forget your guidance, your leadership, and how you allowed me to grow. It's been one marvelous ride. I hope my next stop in life will match up."

"I'm sure you'll make it match up, Vicky. I wouldn't expect anything less."

Commencement day was even hotter than predicted. The cloud cover hoped for thinned out and 90 degrees was the result. The principal, Alfred Larson, gave the introductory speech, trying to keep it relatively short due to the heat and the pending address by Secretary Reese. Allen Anders, the class valedictorian with a grade point average of 3.94, spoke next and gave the standard valedictorian speech, encouraging the graduates to work hard at whatever their choices and to remember their good times at NuWalk High. He then added a postscript that was quite unexpected. He turned toward Victoria on the podium, and said, "It was an honor to be the classmate of our President, Victoria Magnuson, for these past four years." The student body clapped robustly with some hoots and hollers. Victoria was taken aback. Principal Larson strode toward the podium to introduce her but decided she needed no introduction. As she walked close to him he shook her hand, put his arm around her shoulders at the microphone, leaned in to the microphone, and emphatically announced, "Guests, graduates, and faculty, class president, Victoria Magnuson."

The graduates stood, clapping and cheering loudly. She couldn't remember when she was this nervous. She squeezed the edges of the lectern until her hands turned white. The class maintained their utmost praise of her until their hands and throats must have been beet red. Many of the faculty, led by Principal Larson, Vice Principal Stafford, John Snyder, and Mrs. Phillips joined them initially then sat, enjoying the pure outpouring of praise for her. Congressman Woodson and Secretary Reese, taking it all in, were amazed at this spontaneous and lengthy acclaim. Two people, now the proudest on the planet, Vanessa and Gene Magnuson, were not. Victoria finally released the lectern from her death grip and with both arms extended into the air waved to her classmates and then threw a huge kiss to all. They gradually began to sit. She realized nothing she could say would ever come close to the praise she had just received. But from the bottom of her heart she began "Thank you all. I love you all. I will never forget you and NuWalk High." She took a deep breath, looked out at Mom and Dad, said a prayer to herself, and began.

"Well, we finally made it. At times, it may have felt like forever with all the reading and studying and tests. But, my friends," she paused and looked out toward her classmates who were seemingly transfixed on her every word, "It really has just begun. We now have a much longer road ahead of us. It's known as adulthood. A road that our parents have traveled before us."

She attempted to focus her eyes where Vanessa and Gene were sitting, absorbing every word. "Now, not only do we have a much longer road, but one that has steep hills, deep valleys, and sharp curves. A road that will take a great many years more than four to travel. We need to ask ourselves this question. That is, how will we travel this road—with whatever will be will be or *will*," she emphasized, "travel it with goals, purpose, and conviction. You have this choice to make. If you have already made this decision, you will be headed in the right direction. If you are undecided, seek the counsel of your parents and turn to those who you have held in esteem to give you guidance, encouragement, and affirmation. Whatever choice or choices you may decide upon should then be pursued with all the diligence you can give. Remember, half-hearted pursuit will not allow you to achieve your goals."

She paused briefly and took a deep breath.

Praise came from friends standing next to Vanessa and Gene. "You have a very special daughter there." The proud parents nodded and expressed their thanks.

Then with her hands raised, Vicky looked out over the graduates. "My greatest of wishes to you all. I thank you for electing me class president these four years. I will never forget NuWalk High, and especially you, my classmates. It's been one heck of a trip, my friends. God bless you all," and her tears flowed, as did Vanessa's. Gene also wiped more than a tear from his eyes.

The entire class, parents, faculty, and honored guests, including Congressman Woodson and Secretary of State Reese, clapped for a considerable time. Secretary Reese turned to Principal Larson "What a tremendous young woman she is."

"That is for sure, Madame Secretary, that is for sure," he agreed. In the faculty seats, her faculty advisors, John Snyder and Mrs. Phillips, were ecstatic. "Edna, we may never see another Victoria."

"I tend to agree with you John. She is really extraordinary." Vanessa and Gene may have been the proudest parents on earth at that moment.

When the applause subsided and Victoria took her seat, Secretary Reese deliberately walked to the lectern after being introduced by Principal Larson. She received much applause herself. She turned toward Victoria, still somewhat tearful. "Thank you, Victoria, for that very uplifting speech. I trust all of your fellow graduates will remember it."

# Chapter 10

# KEITH FREDERICKS' CLOSE CALL

Nick and Nelson only heard about the accident a week after it happened down south. Keith was traveling Route 95 on his Harley to see his aunt, uncle, and cousins in Clearwater Beach. In South Carolina, on a clear expanse of pavement, his bike blew a tire. His bike, all his belongings, and his body went flying. Fortunately, other drivers with car phones pulled over and dialed 911 for an ambulance. People tried to make him comfortable but could do nothing more to assure him that help was on the way.

Richard and Barbara Fredericks were called when the hospital staff found their information in Keith's wallet. In their grief, they rushed to reach the South Carolina hospital overnight. As fate would have it, Nick and Nelson called late in the day responding to a letter Keith sent. He was planning to visit with them before they enlisted in the service and he entered college. They were hoping to try and convince Keith, one last time, to enlist with them. This accident would squash any chance of that, they realized as they prepared to drive to South Carolina the next morning to comfort their friend. They were praying Keith was still alive and would recognize them.

"Boy, I can't imagine how I would feel all banged up like that", Nick shook his head.

"I can't either," Nelson murmured.

"He's probably on a lot of medication and won't even know us," Nick rubbed his head.

"Wow that would be weird. I hope he does know us," Nelson added.

"His folks didn't say he lost anything, so that's a good thing," Nick kind of said under his breath, shuddering at the thought.

"Yeah, Nick, that's a *good* thing."

"It's a good thing, too, that we contacted Pastor Wagner to call a Lutheran church down there near the hospital," Nelson continued. "We'll need to stay a while and we can't afford a motel."

"I guess if we slept in the car, the police would arrest us as vagrants or bums or something like that," said Nick.

"At least we will be warm and have a bathroom and find a diner or eat at the hospital. When we get to the hospital, we'll have to call Pastor and get the scoop," Nelson added.

For a while they kept their thoughts to themselves as they cruised I95, and taking turns driving.

Obviously, Keith was totally out of it. He had more medication in him than he had taken in his previous 18 years combined. Although he had broken his arm and leg when he was younger in his tomboy antics, this accident far surpassed those incidents. This accident involved broken ribs, feet, and both legs and arms. Thankfully his heartbeat and blood pressure were stabilized. He was still unconscious, thanks to the meds. The doctors were waiting for him to awaken to see if he would respond and show recognition. It would definitely be more than a few days to see positive improvement.

Richard and Barbara stayed at a local motel for several days, then talked the hospital into letting them stay, for a modest fee, when vacancies occurred. This enabled them to be with Keith when he wasn't being examined. Every once in a while, Barbara would stroke his thick brown hair, or touch his hand where there were no intravenous tubes. Richard kept praying to himself, and once in a while embraced Barbara as she stroked their son.

Dr. Nickle, the lead surgeon, sat down next to them. "His vital signs are all strong. We have seen improvement, and we have repaired all that was broken. In these cases there is no way to put a time constraint on his complete recovery. It's probable he will need a wheelchair for some time, but it appears that he will not permanently need one. Any day now, he will recognize you, and smile or wink, and later on squeeze your hands with his." Dr. Nickle knew that a full recovery was possible. It would take a long time with much tender loving care and rehabilitation on Keith's part.

On their way to South Carolina, Nick and Nelson stopped to gas up, eat, and make a call to their minister to see if he contacted a minister near the hospital to find out if the two men could sleep at his church. Nick made contact with Pastor Wagner, who gave them the name of a church near the hospital, as well as the pastor's name and phone number. He then told him to wait and he would call the pastor directly and get back to Nick right away with more specific directions and advise him about when he and Nelson would be arriving.

Nick relayed this information to his brother. "Nelson, we're in luck. Pastor Wagner is going to call a pastor at home whose church is very near the hospital. Let's hope he reaches him. He's going to call me back, so we have to wait to hear from him."

"Let's hope," and Nick held up both hands, to Nelson, with fingers crossed. It was only about twenty minutes or so when their phone rang. Nick answered.

"Hello, Nick—good news. I contacted Pastor Schnell of Advent Lutheran in Conway. He offered to have you sleep in his home, which is right next to the church. He and his wife will be expecting you later this evening. Here's their number so you can keep in touch with them."

"Wow. Thanks a lot, Pastor."

"Sure, Nick, and my regards to Nelson. I'll continue praying for your friend, Keith."

"Wow," Nick said, turning to Nelson, "We can sleep at the pastor's house by the church, and it's near the hospital in Conway, too."

"How's that for luck," said Nelson.

Nelson responded, "Unbelievable! Let's get going, then."

Nick called Pastor Schnell and gave him their location. The Pastor estimated their time of arrival at two and a half hours. They didn't waste any time getting to their destination, fixed on seeing their buddy. Nelson drove while Nick looked at the map to approximate the mileage. "I guess it is about 200 miles. We should be there by 9," Nick figured.

"Visiting hours will be over by then," Nelson said.

"That's O.K., we'll need our sleep anyway," Nick answered.

"You can say that again," Nelson agreed. They pretty much drove with very little conversation the rest of the way, mostly speaking just to confirm directions given by their soon-to-be hosts, Pastor and Mrs. Schnell. They did a lot of silent praying for their buddy Keith, hoping that soon, he would again be the Keith they knew.

When they arrived, Pastor and Mrs. Schnell warmly encouraged them to stay for several nights. Nick and Nelson were extremely grateful. At Sunday services, Pastor Schnell led a prayer for Keith's recovery.

Nick and Nelson alternated visiting times with Mr. and Mrs. Fredericks, who frequently took their son's friends to lunch and dinner. Keith's parents were very appreciative of the brothers' friendship for Keith, and their efforts to drive so far to be with him in his darkest hours. "We really appreciate you boys coming all the way down here for Keith," Richard gratefully thanked them.

"Yes, thank you so much. He will be so happy to see you when he awakes," Barbara added, taking a deep breath and realizing, yet again, that her son was still comatose. She said a brief prayer to herself.

"It's the least we could do," Nelson said, and gently took her hand. She gave him a grateful smile.

"We would never forgive ourselves if we didn't come. He is our best buddy. We need him to be Keith again," Nick emphatically added. He wasn't ashamed to wipe a tear from his eye. Barbara reached out and took his hand with her free one. Richard stood up and silently hugged the three of them as his tears began to flow.

At one of their bedside visits, Nelson thought he saw Keith clench his left hand into a fist. It was the first sign of movement since Keith was sedated. "It happened so fast. I couldn't believe it. Was that a good thing?" Nelson asked, pleading for a positive answer from anyone.

"I hope God is working overtime for our boy," Barbara said as she wiped a tear from her eye.

"I'll look for Dr. Nickle or someone who can give us an answer," Richard said as he left the bedside.

"It will be a week tomorrow since the accident. I pray this is the beginning of recovery," Barbara said to the boys. Both Nick and Nelson squeezed her hands for support. She smiled in recognition. The boys looked at all the greeting cards and flower bouquets. Some of the flowers were withered and dried. They were from aunts, uncles, and cousins. One, in particular, drew the boys' attention, from a woman named Suzanne. The card read, "I'll always have a spot in my heart for you" written on the inside.

"She and Keith were an item for a while. We thought she should know of the accident," Barbara explained.

"I guess we moved away before that," Nick said, turning to Nelson.

A few minutes later, Richard returned with a nurse and a doctor. They took Keith's vital signs and read the monitors. "That movement, however small, is a good sign," the doctor advised. "Recovery will be slow. This is just the beginning of the recovery phase."

The doctor's response was cautious, but Barbara and Richard felt it was positive. Nick and Nelson stayed through mid-evening to give Keith's parents a dinner break, then hugged them goodbye to spend their last evening in South Carolina. They were leaving for home early the next morning. They left cards and messages for Keith, praying and lightly squeezing his arm when they left.

It was two weeks before Keith was well enough to return home to recover. He continued to rapidly improve. Keith tried to encourage Nick and Nelson to enlist in the Air Force right away, but they insisted on waiting until they could see him at 100% or, as they put it, "So close you can spit on it."

They visited twice and called him often. Mom and Dad were very appreciative. His recovery nearly complete, Nick and Nelson visited for the last time just prior to enlistment. Keith still did a good deal of sitting, but he was able to get around a bit using crutches. The conversation was a good deal livelier at this visit.

"You sure did milk this, Keith," Nick chided to get him laughing.

Keith tried to laugh but still had some deep breathing problems. "Yeah, we saw that blond nurse. Now we know why you slow motioned your recovery," Nelson added for good measure.

Keith just smiled to avoid discomfort and pointed his finger at both: "You got that right guys. She did perk things up."

They continued their banter for quite some time. A few minutes later, Barbara intervened. "Guys, I hate to rush you, but he needs his rest. How about another fifteen minutes?" They agreed reluctantly, realizing that it was in Keith's best interest. "Keith's dad and I really appreciate your coming, it has meant so much to Keith," she said. "It really boosted his spirit."

Nick and Nelson nodded. Then Nick said, "Keith, we have finally decided to enlist. Our mom said O.K. last week. We wanted to tell you in person. With boot camp and Air Force school we won't be seeing you for a while."

"Yeah," Nelson added, "and who knows where we will be stationed." Keith made a face but realized they had to get on with their lives. They shouldn't wait for him to get better. Besides, he still had a strong inclination toward the Secret Service, and knew he needed a full recovery, then at least four years of college and maybe graduate school. He held up his arms and waved them to come next to him on the couch. He put one arm around each and pulled them to him." "Guys, I wish you the best. We may not see each other again for a long time, maybe years, but let's write to each other. I promise not to forget our friendship."

Nick and Nelson's eyes teared up. "We won't either, Keith," Nelson answered.

"You can bet on that," Nick quickly added.

They left after Barbara took a few pictures for them to always remember this moment. She would be sending copies to their parents' address. Keith watched from the window as they waved and drove away. Barbara silently hugged him as both shed a few tears.

One quiet evening at home with Mom and Dad, Keith began to tell them for the first time, of a beautiful dream he had weeks ago in the hospital.

"I thought I was in heaven," he began. "I don't know how long it was but I had a beautiful dream and it must have been heaven."

Both Barbara and Richard lightly stroked him and propped up his pillow. They both had tears in their eyes.

"My sweet son. I'm not surprised to hear of this dream, but I'm sure glad you came back to us," Barbara said through her tears as she lightly stroked his face and hair.

"Heaven can wait for a long while. I guess that's what God decided, and we're darn glad he did," Richard added. Keith went on to recount the images he remembered and mentioned relatives that passed away before his time. Mom and Dad were fascinated by what he told them.

He also recounted another special dream that he had. "I was a Secret Service Agent and saved the President's life." It was a truly remarkable story, and it gave all of them a newfound joy and inner strength. Keith believed that, for all this, he was someone special and wanted to prove to God that he was worthy of being spared. He would spend the rest of his life with that in mind, hoping he could deliver on that promise.

# Chapter 11

# GENEVIEVE AND DAVID ENTER STATE UNIVERSITY

Genevieve's summer was truly a fantasy. She wanted to complete four years at State University, but concentrating on her studies was extremely difficult. In a few weeks after her last summer performance, she was finally able to refocus. She made a valiant effort not to interfere with the instruction from her drama coach, Mrs. Lovett. Her problem was that her fellow students were aware of what she had already accomplished at nineteen. She attracted attention like bees to honey. The one sure way she found to guarantee quiet and privacy was by sitting in the University library. She and Mom and Dad also decided she should rent an off campus apartment so she could be more independent. Her red convertible sports car, however, often attracted a cluster of girls, as well as some guys who practically mobbed her on the walk to and from the college buildings. In her first month back, she signed literally hundreds of autographs and was still being gracious about it. Her Mom and Dad were more than a bit concerned that her college years were, in a way, negatively affected. A clear example of this was when she attempted to be involved in activities other than drama or music, her presence so detracted her fellow students that, albeit reluctantly, the faculty leader would suggest she consider another activity, and Genevieve reluctantly obliged. It was beginning to make her a bit distressed.

Mrs. Lovett was truly a gem. She saw what was happening and asked Genevieve to be a guest lecturer and tutor from time to time as her classes were larger than in past years. The increase was partially due to Genevieve's presence. Genevieve made sure to adhere to Mrs. Lovett's teaching methodologies, as well as sequence, to insure the proper curriculum timing and flow for the students. She also gave Mrs. Lovett some of her free time, because she truly enjoyed what she was doing, as well as the respect she had for her instructor who, in her twenties and thirties, also had a stage career with several Broadway parts in the mix. It did put a strain on her in so far as maintaining the rest of her studies, but it gave her a valuable outlet she needed.

The drama department had planned a production for just before the Christmas break and a decision was needed quickly to properly prepare and rehearse. Genevieve gave the idea to Mrs. Lovett for each drama and music class to pick two or three reasonable choices, and vote on them as a group. The faculty would have the final decision on the choice. This would assure the students' and department capabilities would not be unduly stretched. The time to prepare was the main issue.

Mrs. Lovett and other faculty tried to convince Genevieve to take the female lead to assure sellout audiences. If the response was as great as they expected, they thought two back to back performances could be scheduled. This would be a first, and provide additional revenue for the Drama Department. Mr. Arrington, another professor, took the lead in trying to convince her.

"I just wouldn't feel right about that," she kept insisting. "I think several of my classmates should audition. That's what it's all about in the real world and I would be remiss if I prevented a realistic process for them."

Then she had a revolutionary idea to satisfy all. "What if I offer my opinion, only to the faculty, on those planning to audition? My thoughts would remain with me but it's the faculty's decision."

Mrs. Lovett smiled. "Genevieve, that was an answer I'm proud of. Great idea. If there is a strong character actress part in the play eventually chosen, I hope you will audition."

Genevieve shrugged her shoulders. "What if we wrote in a small part for me, as a compromise, with a song or two, assuming we do a musical, of course. That way none of my classmates would feel cheated and I would be a lot more comfortable."

Mr. Arrington was as impressed with Genevieve's humility as Mrs. Lovett. "That, young lady, is a super approach. Sort of like we can have our cake and eat it too. Hopefully, no one's feathers will be ruffled," Mr. Arrington said. "Also, we get the star power and the objective of the sellout crowd for two shows. I think it's definitely attainable."

"The Board of Trustees and President Hall will, I believe, be thrilled with the idea," Mrs. Lovett agreed.

Well, if they had any doubts concerning the enthusiasm of the 125 drama students, they were quickly dispelled. The students were appreciative and thrilled that they were asked to recommend plays, and that the four most suggested would be considered. The dates of December 17th and 18th, Friday and Saturday, were set for the shows. A two week decision process from the date student recommendations were requested, providing a lead time of almost two months when the time off for the Thanksgiving holiday was factored in. In the end, 110 of the 125 students made recommendations. The final four were *Damn Yankees*, *Gypsy*, *Anchors Away*, and *Mama Mia*. The faculty and Genevieve eventually decided on *Damn Yankees*, based on the talent they felt to be present with the students. The announcement was made immediately, and the roles were written up and distributed to the entire drama student body to apply.

Genevieve took as active an instructional role as her schedule allowed. Mrs. Lovett and Mr. Arrington were, together, developing a role for Genevieve to fill, so she didn't have to concern herself with that except for rehearsal later on. However, both of them hoped that Genevieve would agree to play Lyla. It would guarantee a superlative performance and more importantly, attract an overflow audience, which was an important financial consideration.

Elsewhere on Long Island, another serious discussion was taking place. It was a difficult choice for David, but he listened to his mom and dad and chose to enter State University and play college ball. The New York Marauders General Manager Randy Cameron met twice with Mr. and Mrs. Kelsey and David. The Marauders had preferred that David enter their minor league system upon graduation, but respected the family's wishes. The bonus that he received had a clause holding back a significant portion that would be released upon directly signing with the Marauders. The Kelseys understood that, but felt it important that David go to college first. Besides, he could play and excel with the college team. Randy Cameron understood how they felt, and made it a point to assure that the appropriate Marauders personnel maintain close contact with State University's athletic department, keep a watchful eye on their future and hopefully very valuable star.

David majored in business and began his freshman year with a B average. He might have done better, but part of his concentration was on spring training. He had meetings with his baseball coach, Ed Wood, soon after admission and guidance learned of his abilities and desire to join the team. State U. last won a division championship 11 years ago, and sorely wanted another right now. They gave him a four-year scholarship, after learning of the Marauder's interest, to keep him in school. They fully expected he would greatly enhance their chances of a championship. It helped David that his buddies, Stan and Chad, also entered State U. and planned baseball tryouts. He still had some misgivings about not immediately entering the Marauders organization. Little did he know, however, that entering State U. at precisely this time would greatly impact and shape the rest of his life.

Mid November of David and Genevieve's freshman year brought beautiful weather and a change in classes to the State U. campus as Genevieve walked with her friends, Jo Ann and Colleen, toward their new Economics class. Rehearsals were moving along on *Damn Yankees*. A major concern, however, was that some of the roles were not cast. This included the lead male role of the baseball player. Several students tried out, but either bowed out, or were discouraged from continuing. Genevieve was asked to look outside the drama classes to find a better fit for the baseball player, which put a lot of pressure on her. She sought the advice of her drama student friends, who suggested she might actually look toward the school's real baseball team to find a "hunk," as they put it, to fill the role. They all felt that the acting part in this role was less important than the athletic presence of the actor. She was feeling the pressure and expressed it as the three of them walked across the campus to economics class.

"Why don't you go to the Chairman of the Athletic Department," suggested Jo Ann.

"I guess I could, but I'd have to find a way to interview them and have the drama department hold additional tryouts. How would the Chairman even know who to suggest? It all gets very involved and complicated, and there isn't that much time left," she added dejectedly.

Colleen put her arm around Genevieve. "I have a feeling, I don't know why, but I have a strong feeling that everything will happen for you to figure this out," said Colleen.

"I sure hope you're right, Colleen," sighed Genevieve.

"I have the answer," Jo Ann chipped in. "You can change the play to a woman's softball team and have the lead be female—how's that?"

The three of them laughed all the way to Economics class and didn't stop as they entered the classroom. It momentarily, at least, put Genevieve in a relaxed mood.

Robert Dougherty, the Economics Professor, smiled as he saw the three young women walk in laughing. He was very aware of who Genevieve was, being interested in the theatre. It took a few more minutes for the large class of more than 40 to fill the room. Genevieve found herself staring at the guys, hoping to spot one to fit the baseball player role in *Damn Yankees*.

"Good morning," Mr. Dougherty addressed the class and introduced himself. "This is a class on World Economics and how all the countries in the world, no matter size or stature, interrelate economically and have an impact on how goods are produced, why they are produced, how much is produced, and the cost to produce. It will, hopefully, by the completion of this class make you keenly aware that even such a great country as the U.S. needs to concern itself with market shifts, resource availability, adequate labor supply, and currency value fluctuation among other key factors."

Genevieve thought to herself, *Oh my gosh. This sounds very complicated. With everything else on my plate right now maybe I had better drop this course.* She took a few deep breaths and tried to concentrate. The professor handed out an outline of the semester, and advised which textbooks to purchase. He also suggested additional readings from the State U. and public libraries.

"Wow this course is heavy lifting," murmured Colleen.

"Yeah, I thought it would be a slam dunk. Anyone for a switch?" Jo Ann asked.

"I, for one, think it will be interesting, although a lot of work, to be sure," Genevieve chimed in. "Maybe I will learn how performing arts affects economics or vice versa."

"Yeah," Jo Anne retorted. "Maybe we will learn how to get big city play tickets for half the price," and the girls all tried to stifle a laugh. That caught the attention of Mr. Dougherty.

"Miss Carter," he said, knowing who she was, "Let us all have the benefit of why you ladies are having a nice laugh." Genevieve's face turned beet red, but Colleen came to her rescue.

"I started it Mr. D. I said maybe we can, by taking this class, learn how to buy New York show tickets at Eastern European prices." The class got a kick out of that, and so did Professor Dougherty.

"If you learn that, I want to be the very first to know," and the class joined in the humor. "Now," Professor Dougherty got back to his class plan, "Beside weekly assignments and some quizzes for this semester, I have prepared some twenty different topics for a pair of you to complete by the end of the semester. If any of you should drop out I will assign the remaining student on the project to another group, unless you wish to complete the original assignment." He took a small box from his desk and shook it up. "Each of you take only one ticket out of this box and pass it on. Beside the topic name there is a number on each. That is the project number. I suppose you college folks have figured out the rest." Many in the class chuckled. "Anyway after all have been picked I want you all to meet your partner and begin making plans to work on your subject. Of course, this is also the time to know your partner a little bit. This assignment is worth 25% of your grade. The assignment for the next class is on the board. O.K. class, meet each other."

The students began holding up their assignment numbers and shouting them out.

David spotted the attractive blonde holding number 12 up high. He did a double take, checking his number again. Then he slowly moved toward her, holding his number 12 well above his 6'4" frame so she could readily see it. Genevieve saw him coming her way, and immediately noticed his smile, physique and, importantly, his number 12. She decided not to maneuver through her classmates but to wait for him to reach her. Jo Ann noticed David also. "Wow, you hit pay dirt Genevieve. He looks like a winner."

Genevieve just smiled. "Where's your partner, Jo Ann," she asked.

Jo Ann replied, "I see a her, not a him. That's the way the cookie crumbles. I can't wait for your report. See you later kiddo."

"See ya," Genevieve half answered, keeping her eyes focused on David.

"Hello, I'm David Kelsey." He held out his hand and shook hers gently with a big smile.

"I'm Genevieve Carter. It's nice to meet you, David." Like most State U. students, David knew of her, but he decided not to make a big deal of it. Let time do its thing, he thought. Being low key would be the best approach.

"Any ideas on how we get started on this subject?" he asked as he looked at the paper in his hand again. "The effects of a country's devaluation of its currency on the country and how it impacts its financial position when importing and exporting with other countries. Provide at least a fifty-page analysis with charts and graphs as well as actual historical case examples. Include an appendix of all research material utilized. This is going to be some heavy lifting. I'll need help," and he gave her an infectious smile.

She thought, *I think I'm going to like this guy.*

"How about discussing it over a snack at the café," he suggested. "I didn't get a chance for breakfast and I'm famished."

"Sure, we can do that," she agreed. David thought this is going to be a much more pleasant assignment than he ever imagined. So did Genevieve.

Colleen and Jo Ann noticed her leaving with David. "She hit the jackpot," Colleen said, shaking her head.

"You can say that again," Jo Ann added.

As they walked to the café, Genevieve was thinking that Economics may now turn out to be her second most favorite subject, after Drama, of course. The two exchanged pleasantries, such as which high schools they attended and their favorite subjects. David knew she was the buzz all around the campus since September. He did his best not to query her at all concerning her campus notoriety and status. At this point she was oblivious to his status, as were many on the campus until baseball season rolled around. Football had everyone's undivided attention, and that was fine with David. It was ironic that they were brought together by mere chance, and both would be even better known on campus, once spring rolled around. Some would call it fate.

The snack bar was fairly busy. It was a great meeting place for lattes and sweet munchies. Although both Genevieve and David were physique-conscious young people, an infrequent small latte wasn't past either. David offered to buy, and Genevieve found herself accepting where normally she would be independent and gracefully refuse. She was still assessing how all this happened, and she felt both happy and curious to see where it would take them. "Let's sit over there in the corner," David said as he pointed to a small table with two chairs out of the main traffic area. He pulled out a chair for her.

"Thanks, this will be a nice break before next class" she sighed.

"There's nothing like a latte break—well almost nothing," David laughed, and so did Genevieve, who found his manner very pleasant and infectious.

"What's your major, David?" she asked.

"Business Management. Although I hope I won't need to get into it," he laughed.

"What do you mean, you hope you never get into it?" she asked, amazed.

"Well, I have another profession in mind, first. Then if that doesn't work out, I'll hopefully be better prepared for a real career," and he laughed heartily as he threw his head back and rubbed his wavy light brown hair.

She truly liked what she saw. She had a tingly feeling—a real one, not an acting technique she was used to using. It startled her and she shook it off. "Please explain what exactly you mean, David. What profession are you talking about?"

"Well, I want to be a professional baseball player. I'll be playing on the college team this spring."

Genevieve's eyes opened wide. "Oh, I see. I would never have guessed. I mean, I have never met a baseball player before."

"Well, I guess we're even. I never met a professional actress before either," and he reached across the table to shake her hand. "I'm really looking forward to seeing you perform. I understand you were on Broadway last summer."

She had wished he wasn't aware, but responded in kind. "Yes, it was truly a marvelous experience. I can't begin to describe it."

"I'll bet. It must have been fantastic. It's not the same thing to be sure," David continued, "But I went to a Marauders training camp the summer before last and batted against former major league pitchers and did well They gave me a bonus for me to start in their minor league system. My parents wanted me to go to college first. State U. gave me a scholarship to play here. Hopefully I'll help them. They haven't won a championship in 11 years."

"Wow, that's quite a story." Genevieve was wide-eyed, admiring this young man she had just met. "I have a scholarship also and I'm trying, as I have time, to assist the professors and help the students in the Drama Department as part of an agreement my parents and I made. So we have a lot in common it seems." She gave him a dazzling smile. David just stared at her, transfixed in time, admiring her beauty and poise. He came back to earth in a few seconds although it felt much longer.

Finally, he spoke up. "Oh yes, we share an economics assignment we have to complete," and they both laughed, enjoying each other. Then they fell silent, trying not to stare at each other feeling rather conspicuous.

Genevieve broke the silence. "Well, I guess we should plan to meet on *that* assignment."

"Yeah," he sighed. "I guess so. Let's take a look at our calendars" David was reluctant to have this marvelous interlude come to a close. They agreed to meet in three days at the library to begin the assignment, and exchanged cell phone numbers. Standing up, they shook hands kind of awkwardly, and took a few moments to stare into each other's eyes.

Genevieve spoke first. "I really enjoyed this meeting, David, and look forward to working with you."

"So did I, Genevieve. This project has become more of a pleasure than a pain—if possible."

"I agree," she answered with a beautiful smile. David watched her leave and took a real deep breath. This was no dream. He forcefully pinched his arm to be sure. He didn't know it then but his life would be forever changed.

Genevieve couldn't wait to return to the dorm after her next class. She would have to wait until after Math to pour out her thoughts to Colleen and Jo Ann. They were both eagerly waiting for her to return. She was out of breath as she trotted from across the campus. She burst through the door and plopped on her bed.

"Well, what a day ladies, what a day!"

"O.K., tell us about that hunk you deserted us for," screamed Jo Ann as she and Colleen plopped on their beds.

"He is absolutely the sweetest guy. I could hardly believe it. He's a baseball star on a scholarship. The New York baseball team, the Marauders, wanted to sign him up right after high school but his parents, like mine, insisted he go to college first."

"Wow, what a hunk," cheered Jo Ann.

"Amen to that" added Colleen.

Genevieve continued, "He's really laid back, very thoughtful and polite. We just hit it off. Our personalities, just meshed, I guess," she said, shrugging her shoulders.

"When will you see him again?" asked Jo Ann.

"Well, I'll see him in class of course" she answered.

"That doesn't count," laughed Colleen.

"Well, in three days we'll meet at the library for our project," Genevieve laughed back.

"That doesn't count either," shrieked Ann.

"I don't want to be too aggressive here, ladies. He needs to make the first move."

"Yes, but you can give him some hints and encouragement," added Colleen.

"Well, who says I won't," Genevieve shot back, and they all laughed.

"Something else also crossed my mind," she added.

"What?" they both asked in unison.

"Well, remember I told you about the Drama Department producing *Damn Yankees* as the fall play?" They nodded and sat up quickly.

"Wow," Jo Ann guessed. "Are you going to suggest he be the male lead?"

"Why not?" Genevieve shot back. "He would fit perfectly. After working with him on the assignment I would know if, well, we would be a good fit together. What do you guys think?"

"Well, he's not an actor," Colleen shot back.

"But he is a baseball player, and he will have a real feeling for that part of the role. I can help with the rest. Besides, it will bring us closer for the next two months or so," she said with a dazzling smile.

"We get the picture," they squealed almost in unison.

"That's a great plan, kiddo," Colleen shook her head and Jo Ann added, "A great plan indeed."

"He is really a hunk. That's what he is. Oh God, I can't believe I really said that," Genevieve covered her mouth and plopped on the bed.

"Sounds like you have it bad," Colleen laughed.

"Amen to that," Jo Ann chimed in.

"I need you two to keep me under control. That was no act. My emotions just took control over me. I guess he had more of an affect on me than I realized." Genevieve covered her face and rubbed it. "I never felt this way about a guy before. Have either of you?"

"Well, I thought I did once in high school, but it ended my freshman year when he started cozying up to someone else," Jo Ann recalled.

"I still haven't hit the jackpot," Colleen sighed.

They headed out to the main dining hall after reluctantly reviewing some course work. A major hub of activity busy with conversation and laughter, there were long lines for food and students moving from table to table to interact with each other. David, Stan and Chad were at a table with some others. David had told the guys about the Economics project and what a fortunate guy he was to have been assigned Genevieve as a partner. He spotted her and pointed her out to the guys as she disappeared into the food line.

"She sure is a beauty. Your words didn't do her justice," Stan admonished him.

"You hit a grand slam with her," Chad added.

Genevieve happened to see their table at a point in line. She gave some thought to saying hello, but she couldn't think of more conversation with all the guys staring, and thought better of it. David took a good look at her and his heart beat faster. He said, only to himself, *I have it bad and that's good, I think.* The guys saw him sneak a peak, and stifled a laugh or two. He heard them, but chose to ignore. Peeks were also coming from the opposite direction, as Colleen and Jo Ann were surveying the view.

"Wow, he is a hunk, and his friends aren't bad either," Jo Ann added.

"I may be lousy at Math but I believe there are three of them. I know there are three of us. Quite a coincidence, don't you think?" Colleen contributed to the mix.

Genevieve couldn't help but laugh out loud. "O. K., you two. Let's behave."

"Only if you promise to get us introduced to his friends," Jo Ann teased.

"O.K., at the right time I can do that, but I have to be introduced first."

"Make sure you get introduced soon," Colleen suggested, and they all laughed as they came to the cashier. Unfortunately the only available tables at that time were across the large room, so meet and greet would have to wait. Genevieve wanted to move a bit slower with this blossoming romance, and was glad it worked out that way for now.

The table at the library had more than a few books spread out, as well as several newspaper articles and their own textbooks, as David and Genevieve split up their assignment. Other students from their class were here and there working, probably, on their assignments. The small groups waved to each other. Genevieve and David agreed they would read each other's drafts to critique each other's writing, and try to mold them into a unified draft for further review and modification as they felt necessary. She couldn't help it, but she was distracted as she was searching on how to ask him if he would consider the part of Josh in the *Damn Yankees* production. She had talked to Mr. Arrington and Mrs. Lovett, and they were all for it. She was concerned that he would flatly refuse and that her asking would put pressure on him and their budding relationship.

"Just use your fabulous smile and your sweetest voice to ask him," both Colleen and Jo Ann urged. They felt that David would just melt if she did. She wasn't so sure he would and might see right through that and be upset. She really cared for him and didn't want to risk their relationship by using her feminine wiles as if it was scripted. She decided on a natural, mature, straightforward approach.

"David," she started and paused briefly. Forging ahead, she said, "the Drama Department has decided to do *Damn Yankees* for our December production. Have you heard of it?" She paused for his answer, holding her breath for what seemed like an eternity.

"Yes," he emphasized his answer. "If I am correct, it is about the devil using a beautiful woman to corrupt and seduce the star of the Yankees." He gave her a big smile. She was surprised at how well and concisely he described it.

"Right on. You're correct." Then she came right out with it. "Would you consider being the baseball star?"

He just stared at her. She had to do something, so she rather timidly, as her bravado began to wane, she added, "I'd like you to think it over if you don't mind," and again held her breath. She couldn't read his expression as he just looked at her rather passively.

After what seemed forever, she broke the silence. "David, I'm asking because it's just a possibility right now." He remained remarkably expressionless. "We don't have a male in the department that really fits the role."

Genevieve then decided to quit talking and let whatever happens happen. The silence was deafening. She didn't take her eyes off his, but if she looked at her hands she would have seen her knuckles turning colors as her hands had a death grip on the oak library table, which if it were pine, would have lost a couple of inches by now.

Finally, David leaned forward ever so slightly and his hazels looked straight into her blues. He rubbed his chin, took a deep breath and slowly rose to leave the table. However, at the last moment, with his warm breath on her face he whispered, "Only if you are Lola," and gave her a soft but firm kiss before sitting back down.

She was motionless for a few seconds; it was like a silent movie. To both of them, the moment felt much longer than it really was, as he waited for her reaction. Genevieve realized he cleverly reversed their roles. Her smile told it all.

"I would love to be your Lola if the advisers agree. They may want to give someone else the opportunity. But we can rehearse together if you can stand it."

They both laughed heartily, attracting the attention of an Assistant Librarian. Their four hands joined and squeezed to accentuate their feelings for each other.

"O.K., kids, no smooching in the library," the Assistant scolded them as she passed by. They again tried to be serious and concentrate on Economics, but it was difficult.

At first, they tried to keep their relationship a secret on campus, but Chad, Colleen, Jo Ann, and Stan were not so discreet about spreading the news, so they gave up and began holding hands as they walked the campus, but never kissed in public. Given their stature they were extremely popular and, by far, the most infamous twosome on campus.

David was a slam-dunk approval for the Josh Borden lead role. He felt a bit pressured and nervous, between learning the part and keeping up with course work, but Genevieve was superlative in her support and assistance. At times their four friends would visit rehearsals, as they were extremely curious as to how they would be together.

"They look like they have been a couple for years," Colleen surmised.

"Born for each other," Stan agreed. The four friends also became items. So much so that Genevieve joked around when the six friends were all together, "If our primary careers don't pan out, David and I can hire out as matchmakers." Between the three couples, that became their nicknames: the matchers and the matched.

Mrs. Lovett and Mr. Arrington carefully monitored the play rehearsals, and it would be a certainty that Genevieve would be cast as Lola. There was a magic everyone could see between the two. It was certainly good news to the Administration and the Board as they wanted the publicity of Genevieve in the lead to assure capacities for both evenings.

December came around as quickly as a wink. The rehearsals went well, and David really got into it as their relationship grew even stronger. Genevieve sent complimentary tickets to Ron Bannister, Dana Biggs, his assistant, both her and David's parents, Eve Truitt, Ron Bannister's sister who introduced her to him, Mr. Truitt and their son and high school friend Johnny.

Finally, opening night arrived. David had rehearsed almost non-stop with Genevieve and cast over the last several weeks, but still had opening night jitters. He remarked to Genevieve, "I would rather be facing a great major league pitcher in a game saving situation right now."

"I know, honey, but you'll be great. What if I wink at you once in a while or even squeeze you to divert your attention," she smiled.

"Funny," he shook his head. "Off stage I'd love some squeezes, though."

She grabbed him and planted a big kiss on his lips. "You didn't have to tell me twice." They laughed as he removed Lola's lipstick and she replaced it on her end.

Then Genevieve thought of a baseball metaphor. "Just think of it as a fastball coming in belt high in the middle of the plate. You calmly unleash a mighty swing and the—" she didn't finish as he laughed a little and squeezed her again.

Choosing his own metaphor, he murmured, "How about a curve or two—you in your 'uniform', so to speak." She laughed and reminded him that he wouldn't see her until Act 2, Scene 5, and then Act 4, Scene 6. "O.K. give me something to remember," he said. She put her arm around his neck and pulled him tightly to her and they kissed for what seemed an eternity. Then they heard the final buzzer for the cast to be ready. They gently separated.

"For good luck sweetheart."

"That ought to hold me," he said, cupping her face in his hands.

"Remember," she teased, "Whatever Lola wants, Lola gets."

He tapped her gently.

"O.K., you two, save it for later. Let's break a leg." It was Professor Lovett, prompting them to get ready for the opening curtain. She had a great feeling of success tonight as she peeked out at the capacity audience with the band doing overtures.

The play moved along well. The audience was very responsive. Their first meeting in Scene 5 was passive in Mr. Apfel's home. Scene 6, in the locker room was torrid. Genevieve was in top form, in more ways than one, and David gladly played her victim. At the end of the show, the curtain closed to resounding applause. Two additional curtain calls, prompted by the audience, were made.

Genevieve and David hugged each other tightly. "Well, we made it sweetheart, we made it. For a while I had some doubts about me, not you," David admitted with a sigh.

"I never doubted you. You were marvelous. In baseball terms, you hit a grand slam to win the series. If our shoes were reversed, I would have struck out to lose the series," she humbly responded.

"If I hit a grand slam you must have broken the all-time record for slams. You were just mar—vel—ous," he shouted. They kissed and got several oohs and aahs from other cast members headed for the dressing rooms. Professors Arrington and Lovett took it all in.

"Tomorrow will be anti-climactic. There's no way we will top this," Professor Arrington said, turning to Professor Lovett, who nodded.

"You can say that again. I was just thinking well ahead. We have three more years to enjoy this talent and enthusiasm. It will be a great run for the Drama Department."

"You're right. We are quite fortunate to be here at this time in our careers," he added.

Their entire entourage eventually made it backstage to congratulate them. Their parents met for the first time and hit it off right away. They couldn't be happier that their special children met each other and fell in love. Ron Bannister and Dana Biggs suggested he might produce it on Broadway, and they could wow Broadway audiences, also. Ron and Dana quickly added, "For the summer of course so it wouldn't interfere with college." David mentioned it might have to wait until he retires from baseball. He recently agreed to play summer ball in the Marauders farm system to keep his skills sharp until college graduation. They were on top of the world and didn't want to get off, but it really was just the beginning of the rest of marvelous lives for these two. It would be inevitable that some blips would occur, but right now they were impervious and had the world by "the tail" as the saying goes.

**Chapter 12**

# VICTORIA IN D.C. AND NORTHERN DELAWARE UNIVERSITY

Victoria had a marvelous summer experience in Washington D. C. as an aide to Representative Woodson's staff. She gained their admiration with her tireless commitment and quick wit. His chief of staff, Larry Ogden, was amazed at how quickly she understood instructions and at general meetings offered constructive suggestions. She read and absorbed everything she got her hands on so she could better understand the workings of Congress, something he wished all the regular staffers would do. She wanted to be clearly aware and knowledgeable about what Representative Woodson was responsible for and involved with. In one general staff meeting where proposed changes to the income tax regulations were under review, with Representative Woodson having been appointed to a subcommittee on taxes, she suggested changes that would benefit middle income taxpayers, those that share the greatest tax burden. Her suggestion would have the effect of putting more spending power into the economy.

Another time as a member of a staff committee concerning farm subsidies, she delved deeply into the current regulatory structure and recommended a variation to create a more equitable balance that would encourage farmers to change their planting decisions which would benefit consumer pricing.

At one staff meeting just prior to the end of Victoria's summer internship, the subject of import/export imbalances was heatedly debated as U.S. trade imbalances were continually increasing. Howard Woodson started the meeting with an objective. "I want this committee to assist me in developing a realistic proposal that I can put on my congressional committee's agenda to at least move toward a positive direction before we become a second rate nation." The committee was somewhat taken aback by that discouraging remark. "We are losing business and jobs for Americans at an alarming rate. Therefore our tax revenues to support our great country are also in retreat. It will take more than this meeting, obviously, to develop a comprehensive approach. However, over the next three weeks, hopefully I can put something on the table to motivate the committee to speed up the process, and develop a bill to move along. God knows we need to combat this degenerating trend to our economy." He took a deep breath and glanced at his staff, presently digesting the gravity of what he said.

Larry Ogden, the chief of staff, was the first to respond. "I would suppose, Howard, we can put anything on the table to start the discussion."

"Right, anything goes," he agreed.

Jane Abel asked, "What industries are mostly affected?"

Woodson responded, "Many, Jane. Some of the most prominent are glass, tires and steel. In some cases, some of our most revered and historic companies have all but closed up shop in the good old USA, and others are very close to that."

"Are foreign companies taking their place here?" asked Jeff Crane.

"Not necessarily," Woodson responded, sitting back and crossing his legs.

"Are U.S. companies taking their place in the U.S.?" Jeff Crane asked.

"Our U.S. companies in many cases have set up shop overseas and provided jobs in those countries at much lower wages and left the providing of healthcare to the governments of those countries which, as you know, are only a fraction of our health care costs." Representative Woodson stated emphatically. Nods of agreement and versions of "it sure is" were voiced around the table.

Victoria was taking notes and understood the gravity and enormity of the problem. She realized to slow down and stop this trend some unusual and heretofore rarely invoked policies needed to be seriously considered. After deftly uniting her thoughts, she entered the discussion. "I know I'm only a student with no experience really," she started.

But Representative Woodson interrupted to reassure her. "Don't be silly Vicky. We don't have all the answers. Your opinion is important. So let's have it."

She continued "It seems to me a multifaceted approach can be taken. This can include imposing tariffs on the imports and using government subsidies to help support these industries."

"Subsidizing would eventually affect our taxes and increase our national debt," Larry retorted.

"You're right, Larry. That would happen, but I believe it would only be temporarily, if our domestic companies are able to compete due to our subsidizing. It's my understanding," she continued, "and correct me if I am wrong, that some of the companies we import these items and products from are being heavily subsidized by their governments, especially China, which is a major part of our problem, as I understand it." She turned to Howard Woodson to corroborate her response.

"You are correct, Victoria," he answered with a smile, surprised at her suggestions and her confidence in offering them. "These suggestions need to be put on the table. It may be a 'tit for tat', but they are certainly most logical to try and correct the imbalance we now face."

Jane Abel asked, "Do we have any idea how many jobs the U.S. has lost in these three industries?"

Representative Woodson had Victoria draft a letter some weeks ago asking several companies to respond to several key questions, one of which Jane just posed. "To be prepared I asked our young intern here to seek some vital stats that I can use in committee," said Woodson. "She has received a few and the feedback is alarming."

He nodded to Victoria and she opened her folder. She went down the list slowly and carefully so all could take accurate notes. "The chairman of the glass industry union advised that overall employment has declined 30% over the last nine years from about 135,000 to less than 95,000. One large company now operating in Europe now has more employees than in the entire U.S." She paused for emphasis, adding, "They answered back that almost three quarters of their sales are outside the U.S. Other companies reported employment of as low as 20% of what it was several years ago. I think it's important to add," she turned to the Congressman, "That some of our U.S. companies operating overseas are actually benefiting from subsidies received from those countries, but obviously we receive no taxes and no Americans receive a salary from those operations," she added. "It seems to me we need to level the playing field," she tacked on for good measure.

The staff was amazed at her grasp of the situation, an 18-year-old high school graduate, skillfully reporting the facts she had amassed.

Congressman Woodson gave her a broad smile and turned to his staff. "Any questions?" he asked. "Based on what we have heard and Vicky's report, I certainly agree that we ought to consider subsidies for our companies and charge tariffs on imports even if they originate from affiliates of overseas domestics because we get no financial benefit."

The rest of the staff was convinced. "O.K., then, that's what I'll bring to the committee. It will probably be bounced around a while. That's congress—as imperfect as it is, I wouldn't have any other type of government," he said with a sigh.

Jane Abel laughed a little. "It'll be very, very interesting as to what action they'll take and how long it will eventually be until a solution is finalized through Congress as a whole."

"It could take years until it's kicked around into a pulp, and maybe the four years that our brilliant intern will be in college," Larry Ogden smiled, and put his arm around Victoria's petite shoulders.

"I sure hope not. I sure hope not," Howard Woodson repeated, as he rose and looked at Victoria, raising his water glass to toast her as she starts her college career at Northern Delaware University.

"To Victoria. It was indeed a pleasure having you with us this summer. We truly enjoyed your spirit, dedication, and contribution to our efforts on behalf of our country." Howard Woodson and staff toasted her. "Everyone join me and toast this marvelous young woman as she starts college at Northern Delaware University, majoring in Political Science. I wouldn't be surprised that before the end of the semester she will be teaching the course."

"Here, here," the staff responded, clinking their champagne glasses.

Larry Ogden stood. "I'd like to add something. Victoria, you really surprised me with your energy and quick wit. You were a great addition to our staff and this very busy office. Initially, I looked at you as being a page. I soon realized you were much, much more than that. You were a marvelous addition to this office. We will all miss your contribution, but hope to have you return next year and visit with us when you can and sit in on meetings to give us the benefit of your thinking."

"Here, here," the staff responded again, and everyone headed for the sandwiches and salads.

Representative Woodson and Larry Ogden took her aside. "We both hope that you *will* return next summer," they almost implored.

"Oh, I planned on it, hoping you would want me to return," she answered.

"Of course we do!" Howard Woodson smiled at her. "As a matter of fact, if you can spare the time when you are off and we are in session, come and visit with us during the school year. I have also alerted my Delaware staff to welcome your presence so you can see what transpires on the local level as well."

"That would be great," Vicky smiled.

"Also, I will get you an Amtrak pass so you can travel as able. It's only 2 hours from home and you can stay with Audrey and Jennie like you did this summer."

"Thank you very, very much. I'd like that. It will keep me in touch, and I can start next June, running instead of crawling. I can't express my appreciation enough to the both of you."

"We too, express our appreciation to you. I can't ever imagine you crawling, Vicky," Larry Ogden responded.

Northern Delaware University was a large school for a small state. Many students from surrounding states were enrolled. It was a sprawling campus of over 20,000 students. Victoria's two best friends, Anne Herman and Laurie Fassert, enrolled with her. Anne majored in Education to become an English teacher, and Laurie in Engineering to follow her dad. They were fortunate to be able to share a relatively new apartment just off campus within walking distance of some classrooms with college buses nearby. The City of NuWalk was a typical college town where the permanent residents had a love/hate relationship with the students. There were charming and beautiful homes on the outskirts of the downtown area and college campus, but some rather worn ones closer in. Many were rented to the students. As with other college towns, the student dollars kept business humming, and the University provided entertainment and sport venues to the greater community. Even Uncle Sam got in the act with Army, Air Force, and Navy/Marine recruiting stations.

Victoria's high school Social Studies teacher John Snyder was a friend of Dr. Peter Salman, Dean of Political Science, who received a heads up from him, unknown to Victoria, regarding his former star pupil. The dean was indeed impressed and sent her an intra school invitation to meet with him at her earliest convenience. She was taken by surprise and quite excited as she lunched with Anne and Laurie at the relatively new and modern cafeteria that showcased the meals created by the University's Chef Program. When the three of them finally found a table in the crowded cafeteria, Victoria excitedly pulled Dr. Salman's invitation from her purse. "I received this from Dr. Salman, Dean of Government Studies. He wants to meet with me. I wonder what it's all about," she expressed between forkfuls of her salad.

"He's no doubt heard of you somehow," responded Laurie.

"Probably he wants to promote you to Professor Emeritus," added Anne. Both Vicky and Laurie almost choked on their salad and for a while couldn't stop laughing. When they stopped Laurie agreed.

Vicky took a deep breath and got serious. "I really want to keep a low profile and absorb as much as I can. I think college will be a lot more difficult than NuWalk High. Don't you guys think so?"

Anne shook her head "Vicky I think your pipe dreaming or something if you really think *you* can keep a low profile."

"Besides, we both enjoy who you are and what you do," Laurie added.

"We won't recognize the old Vicky if you change." Anne put her hand on Vicky's shoulder.

"Thanks guys, but I do believe you're prejudiced," she sort of giggled, which was unusual for her. I guess I just need to see the lay of the land first, so to speak."

"Sure, it will be tougher than Longport, but you won't even notice, I'm sure," Anne responded.

"Me too. I'm thrilled to be here with my barely B average. You probably won't miss a beat," contributed Laurie.

"My fan club. Thanks to you both." Victoria gave them both big smiles and squeezed their hands in appreciation.

Dr. Peter Salman was in his mid fifties with almost 15 years at Northern Delaware University and Chairman of Government studies the last 5. Besides knowing John Snyder, he also had more than a nodding acquaintance with Howard Woodson, who wrote a very comprehensive letter to N.D.U. recommending Victoria to the University and the program. His interest was really piqued. He had to meet this young lady with credentials beyond any student he knew. He reviewed the class rosters and noted that she was enrolled in Government 1. His initial thought was that she could greatly add to the curriculum by giving her fellow students the benefit of her Washington, D.C. experience. Hopefully she would be willing.

When she made her appointment with Dr. Salman, she didn't know what to expect. Anne and Laurie encouraged her to keep an open mind. She was making her way to his office with the map of the University in hand. In these first few days, before classes began, she was still learning the very spread out campus geography. In her travels through the halls and across the lawns from building to building, she stopped to say hello and chat with several NuWalk High graduates and former classmates, all of whom recognized her. *It was like homecoming week*, she thought. Of the 20,000 or so students from several states, it was amazing that she would see so many former classmates in one day. Some knew of her Washington, D.C. summer experience and asked her about it. She tried to converse with some, but apologetically had to move on for her appointment. She arrived out of breath and perspiring from the late August 90 degree heat and humidity.

Dr. Salman's secretary buzzed him, and Vicky put on her best smile. He stood up. "Hello Victoria, it's a pleasure to finally meet you. I have heard so much about you. Please sit." He came out from behind his desk and motioned to two very comfortable living room armchairs at a round table with a water pitcher, ice tea, and cups. "Would you care for some iced tea," he asked.

"Yes, that would be nice," she answered after drinking some cold water after her heated walk.

"I guess it is very warm out there. I have been in my office since 8:30, so I haven't experienced the 90 plus degrees."

"Take your time to cool off and relax," he said like a father to a daughter. She saw a very distinguished gentleman in his 50's, with wavy graying hair and mustache, in a summer weight dress shirt and flowered tie with his suit jacket neatly hanging on a clothes tree. He reached for the extension phone near the table and instructed his secretary to take messages while he was with Victoria. She liked his mannerisms and friendly disposition. She hadn't known what to expect, but was betting on stodgy, stuffy and egotistical.

She was very pleased that none of the three traits appeared to be present. Victoria sipped her tea, then she very naturally, to his pleasant surprise, started the conversation. "It sure is warm out there. I didn't realize your office was so far from the cafeteria. I need to catch my breath. I met so many of my former high school classmates on the way and that delayed me a bit."

"No problem," he waved his hand and shook his head with a smile, putting her so much at ease she felt like it was her dad.

"I am just getting ready for classes next week," she added.

"Glad we could have this chat before they start and you would be pressed for time. I have heard so much about you and wanted to discuss, with you, some thoughts concerning how you might, if you agree of course, be willing to enlighten your class regarding your experience with Representative Woodson and his *staff*.

Her interest was immediately piqued. "I'm flattered," she humbly responded. "I didn't realize my enrolling at N.D.U.

would be of such interest to the Department Chairman." She sat back waiting for him to answer. He leaned forward, removed his glasses and cupped his hands together.

"Victoria," he said, looking her eye to eye. She responded by matching his focus. "When I receive letters and phone calls concerning you from two men I admire and know well, I'd be a candidate for the loony bin if I didn't make an effort to meet with you."

Her eyes opened widely. "Really. Who do you mean?" He sat back.

"Why, John Snyder and Howard Woodson." He smiled broadly.

"Wow, I had no idea they would contact you. I don't know what to say," she kind of shook her head, as she normally was in control of her thought process and responsiveness.

"Well, you are held in the highest regard by two fine men so you needn't say anything. They said it all for you. I will say this. It is the first instance I have had a U.S. Congressman make time from a very busy schedule to call me concerning a new student. John Snyder and I know each other from various organizations. He was absolutely incredible with his praise for you."

"Wow," she said again. He just patiently waited for her to respond. "Mr. Snyder was my mentor, teacher, and friend at the same time. He was just super." Her voice and smile told it all. "I really enjoyed my summer internship with Congressman Woodson and his staff. I'm hoping to do it again next May."

"He expects you to. In fact, he told me he would be very disappointed and so would many of his staff if you didn't."

"They were all very nice and helpful to me. It was an exciting and surreal experience," Victoria just glowed as she spoke.

He marveled at her composure. After all, she was just 18.

Peter Salman leaned forward with his hands clasped, smiled broadly, and looked at her straight away "Victoria, here is what I propose you can do at N.D.U. How would you feel about helping your fellow students, with faculty assistance of course?" She raised her eyebrows, wondering what he meant. "I would like you to assist in making their learning experience at N.D.U. more of a real life experience and take the workings of government a major step up from the textbook. I want it to simulate the real thing as much as possible."

A broad smile on her face immediately told him she was with the program. She asked, "What does the faculty think?"

"That's a great question, Victoria. I have discussed it thoroughly with Mrs. Casper, Dr. Alfred, and Miss Cassidy, and they all feel it will greatly improve the curriculum. They are waiting to get started with the semester."

"Well," she took a deep breath assimilating this surprise.

"Do you think you can recreate in the classroom what you experienced last summer?" he hopefully asked.

"I can, leaving out the confidential aspects. We can talk about taxes, farm subsidies, and pork barrel issues, and how the compromise system works. Those were the issues I was most involved in. Perhaps we can divide a class into groups and have each defend their positions and conclusions for our professors to evaluate. Also we can do some role-playing. Each student can portray a member of congress and make a proposal to their fictitious counterparts, a fictitious congress so to speak, who can ask questions and challenge with logical reasoning."

She sat back, waiting for the Chairman's response to her suggestions, which poured out of her almost non-stop. He sat there smiling and astonished. *My God*, he thought, *what a brilliant young woman. N.D.U. had a real gem in their midst.* He let her catch her breath and cleared his own throat. "I must say, Victoria, that sounds like a marvelous plan that may take some time to develop. Perhaps we can start it later in the semester or even wait until the second. In the meanwhile, to prevent you from feeling pressured, I will alert the faculty to also provide ideas, and I can set up a joint meeting to plan this. It will be unique, to say the least. It will certainly be an experience for the faculty and the students."

He then sat back. Victoria reached out and shook his hand. "Thank you for this opportunity," she said.

"Thank you, Victoria. It's a pleasure to have you at Northern Delaware University and especially in Political Science."

It took him more than a few minutes to absorb his first meeting with Victoria. Over the years he had many excellent students but he could not remember any so gifted with such intensity, articulation, and logical reasoning residing in the same person and such a young person at that. He could only wonder what her future would hold.

Anne and Laurie were impatiently waiting for Vicky to return with the details of her visit with Dr. Salman.

"Well," they asked together wide eyed.

"Well," Vicky exhaled and flopped backwards on her bed, kicked her legs into the air and pedaled as if riding a bike, she was so excited.

"What did Dr. Salman want of a *mere* freshman?"

"He asked me to help start a new program with the faculty. He wants me to implement and choreograph simulated sessions of Congressional staff and committees discussing various topics."

"Wow, and you wanted to keep a low profile," Laurie gasped.

"If that's low, I can't even imagine what's high," added Anne.

Laurie turned serious "Vicky how will you manage all that and your classes also?"

"Well, Dr. Salman said he would have the faculty help me put it all together. I can direct the discussions—it will be a challenge, but so much fun." She raised her hands high in the air as if she had it all figured out.

"Sounds simple when you put it that way," Anne shrugged.

"There is one thing I am concerned about, though," Laurie interjected into the conversation with her finger tapping her chin. Anne and Vicky sat on the edge of the bed and looked at Laurie intently.

"When the heck are you going to find the right guy with such a hectic schedule? College is a lot of work, you know." They all laughed for what seemed like several minutes.

Vicky took a deep breath and shook her head. "I have so much that I want to accomplish that I don't know either. I probably won't even recognize him when I meet him. Time will tell, I guess."

"Well we have about 9,000 or so to look over here at N.D.U., so we will have to start the weeding out process in a hurry—we only have four years. Let's see. That's 2,250 plus a year to check out, unless many are snatched early before our very eyes," Anne contributed and they all laughed again.

Laurie then suggested "We should start the weeding out process tonight at dinner. We have no time to lose ladies." They slapped their hands together in agreement.

# Chapter 13

# KEITH ENTERS NORTHERN DELAWARE UNIVERSITY

Hours turned to days, days to weeks, weeks to months. Winter came and went, spring bloomed, the heat of summer burned brightly, fall colored the landscape and time started the cycle all over again. Over one year later had passed and Keith was working hard to rebuild his body and strengthen his mind. He went to school part time and spent most of his days laboring in a gym. It seemed like forever to him. Barbara and Richard kept encouraging him on, praying and hoping he would regain his strength, coordination, and will to succeed to eventually live a full, productive adult life. He was now well on his way. It was now time to take the next big step in his life.

Keith took the advice of his Dad and enrolled in the Criminal Justice Curriculum offered by the local Community College after his doctors told him he could, in time, be 100% of his former physical self. He thought that beginning the program on a part time basis, while he was rebuilding his body, then switching to full time days would be a good plan. If successful he could continue on toward his Baccalaureate Degree and then apply to the Government for Secret Service training, which he ultimately decided on rather than the military. He sat down and penned a letter to Nick and Nelson. They had been corresponding off and on since the brothers joined the Air Force.

"Hi, guys. I just wanted you to know that I have made a final decision concerning my career. I know you may be disappointed, but I have decided on the U.S. Secret Service. I am enrolled in the County Community College part time. I am also hard at work trying to get my body back in shape. Boy, is it tough to get up every morning and workout. But I have to do it or I will never, and never is a very long time, get my strength and coordination back. I hope, once I am more physically able, to enroll in a four year college with a Political Science program which is very acceptable to the Secret Service. I sure hope you guys like the Air Force. Write soon."

The brothers each received a copy. They had been separated, themselves many miles apart at different schools, and responded separately, in their own time, wishing him well and asking him to keep the letters flowing.

Barbara Fredericks was looking at various college catalogs they had sent for to help Keith decide on where to apply. "Rich," she turned toward her husband, "It appears that Northern Delaware University in NuWalk, only about 50 miles south of us, has what looks like a very good Political Science Program."

"Really?" Richard responded, "That's great. It would be real handy for us to see Keith more frequently than if he was across country somewhere, and I understand they have a good football team too."

Barbara laughed. "Well, that that's even more in their favor."

"Does Keith have any preference?" he asked.

"Not that he has told me. He's so intent on just going to Community, he hasn't thought of a University. He's so happy that physically he'll be ready to go full time anywhere."

"A University education would greatly approve his chances of being accepted. We need to give it a shot," Richard expressed.

"I agree," Barbara chimed in.

"Does the catalog say he can enroll at N.D.U. in the spring, or must he wait for the fall semester?" he asked Barbara.

"I don't know. Let me read that section of the catalog," she thumbed through it. "I don't see where that question is addressed."

He reached for the phone. "Let's give the Admissions Office a call." He connected with the Assistant Director. She advised him that certain courses in the program had prerequisites and that it would be difficult for Keith if he started mid year. Doing so might require him going beyond four years to complete the program. While a couple of his Community College Courses would qualify, some would not. After explaining Keith's long recovery period, he advised that a wheel chair would be necessary for at least one semester and perhaps longer. She gave assurance to them that it would be no problem at all as they were totally handicapped accessible, including dorms and apartments, with more than a few handicapped students requiring wheel chairs.

He apprised Barbara of his conversation. "We will have to go over this with Keith and see how he feels about it. He needs to make the decision, after all," she said, and sat next to her husband. They hugged for the longest time, both of them shedding some tears, thankful that they, but mostly Keith, reached this point leaving misery far behind. He needed to get on with the rest of his life. He and his parents firmly believed God chose him to do some wonderful things.

Keith finished his last semester at Community College, excited to enter Northern Delaware University. He was careful to take courses that met the prerequisite requirements. Fortunately Richard and Barbara were able to arrange for a handicapped accessible dormitory close to many of the classrooms where Keith could catch the special bus for the handicapped. Keith was both ecstatic and nervous about all that was happening. It wasn't so long ago that he was wondering if he would ever be normal again. His desire and willpower to recover, excellent medical care, and his parents' love and encouragement all contributed to his chances of living a full and vibrant life. He was, perhaps, a year away. Being admitted to a major university gave him a huge emotional boost to work his mind and body extra hard, enabling him to recover his independence and rely on himself once again.

Mom and Dad helped him move in by unpacking boxes, hanging up clothes, setting up the stereo, and accompanying him around the sprawling campus to learn the lay of the land. An important part of that was the gymnasium and exercise center. Keith needed to maintain his exercise regimen so not to delay full recovery. Before Richard and Barbara left for home on Sunday, they watched him leave the wheelchair and maneuver with a cane to a stationary bicycle to strengthen his legs. There were approximately two dozen students working away on various machines.

"It looks like these students are taking in the last few days of summer at the gym rather than the beach," Richard observed.

Barbara looked around. She laughed, "I was so intent on watching Keith that I really didn't notice. Keith, hopefully, will be one of those students at the beach next year," she added.

"Let's hope so sweetie. Let's hope so," said Richard, putting his arm around Barbara's waist as they both focused on Keith.

Two female students were about to pass Keith's machine on their way to the exit when, noticing the wheel chair, they stopped. The blonde woman walked up to Keith and held out her hand. "Hello, welcome to N.D.U. I'm Victoria Magnuson—Vicky for short."

Keith stopped his workout and took a deep breath. "Hi, I'm Keith Fredericks. It's nice to meet you. Hope you don't mind me not getting up."

"No, of course not," Victoria responded, having noticed the wheel chair and cane. She also nodded and smiled at

Barbara and Richard, who were extremely pleased that she took the time to introduce herself.

"Hello, I'm Anne Herman," and Keith nodded to Anne also.

"We haven't seen you here at the gym before or perhaps we have been here at different times?" Vicky continued.

"No, I only registered this past week and only learned of the gym. This is my first visit. I am sure glad it's here. I'll make good use of it. I need to step up and maintain my therapy," he answered.

Vicky thought of asking how he became disabled, but thought better of it. She didn't want to pry. "We would be happy to show you around the campus. We're old hands, having been here about two weeks." She and Anne laughed. So did Keith, Mom and Dad who were so pleased at her friendliness and easy manner.

"We will see you around, Keith. Keep up the good work," said Vicky. She and Anne smiled and nodded to Keith's mom and dad as they left the gym.

"That was nice of them to introduce themselves. Victoria seems especially interesting, like a . . . I can't quite describe what I mean," Richard rubbed his chin.

"You're right, Rich. I had similar thoughts. How about unique or special?" Barbara offered.

"That's it—special," he agreed.

"How about beautiful too," Keith added.

Mom and Dad both smiled, glad that he responded as a young man should. Then, he became somewhat solemn. "I guess the wheel chair got her attention," he said dejectedly.

"Well, Keith, it was still special. Most people would look but go right by, thinking 'there but the grace of God go I,'" Richard responded, trying to keep things positive. Richard put his arm around his son's shoulder.

"Besides honey, you will be rid of the chair and on your own legs, hopefully by spring. Just concentrate on what you need to do—keep working to get better." Barbara leaned into him on the machine and gave him a long loving hug.

The first day of classes saw heavy rain after a few days of sun. Keith looked out his dorm window at the students scurrying about to get out of the rain. How he wished he could scurry about. *Oh well—it will happen—it will!* He thought to himself positive thoughts. Mom and Dad would be proud. Coming back to the present, he realized his first class was Political Science 1 at 9:00. It was now 7:30. He hoped the rain would stop or let up when he left the dorm for breakfast, then catch the disabled student bus at 8:30 or so.

Unfortunately, it was raining even harder as he struggled with the wheel chair to the bus stop. He huddled in his poncho with a heavy text and notebook on his lap. Two other disabled students were also there. They exchanged greetings. *Only they,* Keith thought, *could experience the frustration he felt.* He was getting down again and had to stop that. He had to think positive, remain determined and believe every day was a day closer to freedom from the chair. He could do it. He knew he could!

It was a relatively short bus ride to the Political Science classroom building. It was still pouring, and he had a lot to maneuver going across walkways, around curbs, and through many students all rushing to class ignoring his difficulty, except for one student.

Victoria saw the disabled student struggling ahead of her and wondered if it was Keith from the gym. She stepped up her pace, holding her large umbrella up high so she wouldn't clip another student. Suddenly, Keith realized he no longer had rain pouring on him.

"Hello, Keith. It is surely a terrible morning." He looked up, surprised, and saw her broad smile gracing the hood of the poncho as she held the umbrella over him.

"You bet. Thanks for the protection, Victoria. Right?"

"Right."

"Why don't you hold the umbrella and I'll push."

"No, you needn't," he started to protest.

"Nonsense, it's the least I can do," she insisted.

Keith decided she was to strong-willed to argue with. Besides, he really appreciated the help as it was really pouring.

"I guess you're heading to the Political Science lecture. Am I right?" she asked.

"Right on. How about you?"

"Yes, me too. It's my *favorite* subject," she emphasized. Another considerate student saw them, and held the large door open for them.

"Where do we go from here?" Keith wondered. "Down the hall at Room 120, where most everyone is headed. It's a large lecture hall."

"Wow," Keith uttered, as she pushed him in that direction as he closed and shook her wet umbrella. "Wow," he repeated as they entered 120. "It's larger than any classroom I've ever seen."

"O.K., Keith where do you want to park it?" she asked.

"I'll do it, Victoria," he suddenly was embarrassed. "I will stay here at the back. I can exit easier that way," he turned to tell her and asked, "Where will you sit?"

"Oh," she hesitated "I have to go up front this morning," she muttered. He was surprised at the way she answered, as it wasn't like her. He looked at her but didn't question further.

"Thanks for the help and the umbrella," he called to her. She turned and smiled.

Keith looked around as the room really filled up, and figured there were well over 100 students in attendance. Dr. Salman walked up to the podium and introduced himself. "Good morning, ladies and gentlemen. The weather has not cooperated, but I am pleased to see so many enthusiastic political science majors here this morning. Thank you to our upper class persons, and our first year politicos. Thank you all for choosing political science as your major. It's not a quantifiable science such as mathematics, biology, or chemistry but it certainly will make you think and, depending on your level, will sharpen your debating and reasoning skills. It will not be a cakewalk or, as some might say, a walk in the park," he emphasized, "but if *you* make the effort a lot will be learned. We cannot promise you the presidency, the governorship, or even the mayoralty of your town. However, we will make certain this course, at all class levels, will be invigorating, interesting, and above all, challenging. If anyone has a problem with the word 'challenging' you may tune me out now and leave whenever you wish."

He stopped at that point for a couple of minutes or so and scanned the large room. Keith didn't see anyone leave. He certainly didn't expect the Chairman to say what he did, but he respected what he heard. This was his major, and he would do it justice and himself proud. Dr. Salman continued, "This year we have added a special program which the faculty, my associates Mrs. Casper, Dr. Alfred and Miss Cassidy will supervise." He turned to the other professors, and they stood up and each gave a short wave to the student body. Vicky didn't want to be introduced, to the entire student body of the department, on the first day of the semester, but Dr. Salman insisted. "We have the good fortune this year to have a young lady enrolled this semester with actual experience at the federal government level with Representative Woodson's office. She actively participated in his staff meetings, worked with his staff on position papers to Congress, and listened in on various Congressional committees." He turned, "Victoria, please stand and be recognized."

Keith involuntarily found his mouth opening and then he gulped. Victoria smiled as she turned her head from side to side, then quickly sat to avoid being considered vain.

Dr. Salman added, "Victoria Magnuson will work with the faculty to bring her experience to the classroom via a series of mock debates and discussions similar to those that take place in the offices of our legislators and our congress. It will add much to the traditional textbook learning you will receive. We are very fortunate to have her at N.D.U."

Keith was astonished, to say the least. He knew she was different, given her friendliness and helpfulness toward him. Knowing this, however, clearly added to her persona. She was already a ten in his book. He was now thinking in the hundreds. The faculty took over for Dr. Salman and spent the remainder of the period outlining courses and what they expected. Keith realized the work ahead of him and took a deep breath, resolving to do well.

The student next to him turned his head. "Boy, this sounds tough. Maybe I will switch majors while I still can. We only have a week when we are allowed."

Keith looked at him and smiled. "I'm glad it will be tough. As the old saying goes 'When things get tough, the tough get tougher.'"

The guy seemed not to get it, staring at him, and shrugging his shoulders. Keith smiled and silently, again, thanked God for his life, being at this place of learning, and getting stronger by the day. Bring on his future. He was ready.

The students began to leave before Keith could maneuver his way out the doors. They mostly excused themselves as they just squeezed and rushed past him in their haste, so he patiently waited, not feeling inadequate or sorry for himself in any way. His newfound inner strength was working. He could see the rain had not abated, so he would have a messy trip back to his dorm. Victoria noticed him as she worked her way up the center aisle, now conversing with many students who were asking her question after question. She politely excused herself and walked in his direction.

"Do you mind if I walk with you?" she asked.

"That will be great, if you don't walk too fast," he laughed. He was extremely pleased that she took the time. She smiled, "I promise not to. However, I do promise to give you help in this sloppy weather. Is that O.K. with you, or will you be embarrassed?" she asked.

"No, I really appreciate it." They exited the building, and she opened her large umbrella just in time. As they moved toward the student cafeteria, students were busy asking her about her "Washington experience." Keith was amazed at her poise, intelligence, and her vivaciousness. He thought she was about 19, going on 38 or so. The crowd began to thin out.

She asked him, "How about the snack bar for a hot drink or two?" He was surprised, but responded, "That sounds great—my treat, I insist."

"O.K.," she broadly smiled.

They found a cozy corner table. Keith maneuvered his way out of the wheel chair and with a little help from Victoria plopped into a stationary chair, remarking it felt good to sit like a "real" person. She lightly squeezed his shoulder and went to the counter to get hot chocolates and two doughnuts.

"I hope you like these. I ration myself to only two a week. It satisfies my sweet tooth," she smiled.

He, for the first time, really stared at her and marveled at her green eyes and blondish hair. He was truly amazed that she wasn't surrounded by guys, and even more truly amazed that she paid him so much attention. It quickly flashed across his mind that she just felt sorry for him, but he didn't want to go down that road. He wanted to be liked for who he was, and not because of his current disability. Maybe he was being unfair to her. He shook his head to clear it, lest she realize his momentary lapse and question her sanity in befriending him. She noticed his longer than usual silence, and started the conversation with a common thread they enjoyed—their major, Political Science.

"What made you choose *my* major?" she teased.

"Yeah," he began, "it's easy to see why it's *your* major," he teased back. "Well, I suppose as a kid I was always fascinated with cops and robbers, then the military. As a teenager through High School my two friends, Nick and Nelson, and I imagined being in some kind of heroes in the Army, Navy, or Marines."

"A typical boy's dream," she added with a smile.

"I suppose it was sort of a Hollywood fantasy," he continued, "We were all going to join after graduation, but my parents were not happy at all that I would directly enlist in the military and then maybe, just maybe, go to college some day in the distant future. Then I had this gosh darn (he was thinking God damn but thought better of it in her company) motorcycle accident that came damn (he thought damn was very appropriate at this point) close to ending it all for me. My parents worked on me to go to college, thank God, during my recovery." He took a moment to pause.

Victoria was listening intently, and then asked "What made you choose Political Science then?"

"Well, I suppose in my mind it was the closest connection to the military. I thought I could serve my country in another way by protecting the president as a Secret Service Agent. In addition, besides it being an honorable profession, it includes travel, good salary, meeting and dining with or, at least, close to, famous people," he laughed and so did Victoria. "Not to mention a great pension and lots of memories."

She was impressed with that instantaneous and rather thoughtful response. She liked this guy.

"I must say, you have me convinced that you will be successful."

He took a large bite of his doughnut compared to her small one and a gulp or two of hot chocolate to her sip and added, "If I fully recover from my injuries, that is."

She felt his concern. "I'll pray for you. You seem to have come a long way. What do the doctors say?"

"They agree that I will walk again, but I may always have a limp."

"Will that prevent you from qualifying for the Secret Service?" she asked.

"Probably. I am afraid to inquire. Obviously as an agent I will need to run, maybe jump fences and all that. A limping agent would be a liability. So I intend to overcome that. It is my big number one goal in life right now," and he raised his cup. She raised hers, too, and they met with a solid clink.

"Keith, I truly believe you will overcome—be judicious about it. Don't slack off one bit. I will be looking for you at the gym."

"I will," he emphasized, "do my best, but getting busy with class work may interfere and it will be harder to do as time goes by."

She looked at him eye to eye "I will tell you what. Let's trade room phone numbers and promise each other to once a week bug each other to meet at the gym, and more often if possible."

"Easier said than done, but I really appreciate this pep talk. You are a really special person," he added.

She put her hand on his shoulder "Keith—you must not give up. You must meet your goals." He was really quite amazed at her tenacity, and extremely flattered at her concern for him. Actually, she surprised herself that she became immersed in this fine young man given her very ambitious agenda. She needed to slow down any potential of a galloping romance. It was not in her game plan at this point in her life.

"Well, enough about me. How about you answering some questions." He playfully pointed his finger at her chin with a smile. She smiled back after a sip of chocolate, getting colder, and a larger bite of the doughnut.

"O.K. Shoot some my way."

"I guess I know what you plan on doing—going into politics, I presume."

"You guessed correctly but you were at the lecture so you had a good chance to get it right." They laughed.

Keith then seriously asked, "Tell me something of yourself."

"Like what?" she asked. "Well, for instance, what did you do in high school?"

She sipped her now cool chocolate and took a deep breath. "I certainly hope I will not be boring you."

"I have a feeling that I will not be bored," he said, smiling.

She looked briefly at the clock, realizing the next period was fast approaching, which permitted time for the short version for which she was grateful. The last thing she wanted was to appear vain to him. It could put a damper on their friendly relationship. "My four years of High School were truly a treasure. I just loved the school, had many friends, two of whom are also freshman here at N.D.U.. I was fortunate to have been elected," she hesitated, "class president for four years. I had two summers in Washington, D.C., as an aide to Representative Woodson's staff and requested he ask Secretary of State Colleen Reese to give the commencement speech at my high school graduation."

"Holy smokes," Keith blurted out, amazed. "Four years straight. What an amazing feat. Incredible." She just looked at him as he continued to shake his head.

Time was of the essence, so she was grateful not to go into any more detail. "We need to move on, Keith, I will help you to your bus and I will see you regularly in Government and Economics."

"I will be looking forward to it. You can bet on that, Madame President," he said with a large smile, so pleased to have met and talked with her at length. He knew she was special. Now he realized that she was even beyond that.

They remained friends in their four years at N.D.U. Keith really enjoyed the mock legislative sessions Victoria held in class and participated actively. She involved him in role-playing, which he enjoyed immensely. He had, for a while, a definite crush on her. For her part she remained very fond of him, but was fixated on her studies and future career. Anne and Laurie tried to nudge her to increase her social activity, especially special dances, but she responded infrequently. Keith had initially wished for a personal relationship but, realizing it was not to be, also became immersed in his studies. Now that he was finally physically sound, he could pursue his career also.

# Chapter 14

# THE CHAMPIONSHIP GAME

It was a beautiful day for the game that decided the conference championship. Genevieve gathered as many of her friends as she could, and packed a section of the stands to assure a loud cheering section. A lot more than the Conference championship was at stake. If State U. won this game, they could go on to the College World Series for the very first time. State U. was tied with Alpha University, who was playing Hammel College near Richmond. If both won or lost, a one game playoff would ensue. A victory today by one and a loss by the other would ensure the victor would play Northern California U. in the College World Series.

Excitement was at a fever pitch on this beautiful day in early June. For the first time in 20 years, baseball rivaled football in excitement at the University. Genevieve and her friends made sure they purchased tickets early for their strategic seats. An additional 5,000 seats were added along right and left field, increasing the capacity to over 15,000. Busses were ferrying people from distant parking lots all over the campus. Many more refreshment booths and portable Johns were added. Head coach Gene Spencer and his Assistant Coach looked out from the dugout and were amazed at the fabulous turnout, which would motivate the team even more.

Coach Spencer had psyched his players and they felt they could do it. Winning it all was a long shot, but they would take one game at a time. For the seniors, it was their last chance to hold the cup in their hands. They were playing Randolph College, third in the 6 team conference with a record of 13-10. State U. was leading the season series 2-1, but Randolph was a tough team and would like nothing better than to ruin their hopes. Several busloads of Randolph students were in the stands to root their team on.

In the locker room, Coach Spencer had the team gather around him. "Guys, we can win this, but don't take anything for granted. We need to concentrate. Remember in April when we were ahead 6-1 in the 7th and we lost our focus and they beat us. We can't afford that this time. This is our chance to put State U. baseball on a national level for the first time. We can't depend on Hammel beating Alpha. We have to beat Randolph ourselves. Let's beat them!" he shouted.

They all came together around the coach yelling, "Let's beat Randolph," slapping hands until they hurt and they were out of breath.

When the response subsided the coach decided to again instill his philosophy. As he put it, "Randolph has nothing to lose. They would like nothing better than to knock us off. It would be like them winning the CWS. We can't let that happen. Let's play our game—let's go out there and have fun and WIN!" He created a second rousing response. They caught their breath and began their quest.

David and Stan Mars were in the middle of the team as they entered the field for practice, to tumultuous applause.

"Holy cow," gushed Stan, scanning the field. "Look at all these people!"

"I'll say," gulped David. "It is incredible, almost major league." His heart was really pumping as he put two sticks of gum in his mouth to transfer the pressure a bit. He handed two sticks to Stan. David, in his senior year, had set new State U. single season and college career records for average, home runs, and runs batted in. He was now on the brink of leading his team to the College World Series. The anticipation of the students, faculty, and parents was enormous, and so was the pressure.

In addition, the Marauders were closely watching their investment. General Manager Randy Cameron and Assistant General Manager Harold Baker were sitting several rows back off the first base side to avoid being obvious and making David unnecessarily apprehensive. They had recently signed him, true to their word four years ago, when they first discovered him at their Florida summer camp. He would begin playing in their farm system this summer. David had trouble staying grounded with all that was happening. Genevieve was trying to keep him focused but she also had a lot happening; Ron Bannister had her heavily booked in summer stock after graduation. She would be traveling extensively beginning later in June.

David looked toward the first base stands for Genevieve and he saw several coeds, including Genevieve, holding up a long banner while standing on the seats. "BEAT RANDOLPH! WE ARE THE CHAMPS!" He waved and Genevieve waved back.

"He saw the banner. Keep holding it up," she shrieked.

They were all shouting, "State U, State U, we're the champs. We're going to the series, rah, rah, rah."

"If I didn't know better, I would think it was football season," Coach Spencer wisecracked, then clapped his hands and shouted, "O.K., batting and fielding practice. Game starts in seventy five—let's get the cobwebs out." Randolph left the field and the players traded barbs good-naturedly. Randolph was doing what it could to beat State U. They rested their ace, John Fleming, for this game. He gave State U. a challenge every outing. They were 1-1 as he bested them 2-1 earlier in the season, and they bested him 3-2 the last time they met. David was 2 for 6, with two walks, one strikeout, one double, and one single. It should be mentioned he pulled two "foul home runs" well over the right field fence, with one missing the foul pole by only two feet.

State U. would be starting Andy Gibbs, their number three guy, and then use the entire staff, if necessary, even Ron Evans, their ace, who pitched 7 innings only 2 days ago in beating the number two team in the conference, Blanders U. Over the last two weeks State U. was neck and neck with Blanders and needed to push their pitching staff like never before. For State U., if they won this game and Alpha U. won theirs they would have a one game playoff at a neutral stadium in two days, and Ron Evans would be reasonably rested unless he was required today. Coach Spencer hoped he could avoid that, because his number 2 guy, Larry Davane, had some arm tenderness. The best scenario would be for State U to beat Randolph and for Hammel to beat Alpha. Then the CWS wouldn't begin for a week and the pitching staff as well as some position players with minor ailments would be 100% ready to go. Unfortunately other scenarios could occur such as both State U. and Alpha losing, which required a playoff in any event.

Coach Spencer had all this in his mind and just shook his head, saying to himself, *Wake up Gene, wake up. Take one game at a time or you'll lose focus; this is it, right now, for all the marbles. If you win this at least your career will have a milestone and WHEN, not if, we win THIS GAME, we will go all the way!*

Having successfully psyched himself up, he stood alternately in the batting cage, on the infield, and visited the outfield, encouraging his team and coaching staff to help carry the torch he started. Now they needed to execute.

David took some throws at first and fielded some grounders, then jogged up and down the right field line to loosen up his legs. On his third return to first base he spotted Genevieve waving to him by the box seats near first. He jogged over. "Hi, sweet stuff."

"Hi, D," she said, wrapping her arms around his neck and squeezing. They refrained, with all their might, from kissing.

Definitely against the rules, but they were already pushing the envelope and they knew it. Quickly disengaging, the couple smiled at each other. Box seat fans shook his hand, slapped his back, and gave him the glad hand. Several rows back, toward the right and holding score cards in front of their faces and taking it all in were the Marauder's brass, Randy Cameron and Harold Baker. Genevieve blew David a kiss as he started to go to the batting cage.

"For luck, honey," she smiled.

"Can't lose now," he quipped.

This exchange didn't get past Coach Gene Spencer. "O.K., David. I think she's sufficiently revved you up. Let's use that energy in the batting cage."

All the time, however, David was wondering how he would break the surprise he had planned for her. If they lost the game, he would be deflated and it would be anticlimactic, so he might delay it. Of course, winning would make it super spectacular. *Oh, what the heck, we're going to win. Besides, it's super spectacular all by itself,* he decided. He swung at Assistant Coach Dahling's offering and socked it about 410 feet over the right field wall.

"Atta boy, Dave," Stan Mars shouted to his buddy as he waited his turn at the cage.

"Please all rise for the 'Star Spangled Banner,' sung by State University's own Genevieve Carter," the announcement all were waiting for. Genevieve, who had been quite honored by the request, took a deep breath and gave a beautiful rendition, putting her all into it as she was on an emotional high. David's eyes and ears were riveted to her standing at home plate, her beautiful blonde hair waving in the slight breeze, and her melodious voice permeating the stadium by way of several strategically-placed microphones. As she sang the last stanza, the stadium crescendo began and increased to the end, punctuated by loud cheers to "play ball" from the mikes.

The courtesy abated, for the most part, as Harvey Freedman, Randolph's leadoff hitter, was announced with boos far outnumbering the cheers of Randolph College fans.

Andy Gibbs threw his last warm ups and Freedman stepped in. He took a strike, to more cheers. Then Gibbs lost the plate and walked him. Al Grant, the catcher, went out to settle him down and told him to stop trying to thread the needle. "Just rare back and fire," he advised. On the third pitch to the second hitter, Freedman a speedster, took off to steal second, and was successful as Grant's throw sailed into center. The catcher mad, at himself, kicked the ground.

"Settle down, guys," Coach Spencer shouted through cupped hands, then decided to call timeout, and ran out to the mound. David joined them at the mound with Al and shortstop Ben Evert. "Calm down, Andy, and slow down. You're rushing your pitches," Coach said, putting his arm around Gibbs' shoulders.

"Andy, your curve isn't working yet—let's give them more heaters mixed with changeups, and I'll call for a sinker or two to see if it will mess up their minds," Al Grant added.

"O.K., guys, go get 'em," Coach Spencer yelled as he trotted back to the dugout.

Andy walked around the mound and rubbed up a new ball. He took a deep breath, stepped up to the mound again, and peered in for the sign. The State fans were temporarily silent, but Randolph fans, concentrated down the left field side, were not. Al called for a changeup on a 2 and 1 count, and it was smashed past the mound into center. 1-0, Randolph College.

Andy again rubbed up a new ball, circled the mound, and faced the number 3 hitter. On a 2-2 count, he lined the ball deep to left, caught on the warning track for out number one. The State U. dugout and fans held their collective breath. The cleanup hitter, Bill Willis, strode to the plate. He, historically, has hit Andy well. He took a deep breath, deciding to be cautious with him. Ball one was high and outside. Al called for a curve, but Andy brushed him off. They agreed on a change. That pitch was smoked well over the right field wall. 3-0 Randolph.

State fans were stunned as Randolph fans were hooting and hollering. Finally, a share of State fans booed their counterparts, but most knew their team had to rise to the occasion to reverse the current situation, or perhaps the curtain would fall on the season of hopes.

Coach Spencer trotted out again and asked Andy how he felt.

"Sorry, Coach, I just don't have my comfort level yet." Al Grant thought it was poor follow through and suggested Andy concentrate more on that.

"Maybe you should just use your fastball for now—it's usually around 90. Just try to get through this inning," David suggested.

Coach Spencer agreed and they broke up as the ump was striding toward the mound. At this point Genevieve and friends, as most of State's fans, were conspicuously quiet while Randolph's were ecstatic.

Andy and Al followed David's advice, retiring the next two hitters.

"O.K., guys, let's make up those runs. We can get them, it's only the first inning." Stan led the cheerleading while Coach Spencer and Assistant Coach Dahling walked up and down the dugout to energize State's stunned bench. However the comeback, if it was to come, would have to wait as State meekly succumbed 1-2-3 without a hard hit ball. The loud cheering of the fans didn't help.

Andy did settle in for innings 2, 3, and 4. A few balls were hit hard as he allowed just two hits and walked two. There was a momentary scare when, with one aboard, a drive was barely foul as it left the yard. However, to the chagrin of all, State had nine more men up and nine more men down as Randolph's ace, John Fleming, was doing his thing. State's fans were restless as they followed the scoreboard showing

Alpha U. leading Hammel College 1-0 in the second inning. Here, in the fifth, two singles, an error, a walk and a long out made it 4-0 Randolph. A great play by State's shortstop prevented another run. Randolph and Fleming had two more outs in the fifth when Stan Mars batting third, to Fleming's dismay, fouled off 8 pitches and drew a walk.

The crowd awoke as David strode to the plate. "Let's go State, let's go Dave," they clapped and chanted as he strode to the plate. He struck out in the second on, he had to admit, a great sinker. He thought to himself, *no wonder the Los Angeles Hawks gave Fleming a large bonus to sign.* Would he ever face him at the major league level? *Oh, well, wake up,* he thought, *all that counts is I'm facing him now. Make it count right now,* he thought. Fleming, with a 4-0 lead, attacked him and got two quick strikes. One was questionable and the other on a home run swing that created a breeze.

"Come on, Dave, just meet it. Let's get a bingle," yelled Coach Spencer.

"Let's go, State," yelled the fans. Genevieve and crew were parading their 20 foot banner up and down the stands from right field to left, much to the displeasure of the Randolph contingent when the banner blocked their view as Genevieve seemed to direct her troops to pause inordinately at their location.

Over the noise of the crowd, David imagined Genevieve's voice even though it was impossible to hear. He stepped out, and a glance enabled him to see the banner being held up high. He smiled and stepped back in, proceeding to make Fleming throw eight more pitches before forcing Stan at second. Fleming gave him a long look as he left the mound.

"Atta way, Dave. You made him work," Coach Spencer clapped. He succeeded in making Fleming pitch the equivalent of an extra inning. However, Andy was laboring again in the sixth and the scoreboard had Alpha U. leading Hammel 3-1 in the 4th, not what the team and State U. fans wanted to see. Andy retired the first hitter but walked the second. Coach

Spencer jogged to the mound and the rest of the infield joined in. Jake Nelson, a fast balling lefty, was warming up. The coach signaled him in and patted Andy on the back as he left the mound. He handed the ball to Jake as two lefties were coming up. "O.K., Jake. Go get 'em, man," Coach encouraged him.

"O.K., coach, will do." Jake had performed admirably this past season and the team hoped he could continue his success.

Coach Spencer then turned around and emphasized again, "Go right after them. Don't mamby pamby around."

"O.K., Coach, you betcha. I'll hold them."

Jake was State U's most reliable reliever with a live fastball sometimes clocked at 98 mph, and a crisp curve, but he could be wild. Sometimes that wildness kept hitters on edge, and they swung when it wasn't appropriate. The Marauders brass were interested in him and Messrs. Cameron and Baker were pleased to have the opportunity to observe him front and center. After a few throws on the mound, he was ready. He went into the stretch position and fired a 90 plus mph fastball not to the plate, but to first, picking off the base runner as David slapped the tag on him for out number one. David had learned to be ready with Jake Nelson in the mound as this was his 7th successful pick off, a league high. Jake struck out the next two hitters on 7 pitches. Almost every State U. fan joined the team dugout in standing and clapping as he walked to the dugout. The last of the 7th was looming.

"O.K., men, let's turn this game around," Coach Spencer and Assistant Dahling were shouting to the bench, imploring some offense. The scoreboard was still 3-1 Alpha U. going into the 5th when it suddenly changed to 3-2 and a cheer rose in the stands and started a rhythmic clapping to get State U's bats in gear. Robbie Vincent, the number 9 hitter was 0 for 2 with a strikeout and a pop out. Fleming had allowed only three harmless hits and one walk. On a 1 and 2 count Vincent hit a hard grounder to the right of shortstop whose backhanded attempt failed and Robbie reached first on the hit. At the end of the 5th it was still Alpha 3 and Hammel College 2, a little better. Jerry Collins hitting leadoff on a 2-0 count laid down a surprise bunt, catching the third baseman napping. Coach told him to get on any way he could and he did. Barry Harmon, hitting second, ran the count full, fouling off 4 pitches. Fleming circled around the mound, slamming the rosin bag down. His coach and infield came to the mound to the boos of the crowd, who wanted State to continue the momentum.

Genevieve and her friends again toured the stadium with the banner. Those with hoarse voices were immediately rescued by a substitute in waiting as there was no shortage of voices for this vital game.

The Randolph bullpen got busy as a lefty and rightie started to toss. The ump broke up the conference. Fleming peered in for the sign as Harmon pumped the bat. In came a low fastball, and the batter hammered it to deep left center. The center fielder raced over, dove and made a spectacular back handed catch, rolling over with the ball coming out of his mitt. Vincent and Collins held up, then tagged up as the ump made the belated out call. The throw to third was off line and Vincent was able to slide in around the tag. For the first time State U. had two runners in scoring position. The State U. fans were beside themselves as they were shouting, "State U.! State U.!" If one were blindfolded they would have thought it to be a football game. Stan Mars was 0 for 1 with a walk as he stepped in to bat, but he had to wait for another mound conference.

Randolph went to the bullpen for left handed specialist, Gerry Rogers. Stan walked over to David on deck. "This guy is tough. He's got a sinking slider that to us lefties starts out like it's gonna break your ribs, then dives down to your shoe tops."

Stan groaned. "He walked me twice this year to set up double plays so I didn't face his real 'stuff,'" David said, making quote marks with his fingers to accentuate what he meant.

"He may walk me again here to set up a double play at any base," Stan conjectured.

The home plate umpire shouted, "Play ball!" Sure enough, as Stan guessed, Randolph's catcher stood up and he took four intentional balls. David walked toward the plate. The cheering was probably the loudest at this field since this field was named Maxwell field after a WW2 hero and graduate of State U. David took the first pitch for a strike and it was that wicked slider. The runners all took small leads as David pumped his bat. Rogers threw him a fast ball, high and outside for a ball. David stepped out, adjusted his gloves all the time looking at Rogers on the mound. He thought he noticed a change in Rogers' foot position from his slider to his fastball and he paid close attention as Rogers toed the mound for his third pitch. Sure enough he set up much further to the left, as he had for the first pitch slider. The slider came in low for ball 2. If he hadn't read it correctly he probably would have swung and missed for strike two. Rogers' feet changed again. David was thinking fastball or change. David decided to lower his bat just in case. It was a change and with an easy, fluid swing he deposited the ball two feet inside the left field line and it rolled all the way to the wall. Stan was able to score from first and David held at second. Randolph 4 State U. 3. The stadium rocked.

David turned to Coach Dahling, coaching third, as time was called by Randolph, and David ran over for some instruction relayed from the dugout. "Then!" Coach Dahling emphatically stated. "You guys did what we knew you could. Just keep it up."

Unfortunately Randolph kept State from any more scoring, a disappointment, losing a golden opportunity. The scoreboard flashed some good news. Hammel College was now leading Alpha U. 5-3 in the last of the 6th in Richmond. The State U. dugout and fans cheered.

Jake Nelson held Randolph in the top of the eighth thanks to a spectacular throw by Stan Mars and a great block of the plate by Al Grant, which saved a run. The stadium was rocking after that play. In the last of the eighth, State managed a single and a walk but did not score. They held Randolph in the ninth and needed to make the most of their last three outs. This game had reached a pressure level that was unbelievable. Genevieve and pals were exhausted. Their voices were raw. Genevieve couldn't imagine what tonight's dinner with their four parents would be like if State didn't win this game. She sat in between her parents and David's holding all their hands, as she watched Jo Ann and Colleen lead the group with the cheers and the banner. She thanked God again for these two marvelous friends.

It was the bottom of the 9th and Owen Robinson, State's speedy leadoff hitter, decided to lay down a surprise bunt. On a 1-1 count he got a good pitch to bunt and surprised the third baseman, beating the throw by a step. State's fans held their breath, then cheered, hoarse voices notwithstanding. A wild pitch moved him to second, an unexpected break. The second hitter, Brian Oliver, in a slump, popped out to second, throwing his bat down in disgust. Stan Mars, on a 3-2 count, fouled off 6 pitches, then struck out on a pitch in the dirt and walked away dejectedly. David slowly walked to the plate with the weight of the world on his shoulders. A cheer arose. David looked up at the scoreboard. Hammel had retained the 5-3 lead at the end of 7. He said to himself, *it's great if they win, but let's end this game right here and now.* The cheers began as just about every State fan in the stadium stood up. He had only faced this 5th pitcher of the day for Randolph once before, and had struck out. He had a deceptive move but wasn't overpowering so he felt he could stay back and meet the ball. After all, he reasoned, he only needed to meet the ball to get a single and score the speedy Owen Robinson to tie the game. It was a 2-1 count. David hadn't yet seen a pitch he felt compelled to swing at. There it was, a medium speed fastball. He whipped his bat around without over swinging and the ball momentarily disappeared into the sky after a resounding crack of his bat. It could next be seen sailing high and deep beyond right field. State U. 5 Randolph 4.

It was finally over! What a year! What a game!!

David leaped high in the air. The stands exploded with joy, excepting Randolph's fans. State's dugout and bullpen emptied and all 24 coaches, managers, and ball boys were jumping and clapping waiting for him to circle the bases. Genevieve was hugging and kissing all four of their parents. It was absolute mayhem. Oh yes, Hammel College won over Alpha U. No playoff was necessary. Randy Cameron and Harold Baker congratulated each other on the decision to sign David Kelsey and left their seats for the locker room to surprise David and congratulate State U. on their victory.

This college and college town hadn't ever experienced a celebration like this for baseball, and it was 8 years ago for football and 11 for basketball. David was beside himself, trying to get a grip, not only for the victory and a chance to play in the CWS but also for what he had planned this evening. The stage was now set, everything was perfect. Now he needed to control his emotions to execute as he did earlier on the field. This decision, he realized, was for life.

Randy Cameron and Harold Baker finally worked their way through the exuberant crowd. With identification, a surprised security guard led them through and down to State U.'s locker room. David was beside himself as his teammates were hugging and slapping him on the back unmercifully. Coaches Spencer and Dahling were just as euphoric, trying to get their attention. "Guys, take it easy on Dave. We still have a five game world series to play starting next week," the coaches implored. It took a while before they finally settled down and plopped by their lockers, starting to undress for the showers. "Great game, guys. We had an uphill battle but you showed what you are made of. We are proud of you," Spencer told them.

"It was a real major league comeback and victory. Something you will never forget," added Dahling.

Randy Cameron and Harold Baker surprised them when they entered the locker room. "Sorry to butt in on your celebration. I am Randy Cameron from the Marauders," he turned to Harold.

"And I am Harold Baker, Assistant General Manager."

"Great, great game, guys. You should be real proud of yourselves!" Cameron praised them.

"That goes for me too," Baker added.

They both shook hands with everyone and congratulated Coaches Spencer and Dahling. The team members were awed to see these two Marauders executives in their locker rooms. Only Cameron and Baker knew of David's bonus. It was difficult for them to keep it confidential these four years, but they had honored his request. That decision also prevented any prima donna concerns of David's teammates. Stan Mars knew of the bonus, and being the good friend that he was he maintained secrecy as hard as it was for as long as it was.

Cameron turned to David. "Hi, Dave. Long time, no see, young man." They shook hands.

"Thanks, Mr. Cameron. I guess it's four years or so. I received your letters telling me to keep well and fit. It sure kept me focused."

"Harold kept me posted. It pleased me to see how conscientious you were for so long."

David turned to Harold Baker "Mr. Baker, I didn't know you were going to be here," he said.

"Oh, Harold was following my instructions," Cameron advised.

"We were concerned about making you nervous, just like today. That would have been counter-productive," Harold Baker interjected.

"We needed to see how our star protégé handled a playoff game. We expect that he will be in many more with the Marauders," Randy Cameron added with a big smile at David.

"We are planning to watch the College World Series on television. We will be rooting for you from afar," said Harold Baker.

"Go State U.!" Randy Cameron shouted, and the team and coaches Spencer and Dahling grinned from ear to ear.

"We will let you guys celebrate now," Baker added as he hugged David, and Cameron shook everyone's hand, hugged David for good measure, and left.

"Wow. That was quite a surprise," Coach Estes expressed with a deep breath.

"I'll say," David responded. "If I knew they were here . . ." but Coach Estes interrupted.

"Better not to know. You probably would not have concentrated as well as you did, and thank goodness you did, David," he added with conviction.

David absorbed that response realizing that perhaps two of those eyes would be ever present when he wore the Marauders uniform. He took a real deep breath and took shower with water as hot as he could stand it.

*What a tremendous, tremendous afternoon*, he thought. How could it ever be topped? He then tried to unscramble his thoughts to concentrate on the big evening about to unfold that would change the rest of his life.

# Chapter 15

# THE EVENT AND SURPRISE

The team, their lady friends, and their families, as well as many fans headed to the Log Cabin, a local restaurant and tavern of many years in order to celebrate the big win. After a whole lot of hugging and kissing, he and Genevieve went back to the dorms to spruce up, and the four parents took a leisurely drive to the Log Cabin and for a look at the Long Island Sound this beautiful late spring evening. David routinely flipped the sports channel on and enjoyed seeing, for the second time, the reporting of State's victory and Alpha's loss. The next step while he was putting on the glad rags was to take it from the resting place in the dresser drawer. He marveled at its beauty.

*What a once in a lifetime day and night*, he thought. For, probably the hundredth time today, he took a deep breath. He then showered and began dressing for the occasion. The phone rang. It was Genevieve.

"Hi, slugger. When can you come and get me. I'll be ready in less than a half hour."

"Wow, you are a lot faster than me. I just left the shower."

"Oh wow" she gushed. "I sure wish I could be there to see your equipment." He laughed.

"Guess you will have to wait until they invent picture phones, gorgeous."

"Being there in person is still the cat's meow," she laughed back.

"Let's arrange that real soon gorgeous."

"You can bet on that, slugger."

They threw ecstatic kisses to each other.

There had to have been hundreds of cars, the couple agreed, as they drove up to the restaurant. Because of occasions like this, the Log Cabin purchased additional property for overflow parking and ran a bus to and fro. For this occasion, in recognition of the victory, team members and their families were given special parking passes to park adjacent to the restaurant so David and Genevieve, although a bit late, had a guaranteed spot. They parked and wound their way through the crowd, looking for their folks. They heard a whole lot of cheering going on by the patio overlooking the Sound. The crowd recognized them as they inched their way through. "Atta' boy Davey," "Thatta way, some homer," "Great game Dave," "Let's Win the CWS, Dave" were some of the accolades they heard as well as compliments to Genevieve for her dress and how she looked and how they enjoyed her plays. They were the most revered couple on campus. They realized it, but to their credit they remained open and receptive to their fellow students.

As they wound their way through the restaurant, David received some hugs from the ladies. He turned red with all the attention. Genevieve attracted stares from male and female alike. She was dazzling. David saw some teammates intermingled with, he assumed, parents and other students. He and Stan Mars and many more hugged and, to be sure, Genevieve wasn't neglected. They enjoyed and endured many handshakes, back pats and "thatta boys" and "you look beautiful" as they finally got to the other side of the patio "Dave—we're over here," he saw his Dad waving to him. They were all together—their moms and dads. He suddenly realized, even in this euphoric state, he was more nervous than he was in that critical 9th inning. There, he was in his natural element. Here he wasn't. There was no way to prepare for this evening. He touched his jacket pocket.

Finally joining their parents, everyone hugged everyone else. Dad gave David and Genevieve wine and then raised his glass and at the top of his voice trying to project above the chatter and laughter on the patio he announced, "Everyone raise your glasses, please! A toast to State U's baseball team and victory in the College World Series, and may David be the MVP."

"Hear, hear," shouted Kenneth Carter.

"HEAR, HEAR, HEAR," shouted the patrons, many of whom were State U. students, faculty, and their guests as well as local fans.

Genevieve put down her wine glass, reached up and put her hands around his neck. "Oh honey I'm so proud of you," and gave him a huge kiss. The crowd roared their approval as David kissed her back, then seemed embarrassed by all the attention. His mom, Helen, gave him a big hug when Genevieve let him breathe.

"Wow, this is so special. I just can't express it. It's surreal," Helen remarked.

He shook his head. "It sounds stupid, I guess, but every thing is just so perfect and wonderful. Like a dream that doesn't end."

"Just enjoy the moment, David, you deserve it," Mom advised. "Surely you will have more moments like this to help you with life's downturns," and she hugged him and he hugged her back.

"Just enjoy these moments, Dave" Dad added. "You have the world by the—oh well, you know."

"You deserve every bit, Dave, enjoy it to the fullest," Ken Carter added. Kathy Carter squeezed his arm.

"This is a super evening, David, and you are mainly responsible. Thanks." She planted a big kiss on his lips. He blushed with a wide smile and thought how really blessed, both Genevieve and he were, having such wonderful parents.

The six edged their way through the crowd on the patio to their reserved table, though they had to stop every few feet for people to congratulate David. He instinctively squeezed his jacket pocket more often, becoming more and more nervous by the minute. Suddenly, he panicked. It dawned on him that he needed to speak to Mr. Carter in private. In all the excitement he had completely forgotten. For a moment, he was beside himself. His suddenly unnerved state of mind prevented him from thinking clearly. His dad unknowingly came to his rescue by excusing himself for a bathroom break before they ordered dinner. Ken Carter said he would join him. David breathed a giant sigh of relief, which went unnoticed. With a nervous stammer, he stood and said he would go with them. Under his breath, he said a Hail Mary for someone's weak kidneys. The ladies looked surprised at his strange response, but didn't think any more of it, and the three left for the men's room and David's salvation.

The men's room line moved slowly as it was a popular destination at this point in the evening. David thanked God again for this fortunate change in events. His bewildered state had calmed down, and he was trying to rehearse what he wanted to say to Ken Carter as they inched their way forward. He couldn't help thinking that this was a lot harder than hitting a 95 mph fastball or a sinking curve. He had conjured up several approaches, but was afraid his nerves would screw it up so he decided to be short and sweet. The only problem was there would be many other ears, not just his dad's and Mr. Carter's. He didn't want his announcement to be carried across the restaurant and to Genevieve's ears before he even got back to their table. When they finally were able to enter the restroom, David noted some armchairs in a foyer, and immediately resolved that would suffice to inform Mr. Carter of his intention to propose to Genevieve.

As they were exiting the restroom, David moved toward that foyer, ignoring the puzzling looks both fathers gave him.

"We should be getting back to the table, David," his dad suggested.

"I know, Dad. I just want to take a quick breather," he answered nervously.

Ken Carter looked at Fred and just shrugged his shoulders.

As they reached the chairs, David thought to himself, *I should have used an excuse different than taking a quick breather.* He resolved to keep his request to Mr. Carter short and to the point, and decided to do this standing up. He turned to him, took a deep breath, and then with all the assurance he could muster cleared his throat.

"Mr. Carter, I have a good deal of respect for you and Mrs. Carter. I want you to know I love Genevieve very, very much from the very depths of my soul, and I am asking your permission to ask her to marry me."

He took an enormously deep breath and waited for what seemed an eternity for Ken Carter to answer. His parents had more than an inkling that he was ready to ask Genevieve the question, so Fred Kelsey just smiled, also waiting for Ken's response. Ken Carter's face formed a big smile and he put out his hand. "Welcome to the family, David. Katherine and I have been wondering when you would pop the question. You have mine and her mom's unequivocal approval. Genevieve couldn't have made a better choice," he said, shaking David's right hand and squeezing his shoulder with his left. After, he and Fred shook hands, very happily, as they were friends for some four years.

"Well, Dave do you have the hardware to present your beautiful future bride?" David's dad asked with a big grin. David, with the greatest feelings of relief, reached into his jacket pocket and took out the light blue velvet covered box, opened it slowly and flashed the one plus carat diamond.

"Wow, what a Marauders signing bonus can wrought," Dad humorously exclaimed.

"I think it's marvelous. Actually, Genevieve loves you so much you could have given her one from the Dollar Store and she wouldn't care," Ken Carter added jokingly.

"Now I am ready to start the rest of my life with Genevieve. Let's head out before they start a search party. Besides I am thirsty and famished," David humorously added, although still a tad, but just a tad, nervous compared to a little earlier.

"Lead the way," his dad held out his arm and stepped aside for his son and his son's future father-in-law.

It was with some relief that the women saw them returning from across the crowded restaurant. They had needed to send the waiter away twice while waiting for the men to return. As they walked past the waiter, Ken asked him to bring a magnum of their very best champagne to their table, and that they would order soon. David was still getting glad handed every few feet as he tried to reach the table. State U. fans would never forget this day and there were more to come, hopefully culminating in the University's first College World Series victory.

"Wow—you guy's took longer than us to return to the table," Genevieve remarked.

"Yeah, it was a very long line in a small restroom," David quipped, as Ken and Fred just smiled, waiting for the champagne to arrive and the question to be popped.

The waiter rolled the magnum toward the table and passed out the menus. It gave David a chance to calm down from his tremendous high. He only half looked at the menu as he watched the champagne being poured. He planned to have the champagne available for an immediate toast, hoping for Genevieve's acceptance as they had decided to wait until graduation for definite future plans. Graduation would come in a few weeks after the series so she wouldn't really expect this surprise. It felt like an eternity, but finally the cork was popped and the champagne was slowly poured. Each was filled half way. Ken stood up to make a toast. David had to make his move. His moment had arrived. Ken noticed and immediately sat down.

David took the ring box from his right pocket and extended his hand to Genevieve with the broadest smile she had ever seen him give her, and there had been many. She matched it with her dazzling features at their best and stood before him. This did not go without attention by dozens sitting nearby. He flipped the box open with his left hand. "Oh my," she gushed. Katherine and Helen held their breaths. He released her hand momentarily to remove the ring from the satin resting place and gently slipped the ring on her finger, where it fit perfectly. "Genevieve Elizabeth Carter, will you marry me?" She was radiant. Her eyes were sparkling, her smile more beautiful than he could imagine. This was the "real" Genevieve, not the actress.

"You betcha, David Roland Kelsey. I love you so much. I've been waiting for you to—" but she couldn't finish the sentence because he had engulfed her entire body and lips into his. The roar and cheers by dozens of patrons in the enclosed restaurant rivaled, hours earlier, the thousands at the stadium.

# Chapter 16
# THE ROAD TO THE BIG SHOW

David couldn't believe the moment had finally arrived. He was now a professional baseball player. He and Genevieve had finally graduated and were, for the first time in four years, separated for a time. She was in summer stock building her star and touring the country; David was in the Midwest with the Cougars, a Class A affiliate of the Marauders, building his star. He had helped State University win the college world series for the first time. Being separated was hard for both Genevieve and David, to be sure, but each had to fulfill their destiny. They felt it was written for both of them, and they were obliged to follow their star to see how far it would lead.

Only a few weeks ago he was the center of attention, the star of State University's team and the fiancé of the beautiful Genevieve Carter, a budding Broadway star. He was still that person, but only one of many major league hopefuls plying his trade in small cities around the U.S. to less than enthusiastic crowds, sometimes numbering in the hundreds, except for firework nights or Sunday's promoted with giveaways. It was a hard transition.

He had a difficult time focusing and getting it in gear. He was slow to find his rhythm—going only five for sixty for a paltry .083 in his first 16 games. One double and four singles. He realized that Class A pitching was somewhat better than college, but he did hit the better college hurlers pretty well. He took extra batting practice whenever he could. It didn't help. In game situations he was pressing and either overswinging or swinging at bad pitches. His timing seemed to be way off the mark. For the first time ever, he felt overmatched.

Casey Nolan, his manager, sat him down, suggesting he was pressing and needed to relax and made him the major object of his attention since the Marauders had a huge financial interest in his development. David was more than a little concerned as his replacement at first base came out swinging and the Marauders investment in his replacement was a lot less.

David became depressed watching the game from the bench and was instructed to take extra batting practice. The coaches devoted much time working with him, hoping to notice flaws he could correct. So far, nothing had worked. While he connected with far more batting practice pitches than he had with actual game pitches, the results were still far from satisfactory. He missed Genevieve, to be sure, but couldn't believe that caused this slump. Neither he or the coaching staff had a clue what to do. After several days out of the lineup and many hours of batting practice, Casey Nolan had to insert him back in the lineup when his replacement was sidelined after being conked in the elbow. David prayed that he would get his swing back.

One morning when he awoke at the motel, rummaging in the bureau drawer for clean underwear, he found the St. Christopher medal Genevieve had given him for good luck. He rubbed it fondly. "Dear Lord, I realize this may not be an appropriate prayer, but I ask you kindly to help me find my rhythm and have my swing return so that I may fulfill my destiny. Amen."

He kissed the medal and lifted Genevieve's color photograph from the bureau, kissing her smiling lips. He then realized he was missing her terribly, and wondered if she felt the same way. The realization also set in that this would be their life, if he eventually succeeded at baseball and she as an actress. *So far,* he thought, *she was having a better time of it than he.*

Genevieve finally reached him by cell phone when she arrived at the Indianapolis Airport. As luck would have it she would be near him on a Midwest tour. They had been missing each other for weeks with her touring and he on road trips, with the team arriving in Jenkintown on Monday to open a three game series on Tuesday evening.

She greeted him, "Hi, sweetie. I miss you so much. How is everything?"

He just came right out with it. "I sure miss you, honey.

I'm in a big slump right now. I need something to change my luck. I've been on the bench for almost two weeks. Casey Nolan has me back in the lineup Tuesday night only because my replacement is hurt."

"Wow—my David on the bench? I hope I can perform some magic for you."

"Well if anyone could, darling, it would be you. It sure would be you," he replied.

"I'll be heading to Indianapolis within the hour, so be ready, because I'm *really* missing you," she said.

"Where are you staying, anyway?"

"I'm at the Globe Motel on 4th and Main, Room 402. I'll have my roomie spend the night elsewhere."

"I sure hope so," She quipped. "And I hope your manager won't mind."

"Well we are *almost* married. I'm willing to take the chance. I'll leave the door open darling. What's your E.T.A.?"

"Normally, it should take three hours, but I have a feeling I will be there quicker than that. My motor is all tuned up," she said amorously.

"Surprise me and wake me gently, darling," he said, kissing her through the phone. He closed his eyes thinking of her, and kissed the gold framed 8 x 10 he had placed on the nightstand. Before falling asleep, he turned on the night light for her to enter the room in the dead of night.

He reached for his cell phone to call Buddy Lenhart, his roommate, who was playing poker in another room, and asked him to fold his cards for a few minutes as he needed to speak to him.

"Why can't you tell me what you want over the phone? I've got a good hand here," Buddy pleaded.

"O.K., play out your hand."

Buddy grumbled but agreed. In a few minutes he came crashing through the door. "I hope this is important and short. I've had some hot hands. This may cool me off," he uttered.

"I need you to sleep in another room tonight. My fiancée just surprised me. She's flying into Indianapolis and she's going to visit. Luckily her tour schedule just worked out this way. We probably won't see each other for another two months. I would really appreciate it, Buddy."

"Wow," Buddy, exclaimed wide-eyed. "But Dave, that's against the rules unless it's your wife."

"Well, she's my fiancé. We're getting married this fall. That's pretty darn close to being married," David retorted. "I hope, though, that you won't blab this on me. I'll have to deal with Skipper Nolan myself. Besides, she has helped me out of slumps before. She has made a science out of studying my mechanics. It worked in college and sure as heck should work again. I'm hoping Skip will accept that."

"Well, for your sake, I sure hope so" Buddy shrugged his shoulders. and started out the door.

David put his hand on Buddy's shoulder "Remember Bud, mum's the word."

Buddy shook his head but then rubbed his chin. "I think we've forgotten something though."

"What?" David asked.

"Where do I sleep tonight? If I ask to bunk with anyone else they'll be all over me wanting to know why."

"How about I have a bad cold, and you don't want to catch it" David realized it was a stupid excuse as he said it.

Buddy laughed, "Boy, is that dumb. These are two bedrooms with plenty of ventilation. Try again."

David shook his head and tapped his temple as to shake up his brain then reached for his wallet. "Here's a C-note. Be my guest. Get yourself a luxury room and have the best breakfast you can buy and keep the change."

"Wow, roomie. Now you're talking. It's sure great to get a big bonus."

David laughed. "It does come in handy. Book the room first before you lose that money at poker."

Buddy threw some clothes and shaving gear into a canvas bag and as he was leaving he couldn't resist. "I'll be thinking of you tonight, you lucky, lucky dog."

David put his fingers to his lips. "Remember, mum's the word."

Buddy smiled with a finger on his lips to show the signal to be silent, hoping he could maintain such a titillating secret. So did David.

Although they had only been apart for a few weeks, it felt like a few years. David and Genevieve would make the most of their free time this Monday until Tuesday morning, when the team traveled to the ballpark for practice. Genevieve had to join her troupe on Wednesday to rehearse and get used to the Indianapolis theatre conditions.

After a considerable time devoted to intimacy, David joked, "Now I need another week to revitalize."

"O.K I get the message; I'll maintain my distance, but only if you will." She leaned over, planted a kiss, and bounded out of bed before he could grab her.

"You sure know how to tease a guy," he countered.

"Just remember that kiss until later tonight and let it be an incentive for you," she laughed, running to the shower.

"I'll join you to save time—we have about an hour to make our dinner reservation time," he offered.

"O. K., but no funny stuff," she replied.

He stepped into the shower and was immediately captivated once again. They had one of the warmest showers on record to be sure.

They drove in the Porsche Roadster she rented to a nice cozy Italian restaurant that some of his teammates found very charming. "So, tell me sweetheart, what's with this slump?" she asked as they sipped their wine and nibbled at their appetizers.

"It's awful. I just can't seem to get my rhythm. I have adjusted my stance and tried to cut down on my swing but nothing seems to work."

"Remember at State U. two—or was it three—years ago?"

"It was three years ago. I remember it well. You had a very lazy and somewhat lengthy swing and your timing was way off."

"Right, you remember. You watched me closely and you reviewed film of my at bats you took then, as well as film from when I was hitting almost everything hard. I need you to closely observe me tomorrow. I hope you can detect the problem. I have been benched for eight games now, but I'll be back in the lineup tomorrow night only because my replacement got hurt. He hit about .260 in those eight games to my .083 for the first sixteen of the season. Really disgusting," he flinched.

They heard lots of laughter and chatter, and turned to see about 10 of his teammates, including Buddy Lenhart. David's teammates saw him, too, and quickly registered that he had company at his table. They loudly acknowledged Genevieve's presence with good-natured comments such as "Thatta way, Davy," "How's the Honeymooners," and "Save your energy."

He waved at them. He turned back to Genevieve, shaking his head. She was laughing.

"You should have expected the teasing. In retrospect, we probably should have ordered in. Do you think your manager will know I'm here?"

"I'm sure he will. I asked my roomy Buddy Lenhart not to tell, but even if he didn't, us being spotted certainly assures that he will."

Genevieve leaned forward. "David, what really matters is you coming out of your slump. Even if you get fined, it will be worth it, and your manager, the team, and the Marauders will be ecstatic and feel they made the right decision to give you that bonus." She took both his hands in hers and squeezed. "I love you, Davy boy, and don't you forget it."

He smiled. Then their food arrived. "Good, the foods here."

"I'm hungry myself. I last ate on the plane over seven hours ago, and they don't feed you well these days."

The couple didn't rush, but were cognizant of the stares from the guys. They decided to have some of the dinner boxed for later in the evening as the servings were quite ample.

"What do you say we take in a movie since it's still early? We can stop at the motel and put this in the fridge."

"Great idea," she agreed. "We need some privacy."

Buddy just quietly sat there. He was true to his word. How did he know David and Genevieve would choose the same restaurant as the guys—oh well, he thought, it won't matter if David starts hitting the way he should.

They awoke around 7. The team bus would be boarding and leaving by 9:30.

She planned to leave early, go for a quick breakfast, and head for the ballpark. She would explain to the grounds keeper that she was David's fiancée and hope that she could just sit and observe. Otherwise David would have to appeal to manager Nolan to get her in and explain why she was here. David suspected, however, that Casey Nolan knew that she had come yesterday, and that he would confront him.

David sucked in his breath and remembered what Genevieve said. In a nutshell, he had to start hitting and he employed the best methods to ensure that and that was it. Let's have at it.

Genevieve came out of the bathroom, pretty as a picture. They hugged and kissed goodbye.

"See you around 10 or so. Have a good breakfast. I'll see you at the park, sweetheart," she promised.

"Remember—don't hesitate to be honest with Mr. Nolan. Emphasize that I can help, that I have before. So what if you get a fine? It may be the only one you'll ever get. The team may even refund it when they see the results." They both laughed, knowing that was unlikely. It did, however, put them in a better frame of mind. He watched her get in the roadster and slip away into town. He was certain she was seen by teammates and he would be razzed unmercifully. But it was Casey Nolan he had to convince. He sucked in his breath, envisioning his bat to be the ultimate convincer.

David's cell phone rang. "Hello, Buddy," he answered.

"Morning, Dave. Can I come back to my room now for my gear?"

"Sure. Come on ahead." Buddy entered with his hands up.

"Honest, Dave, I swear, I didn't spill the beans. It was a quirk of fate that we wound up at the same restaurant. The guys kept asking me if I knew she was here and I kept saying no. I have to tell you though. Greg Wallace saw me go into my new room and asked me why. Would you believe I told him you and I had an argument? When we got to the restaurant and he saw Genevieve, he really ribbed me about that."

Dave put an arm around Buddy's shoulder "I know Bud. It was impossible for no one to find out. There are only three decent restaurants in this town and I suppose we would have been spotted no matter where we ate."

"I hope the skipper isn't hard on you," Buddy offered.

"If I get my swing back, it will be worth it. Gen's helped me before. She can help me now."

"Well, we have about 25 minutes to board the bus. I'll see you out there," Buddy put an arm around his shoulder, grabbed his bag and headed out.

The phone rang. It was probably Genevieve, "Hi," he said in a sweet voice.

"Hi my backside. Stay put. I'm coming over to you," Casey Nolan yelled into the phone, definitely angry. Most of the team were standing around and stowing their gear on the bus. They were staring at the hotel room door expecting an explosion. It surely jazzed up an otherwise routine morning in a quiet little burg.

"David, you broke the team rules having an unmarried female, fiancée or not, overnight. What have you got to say for yourself and what do you think I should do about it?" David was genuinely surprised that the skipper would even allow him to explain anything. He quickly decided to acquiesce.

"I know it was against the rules, Skip, but I let her come so she could help me with my slump."

"Well, that's interesting. How can *she* help you with your slump?" Casey Nolan asked, impatiently waiting for the answer. David was glad he was given an opportunity to explain himself. He decided not to invoke the fact that he was missing her. He figured that wouldn't impress or carry any weight with skipper.

"Well, Skip," he began slowly, "over my four years of college ball I had a few slumps. On several occasions I've had Genevieve film me when I'm hot and when I'm not. We then analyze the films together and we can usually pick up even the slightest of flaws. During my senior year when we were competing for the championship, I had a terrible slump mid schedule and corrected my swing by analyzing the films. I wound up the last few games hot as a pistol to help us win the championship." He waited for the skipper to answer.

Casey Nolan looked at his watch. *They really should be leaving for practice about now*, he thought.

"David I'll have to fine you, it's team rules, but I'll accept your explanation this time. It cannot happen again. How is she going to help you now?"

"God knows we haven't so far this year!" he exclaimed. David was glad he received only a fine and no suspension and answered, "She will have to closely observe me from a box seat during practice, Skipper. Then she'll be leaving this morning for summer stock in Indianapolis."

Casey Nolan completely understood David's wanting to see his beautiful fiancée and hoped that there would be positive results from allowing her to observe batting practice. He wasn't, however, going to appear sympathetic, but if it ends up working, fine, he thought.

A first for him in all his years in baseball. It had better work as he will have some explaining to do when he talks to General Manager Randy Cameron. He figured the kid would be fined a few hundred or so, a token, to follow team rules. He didn't tell David, of course, but if he starts hitting like David Kelsey, it would be worth paying him back the fine. Nolan reached for the door. "O.K. David, the bus is waiting and so is your unorthodox hitting coach." David stuffed some gear in his bag and walked out into the beautiful sunny morning. Some of the team were still milling around outside the bus. "O.K., team, let's get on this bus, grab some breakfast, and get to practice," Nolan ordered.

On the way to the Class A ballpark, David sat at the rear with Tony Colari and Bobby Lukasi, two players he barely knew.

"What happened with the Skipper?" Colari asked.

"Sorry guys, it's not for public knowledge," David answered, hoping to put a stop to all further questions. He wondered about the reaction when they saw Genevieve at the park. He would probably never live this down, but so what? Then he thought to himself, *How lucky I am to have such a beautiful batting coach.* At the quick diner stop he sat with Buddy and catcher Greg Wallace, the two players he was closest with. They had the sense not to bug him about the events that brought so much revelry to the team at his expense. He was just grateful to talk baseball.

Genevieve asked permission from the head groundskeeper to sit in a third base box so she could view David's practice swings close up. The morning sun was delightful. She had brought a bonnet, sunglasses, and sun lotion for the ride back in the convertible. All three came in handy this morning.

The Cougars were beginning to come on the field to start their calisthenics exercises. She had been here for more than an hour and was glad to finally see the team and wondering, with concern, how David's discussion with Manager Nolan worked out. Skipper Nolan saw her sitting in the sun and walked over to have a little talk. Many of the players took notice and got distracted from their warm-ups until the coaches barked at them. She was definitely a distraction.

"Hello, Miss Carter. I'm manager Casey Nolan."

"Nice to meet you, Mr. Nolan" she responded, smiling at him.

"David tells me you have advised him in the past when he is in a slump. Well he sure is in a big one now."

"Yes. I don't have a camera today, but I can certainly observe and let him know what I see. This will be a good spot. I want to apologize Mr. Nolan. We just got engaged and hadn't seen each other for several weeks with our travel schedules, and I guess we circumvented the rules by getting together on your road trip."

"Yes, young lady you did circumvent the rules. Big time. David has to pay a fine, but if you can help him get back on track with the bat it's easily behind us—the circumvention, I mean."

"Thank you so much for understanding. I know we'll figure out the root of the slump. We have gotten him squared away before and we can do it again."

At 58 years old, Nolan found himself lost in her voice and beauty. He had never been this close to a Broadway star before. He even thought for a moment that he might wait a while to wash his hand because she had shaken it. But he quickly realized he was being foolish.

"Thank you Miss Carter. Enjoy the practice. I'll have David in the cage as soon as possible. By the way," he added, "You may receive some whistles and hoots from his teammates.

Boys will be boys, and I can't stand here admonishing them. I hope you're prepared."

"I understand. I'll certainly be on my best behavior. I have a very important mission here, and I won't let you down."

The Skipper got David's attention to get ready to take some swings. He was plenty anxious to get this "experiment" underway. *Whatever works,* he thought, *was O.K.* He still had some apprehensions. He had to see to believe.

David finished his warm ups and stepped in the cage to face Coach Eric Springer a former pitcher throwing at about 75 mph at the fastest—all straight balls, or meatballs, as hitters called them.

"I should hit these easily, but it won't solve my problem," David said to himself out loud. Skipper Nolan had considered that and waved for Ryan O'Grady, a fast balling lefty with a good curve to pitch to David. "That's more like it, Skipper. Now I have a challenge," he said to himself.

He slowly swung the loaded bat, took a deep breath, and quickly glanced at Genevieve who was transfixed with a laser-like stare. He was determined to offer only at what he thought were strikes. There was no sense in flailing away at anything out of the strike zone, which aptly described the first three offerings. He almost offered at one as O'Grady's curve was sharp breaking and very tempting. The next pitch was a high fastball, which David offered at and missed.

He took a deep breath, pumped the bat twice, and waited. Another fastball came in below the letters. He swung and topped a weak grounder to the right side. The best he could do with the next dozen or so was two fly balls to right, neither of which was particularly deep, and three line drives, one to the shortstop and two that would have been singles, one to center and one to left. He had fouled off more than he connected with.

While watching, Genevieve noticed that his bat was definitely slow, but she was still trying to put it all together.

Actually Skipper Nolan realized that very same fault but wanted to check with his blonde, off the payroll, scout. He laughed to himself when he thought about it. He put his arm around David's shoulders. "You're pressing David. Take some fielding practice, do some laps, and come back here in about 20 minutes, O.K.? I'll talk to my unpaid analyst over there," he said, nodding toward third base, "and get her opinion." David just grinned at that description of Genevieve, but was dismayed at his continued ineptness at bat. Nolan called Coach Springer to pitch batting practice again and walked over to Genevieve, hoping she noticed something he didn't.

"Well, Miss Carter, what did you see that can help us?"

"He's not relaxed at all. I'm used to seeing him very loose. His swing has changed somehow; it's not as fluid as it usually is. May I talk to him a few minutes? just he and I alone?"

He figured there was no harm in letting them talk. *She has seen him hit much more than I so maybe she's on to something.*

"O.K., young lady, have at it. We need to charge him up somehow," and he blew his whistle. He waved David over. A couple of teammates couldn't resist ribbing him.

"Wow, I *wish I* had such a gorgeous personal trainer. Bet she can get your juices flowing, Davey."

David just smiled, knowing he wouldn't ever live this down in the club house. Nolan stopped him midway "Talk to her for a few minutes, then get back in the box. We'll get to the bottom of this." Nolan slapped David on the shoulder. *I sure hope this works*, he thought. He had better have answers if questioned by his General Manager. *God, I hope this works.*

He laughed to himself again thinking that he asked God to intervene for such a mundane reason—a baseball player's slump. But then again who was he to question what God will or will not do?

Genevieve stood up as her fiancée approached. "Well honey, what do you think?" he asked dejectedly.

She stared at him "Are you ready? I'll pull no punches."

He was momentarily taken aback by her no-nonsense attitude, then recovered. "I'll try to be, so go ahead and don't pull any punches."

"O.K. Your swing is long and lazy. Your stride is much too long, and you are slow to react to the pitch. Consequently, the fat part of the bat is not getting out there. I think you should choke up a bit and shorten your swing until you get your rhythm back."

She waited to see what his reaction would be. He just stared at her for a few moments. "Choke up! I've never choked up," he blurted out.

She glared at him. "David, just try it. You asked me to help and so did Casey Nolan. I didn't tell him that I thought you should choke up. I just said that your swing was different and that I needed more time to observe."

She put her hands on her hips and stared into his eyes. "O,K., big guy, go show them you're worth all that money. I want my State U. hero back into the swing of things! You can do it, David."

She gave him her most dazzling smile. He couldn't resist leaning over the railing, almost crushing her in his arms and planting a juicy kiss on her beautiful lips.

The hoots and hollers of his teammates were probably heard well beyond the empty ballpark. The coaches were more restrained with big smiles on their faces. Casey Nolan folded his arms across his chest, put his head down, and waited for his young men to calm down. His first impulse was to scold them like a father, but he ultimately thought better of it. His stronger concern was to see their discussion and amorous behavior translate into the David Kelsey he had expected in his lineup. He laughed to himself and thought he might be the first manager in baseball to have a Broadway star act as an unpaid coach and utilize such unorthodox methods.

He waved David back over and had O'Grady start to warm up again before Genevieve's advice got cold. "Well, Dave, are you ready to knock the cover off the ball? Was her advice what you needed?"

"Well, I don't agree with all of it, but we'll give it a try."

Nolan just shook his head. "For your sake *and* ours, try everything and anything. The Marauders are counting on you big time."

David tossed the lead bat and walked up to the dish while O'Grady rubbed up a new ball. Catcher Greg Wallace was grinning broadly.

"What's so funny, Greg?" asked David.

"Wow, you sure know how to pick a personal coach. Are there any more like her that you know?"

"Maybe, if you get that smirk off your face."

Casey Nolan interrupted their banter "O.K., you two, let's get down to business." He waved to O'Grady to step up to the mound.

"Mix up the pitches, Greg. Simulate game conditions."

"Gotcha, Skip," the catcher replied.

David took one more practice swing and got set. Genevieve crossed her fingers and leaned forward in her seat, cupping her head in her hands preventing any peripheral vision so she could be certain not to miss every aspect of David's swing. She erased everything else from her mind. Greg Wallace decided to start this session off with some sharp breaking curves. The first two were down and dirty and David held back. Manager Nolan correctly called them balls. Wallace signaled for a changeup. David connected with a blistering liner hit right to first.

*At least I got the fat part of the bat on it,* thought David. Genevieve was riveted to every move and realized he was still over striding. To her further dismay, he was holding the bat at the knob. She took a deep breath. *Boy is he stubborn,* she thought.

She decided to watch the result of several more pitches before interfering. The next five offerings from Greg O'Grady, two fastballs clocked by Coach Weathers at 92 and 94, holding the gun behind Manager Nolan, were barely hit foul by David, with one definitely out of the strike zone to boot. Three curve balls produced only a soft fly, a foul tip and a grounder to short.

David was frustrated, as was Casey Nolan. David raised his hand and stepped out of the box.

Nolan shook his head. "Dave, it doesn't seem like you're doing anything different. Am I right or wrong?"

David didn't answer.

Genevieve decided to chime in. She took a deep breath and shouted out, "David, let's go to plan B, please."

Nolan grinned, shaking his head. "O.K., Dave let's listen to the pretty lady and move to plan B, whatever that is. It certainly can't be any worse, I *hope*," he emphasized.

Greg Wallace was softly laughing under his mask. He looked up at David. "Do what she says, my friend. It might work."

David stepped out again, looked at Wallace, choked up about two inches, brought his feet closer together, and dropped the bat to almost shoulder height. He shouted "ready" to O'Grady. A 90+ miles per hour fastball came in a bit high. David checked his swing and the skipper agreed it was a ball.

Another fastball had David taking a short stride and whipping the bat around, connecting for a blistering drive to right center caught only because of all the fielders out there. "That would have been a stinging double," Wallace chimed in.

"'Let's see some more like that," called the skipper.

Wallace had O'Grady mix up his pitches just like a game situation. Skipper Nolan kept close tabs on the next 20. Fifteen were strikes. David hit ten well, with two clearing the 350-foot right field wall with plenty to spare.

*This choking up business has its merit. I'll stick with it for a while until I feel confident to go back to using a full bat,* thought David.

Genevieve was standing, clapping and cheering. She provided lots of attractive amusement to the team. O'Grady signaled that he was tired.

Nolan raised his hands. "That's enough for now. Good job, Dave. It looks like the lovely lady succeeded where we failed. Maybe we can put her on the payroll. Do you think she'll give up acting?" he said, laughing.

"I doubt that," Dave laughed. He realized that laugh was a long time coming and it sure felt real good.

Nolan pulled David aside. "O.K., young man, go say hasta la vista to your fiancée and take a few laps before this practice is over. Be sure to thank her for me." Nolan waved to her and she waved back.

"Thanks Skipper, I will." He trotted over to the box seats. Genevieve was grinning broadly. He grabbed her by the shoulders, said "Plan B, huh? This is what I think of Plan B," and he planted a firm kiss on her beautiful lips, then hugged her for the longest time to the shouts, whistles and cheers from his teammates.

Skipper Nolan and his coaches smiled at the lovebirds. For Nolan, for all his years as a player, coach, and manager, this was a first. *If David pays for his large bonus it will be something. Really something. I only hope he can take this last performance to the game tonight.*

Then he realized that this exhibition had impacted team practice enough; he blew his whistle several times and ordered everyone but David, only temporarily, back to serious practicing and waved the next hitters in to take their turn in the cage.

Greg Wallace was silently staring with envy. "What a lucky guy he is. We may receive residual benefits of sorts."

"That's a good way of putting it Greg—I surely hope so."

"David, I will miss you terribly. Let's call each other as often as we can."

"We can e-mail each other in between," he managed to say between kisses. He gently took a still clean handkerchief from his pants and wiped some tears from her eyes. "Darling, I'll miss you a ton. Thanks for making this trip and putting me back in the swing of things. Maybe when this road trip is over we can find some time when the team comes home. We'll have a 12 game home stand with four days off."

She barely whispered between kisses, "Oh, I hope so, even if I have to fly back and forth for a day at a time." She tenderly stared at him with tears in her eyes.

He kissed her again. "I know, Gen, I know. We both realized that our careers and schedules would get in our way. This is just the beginning. We will just have to stick it out. It's just our destiny, I guess."

She hugged him tightly, kissed him again, and whispered "I love you, Dave. Keep well and knock the cover off the ball, you big lug." She backed away, holding on to his arm, then squeezed his hands and caressed his fingertips as she backed away, both with eyes tearing.

"Drive safely darling. I'll call you tonight to give you the results of your advice. Sorry I was so stubborn for a while."

"That's O.K. Who knows I may have a slump myself and I'll need you to help me."

"Fair enough," he said, as she turned, trotting up to the exit before she started to cry uncontrollably.

He stared after her until he heard Skipper shouting at home: "David, lets get more practice in." He acknowledged Nolan, then turned to catch a last glimpse of Genevieve, but she was gone.

*I have to get it all together and prove to the Marauders that they made a good investment. The quicker I make the big show the happier I'll be and half the time I'll be with Genevieve in the Big Apple.*

He was the last to leave the field, and figured he would be about the last to shower, considering the not very generous facilities of a Class A ballpark, especially an older one such as this. He began to strip off his uniform as he trotted to the locker rooms. They were all waiting for him, and as he came through the door, he got razzed.

"Hi, Davey—how's our sweetie pie?" and "Hello big guy, how about a smooch right here" were some of the greetings. Harry Neville, the team clown, had brushed his long hair to look as womanly as possible, and, with a towel wrapped around his neck, he pursed his lips for a kiss, jumped on a bench did a bump and grind routine to the boisterous clapping and hoots and hollers of his teammates and the coaches. Then he slinked toward David. He reached out with his fingertips to touch David's bare chest.

"Don't you dare, Harry, or I'll deck you," David warned as he raised his fist.

Harry backed away and doubled over from laughter he couldn't control. The rest of them, including Skipper Nolan and all the coaches howled in delight. The whole thing lasted for a few minutes. All David could do was sit in front of his locker and enjoy the show, though it was at his expense. When it finally slowed down and most of them were breathless from all the laughter, he looked at the skipper.

"Did you put them up to this Skipper?"

"Hell no. You had it coming, Dave. You sure gave them plenty of material. It was a good show, and boys will be boys," Nolan answered. "It also loosened everyone up. It's what we needed to win tonight and start a great road trip. Let's hope you come out swinging like you finished practice."

"Amen to that," Greg Wallace added, putting his arm around David's shoulder. "If you hit tonight like you did in that last session we'll be O.K., Dave."

"Thanks Greg. I aim to do just that."

Several hours later, they were in front of about 1,200 fans who were all hoping to see their hometown team whip the Cougars. Instead, they saw a show put on by David Kelsey, who homered, doubled, singled and was intentionally walked twice as the Cougars went on to demolish the Green Devils 12 to 3. He continued to tear the cover off the ball against the next three Class A teams, and his streak continued for several more series, both home and away. He was in a groove and it felt great. Casey Nolan was ecstatic over David's performance, but knew he wouldn't have David with him for very long.

The time came when he had to ask David to meet with him. David had no clue. He was in a super groove, following the rules, not seeing Genevieve since the Indiana trip, and being a good teammate.

Nolan, with a straight deadpan face and voice announced, "Sorry, David. I have to cut you from the team," and sat there just staring as only the Skipper could do. David stared back at him incredulously, without a hint as to what was happening. These last weeks were like a fairy tale whirlwind to him. There was no pressure at all, just fun playing great baseball. Then, out of the blue, Nolan smiled and it suddenly dawned on his star player. "David, my boy, I have heard from the Marauders. They want you to report to Triple A in three days. Congratulations. You sure deserve it. I'll be sorry to see you go, but I'll be thrilled to see you develop and do great things. I have to tell you that you are one of the greatest players I have managed, as well as a fine young man."

David just sat taking it all in.

The Skipper continued, leaning forward toward David. "I knew it would happen. When was the only question. You're only one step away from the big show lad—just keep your eye on the ball." He stood up and shook David's hand.

"Wow," David let out and shook his head a bit. "Wow, I skipped Double A altogether. That's amazing."

"Well, we think you can do it, son. Assistant G.M., Harold Baker, asked me if I thought you were ready for Triple A, and I told him I thought you were, so don't let me down. More importantly, don't let yourself down. I'll be following your exploits, David. Just keep knocking the cover off the ball."

David took a deep breath and shook Nolan's hand. "Thanks again, Skipper. It was great playing for you."

"The pleasure was all mine, David, and best wishes on your coming marriage in the fall. You have a beauty there, young man, as well as an excellent batting coach," he quipped. "Now you have about all a man could hope for. Treasure it, my boy; it only happens to a very few and you were one of those few that was chosen." David shook Nolan's hand again and promised himself to remember, for the rest of his life, what the Skipper said.

When he called Genevieve, she was ecstatic. "Wow, I'm so proud of you sweetheart. This is great news. I *wish* I could find a way to see you," she cheered with joy into the cell phone.

"They gave me three days to report. Where will you be for the next two?" he asked hopefully.

"Would you believe, I'm in Chattanooga. I'll be here for a week. What's your chance of getting here? I can pick you up after rehearsal, about four."

"I'll try. It will probably involve a transfer flight. Maybe we'll get two partial days together."

"Any time at all with you, sweetheart, will be fabulous."

He could feel the love through the phone. "I can't wait. It's been about a month hasn't it?" he asked.

"Actually, today makes 34 days, but who's counting?" she quipped. He laughed. "Well, tonight you can see me perform in the theatre and beyond," she insinuated, pausing for emphasis. "We are doing *Hello Dottie* downtown. After the show I'll show you off to the cast. They've heard so much about you they are just dying to meet you."

"I don't want to be responsible if they do," he joked.

"Then we can celebrate after the show," she added.

"We sure will sweetie. We sure will."

"Be safe, darling. I'll be waiting in Tennessee."

## Chapter 17
# VICTORIA IN WASHINGTON, D.C.

The Magnusons were the center of attention as the bus continued down Route 896 on its way to D.C. They had been invited by their local state representative to the National Foundation, a think tank. It was always a treat to listen to the Foundation's speakers, who were experts on many critical issues concerning America domestically and internationally. The sumptuous luncheon buffet and leisure time walking through beautiful Union Station were added benefits of attending. This year would be exceptionally special since Victoria, Delaware's Congressional Representative, was slated to be the pre-lunch guest speaker.

So, the bus was all abuzz with chatter, knowing Victoria Magnuson's parents were traveling in their midst. Many were asking what she would be speaking about. "The last we spoke to her, she was preparing to talk about our changing relationships with Russia and China and how we may soon see certain advantages due to that," Vanessa responded.

"She may also talk about energy. That is also on her very busy plate right now. She will have a limited time to speak so we'll see how far she gets," added Victoria's father. Both parents graciously accepted compliments, but were glad to finally settle in their seats and close their eyes a bit after thanking most of the bus.

"I guess I never gave much of a thought to us having to answer all these questions and getting all this attention," sighed Vanessa.

"I actually expected some attention," Gene responded. "I like getting to be the proud parents." Vanessa grasped and squeezed his hand, and they tilted their seats back to rest the remainder of the trip to the capital.

They arrived at the foundation doors just before 9 a.m. The two busloads from Delaware, one from downstate, one from northern Delaware, poured into the elegant looking building and took the elevators to the auditorium level. Pat Moier, their State Representative, sat with the Magnusons. "You must be *really* excited."

"We're trying to hold it in. The bus trip down was almost surreal. We had to answer so many questions," Vanessa said.

Gene just nodded in agreement. "We never thought we would be the center of all that attention."

"You had better get accustomed to it. Vicky is a rising star and a real bright light that should shine for many years," Pat proclaimed.

Just then Adele Palmer, the Foundation's Administrator, walked to the podium. It was 9:15. "Welcome, Delaware. It is great to have you all here today, and do we have a treat for you. Delaware's own Victoria Magnuson will spearhead the program this morning." Victoria entered the auditorium in a light gray business suit with a skirt, pale blue blouse, royal blue scarf and medium black heels. Her chestnut color hair was at her shoulders. She was both attractive and professional. Everyone stood, clapping loudly.

"Thank you, Delawareans." Everyone settled back into their seats. "It's really marvelous to see you all here this morning. I trust you all had a marvelous trip," she continued as she scanned the auditorium from right to left before spotting her mom and dad, who were both smiling broadly. She smiled back and gave a nod, which they noticed and waved in return.

She began her formal statements. "There is so much to talk about, and so little time, so I decided to concentrate on our relationships with China and Russia, which should more than consume the time I have been allotted this morning. As you are aware, I am sure, these relationships are drastically different than they were just a few years ago. The threat of nuclear annihilation is, thank God, a part of the dark, dark past. We are now looking at and living through the era of technical and economic competition. In a sense, our future as the greatest nation in the world is being challenged by these superpowers. In fact other countries have greatly improved their status as well." She paused for a sip or two of water.

"Wealth is now being spread more evenly over the entire planet. This is not necessarily a bad thing. Actually for those of us more divinely intent, it could be thought of as God's master plan. For us in the United States, however, it will been a major, major adjustment. I have heard it said by many, including our leaders here in Washington, that they thought years ago when and if the rest of the world, especially Eastern Europe and Asia, wanted televisions, cars, frozen orange juice or you name it they would look to us the good old U.S. of A to provide it. Well, guess what, ladies and gentlemen? These countries are or will be producing these and many more creature comforts, or looking elsewhere in this new global economy rather than to us. There has been a significant shift, and the balance has begun to tilt. In fact, concerning manufacturing, it already has tilted and it's tilted away from us."

Victoria took another swig or two of water as she was just getting warmed up. Her audience was riveted to her smooth, powerful delivery, but concerned, of course, with her message. "Ladies and gentlemen," she continued, "the question no longer is how do we restore our complete superiority, as the rest of the world will no longer permit us to be all superior, but rather how do we maintain reasonable parity and critical area superiority? My colleagues and I hope that responsible Americans, such as you here today, realize that unless these

Communist countries evolve into democracies of the people, our country and our true allies around the world will be greatly diminished in power and influence." Victoria's audience was intently listening to this intelligent, fluent, and attractive 37-year-old member of Congress; Victoria began outlining a number of steps that America must take. In mid-sentence, however, Adele Palmer walked to the podium and whispered something in her ear.

"Please excuse me, ladies and gentleman. I have a very important phone call," and quickly walked off the stage. Everyone in the audience began murmering, wondering what the call could be about.

Adele spoke into the microphone, announcing that there would be a 30 minute recess before Victoria continued her talk. The Magnusons were now the center of attention, as people filed out to the great room for some light refreshments during this unscheduled period. Several people asked them why they thought Victoria had been called away in the middle of her speech. Her parents were as stumped as everyone else in attendance. They repeated, "Beats us. Even though when we're fortunate, these days, to have a rare visit, at home she's frequently called by many different people, even on weekends. Seems the government never rests. Maybe that's a good thing," Gene quipped.

"It really is a 24/7 job, and she loves it," added Vanessa.

Adele sought Vanessa and Gene out after almost a half hour. "I just wanted to let you know that Victoria was driven away in a limo flanked by two secret service cars. She told me to tell you that she will try to call you later tonight or tomorrow."

"Thank you," Vanessa responded. "Do you know who called her?"

"She didn't tell me, but it looks urgent and pretty high up the ladder," she answered.

The audience was called back to the auditorium for the next speaker. He concentrated on renewable energy alternatives. Midway into his presentation, Adele Palmer interrupted again.

She spoke from the podium. "I am very sorry to announce that the Secretary of State has passed away. He was taken to the hospital directly from his office. He had a heart attack, apparently. I apologize again for interrupting our speaker, but the president will be addressing the nation shortly. Let's all proceed to the great room. I will turn on the monitors and we can watch the president's address while we have lunch."

It was now past 11:40, and Gene turned to Vanessa. "Let's take a walk to Union Station after we eat. It will be good for us after sitting on the bus, as well as our time sitting here. It'll help us digest this delicious lunch."

Vanessa agreed. "Maybe Pat will want to join us."

"Sure thing," he said. The buffet was as sumptuous as they remembered from the last couple of years. They were busy serving themselves. Adele walked back into the room.

"We will turn on the monitors for you all. The president is about to address the nation."

President Layne was seen walking out of the White House to a podium, and a large group of news people and staff were gathered on the lawn. He shuffled some papers, then turned and held out his hand as Representative Victoria Magnuson moved to stand next to him. Gene and Vanessa Magnuson gasped and almost dropped their plates full of food. Pat Moier and others noticed their surprised reaction, took their plates and motioned to have chairs brought over to them. Others reacted quickly and helped. Vanessa and Gene joined hands as they sat, staring intensely at the TV monitor. The quiet in the room was defining, the anticipation incredulous.

President Layne cleared his throat. "My fellow Americans, members of Congress, my White House staff, ladies and gentlemen of the press and all others that may be listening or watching, I regret to inform you that Donald Reeder, the United States Secretary of State, passed away this morning. As many of you know, he has been ill for some time. We were praying for his recovery, but unfortunately it wasn't to be. He was a great American admirably serving his country, administratively, in Congress and as my Secretary of State. He was a trusted friend. My sympathy to his wife, Betty, and his children, Eric and Rebecca, and his six grandchildren. He will be sorely missed. I will offer a silent prayer for his soul. I hope all listening will silently or out loud, as you wish, join me in prayer." President Layne bowed his head and closed his eyes, hands folded. The audience at The National Foundation followed suit to a person.

The president raised his head, and put on his sunglasses, as the sun was coming around to that area of the White House. Clearing his throat again, he turned to Victoria, who stood on his left. "All of you listening to me this morning know that my heart is heavy with grief over Secretary of State Reeder's death. However, you must also be aware that the important business of the United States never takes a break, no matter what the circumstance. In that regard, I have asked Delaware Representative Victoria Magnuson to accept the position of Secretary of State, and she has agreed. I have been very impressed with her keen insight and leadership qualities and practices during her time in Washington. She has made a study of international relations, and has served as a valuable member of the Foreign Relations and other committees." He and Victoria shook hands.

Gene and Vanessa were in awe, both speechless as they listened to the president. Some of the attendees came over to give them congratulatory smiles, handshakes, and pats on the back. All they could do, at this point, was smile and nod. They were prouder than proud, if that were possible. It was a feeling they could not express. Their Vicky, their once little girl, would have the ear and confidence of the President of the United States. She would meet with leaders around the world. They remained riveted to their seats as Victoria strode to the microphone at the White House.

"Mr. President, members of the press, other honorable guests, and those Americans watching and listening. This is a great honor and responsibility bestowed upon me and I will not let my country down. I had great respect for Secretary of State Donald Reeder. He and I were in synch on many issues, as you know, and I will carry the torch he lit wherever I go for our great land. It is a difficult time for the United States and the world." She then raised her voice. "I am up to the challenge. God Bless America."

Gene and Vanessa smiled and gave a "God Bless America" salutation as they watched in the National Foundation's great room. All of their fellow Americans followed their lead. Their daughter stepped away from the microphone, and an avalanche of questions were fired at her by the press.

The President stepped up to the microphone and raised his hand. "I can imagine many of you have quite a few questions at this time, but we will be setting up a press conference in the near future. This is not the appropriate time for questions. Thank you all for coming." After only a brief pause, he said firmly, "God Bless America." The cameras followed the President, the Congresswoman, and many aids as they disappeared into the White House.

Some 900 miles south in Florida John Snyder, Dorothy Carter and Elizabeth Phillips, the retired teachers, were in awe of their one-time student. Elsewhere, lifelong friends Laurie Fassert and Ann Herman smiled broadly. Retired Congressman Howard Woodson and University of Northern Delaware Dean of Government Studies Doctor Peter Salman nodded in approval, as did Keith Fredericks, on assignment with the Secret Service guarding the Vice President, all wishing they could congratulate her in person. Hundreds of miles apart, they almost simultaneously decided to sit down and write notes of affection and congratulations.

"Wow, you both must be so proud," exclaimed Pat Moier as she hugged them both. "Adele said we have forty five minutes to take a walk and catch our breath. Let's go to Union Station to digest and revel in Vicky's appointment."

The Magnusons nodded their heads in agreement, took deep breaths, and followed her out the door into the bright sunlight. Several others added their congratulations. They were beginning to feel somewhat self conscious and absolutely speechless and in awe of what they lived to see for their wonderful daughter. As they walked, Pat picked up the conversation. "Did Vicky ever give you any indication that the president would appoint her to a position like this, should the need ever arise?"

"We had no idea, really. We knew that Donald Reeder had a heart problem, but Vicky never mentioned that the President spoke to her directly, or considered her as a replacement," Vanessa answered.

"I would think if she had had any inkling at all, she would have told us," Gene added, turning to his wife. "Don't you think so, sweetheart?"

Vanessa nodded. "I do. I still can't quite believe it. That our daughter—our daughter—was chosen over so many people to be Secretary of State of the United States. Over so many people. It's *unbelieveable.*"

"It's really quite amazing. I've always knew her to be really special," Pat agreed. "When you think about it, it was only five years ago that she was elected to the house and her star burns so, so bright now she'll be conversing with the leaders of the world. Hard to imagine and really fantastic."

Gene and Vanessa impulsively stopped on the sidewalk and motioned to the group walking just behind them to form a circle with them.

Gene took a deep breath and prayed, "Thank you God, for blessing us with Victoria. May she live up to the expectations our President has for her, may she make her country proud and please, oh please, protect her from those who would harm her as she travels the world in the name of freedom."

"Amen," everyone added in unison and continued, uplifted, to Union Station.

# Chapter 18

# TO THEE I DO WED

David's first professional baseball season was a resounding success. He tore up AAA pitching, and received his call to the Marauders in August to help them win a playoff spot. They ended up falling short by two games, but David wasn't the reason, as he batted .385 with six four baggers in the last 35 games of the season. Manager Ken Hohner told him he would be on the opening day roster next season. He was on his way.

Genevieve had a superlative run in the first few months of *The Girlfriends*, playing to capacity audiences with advance ticket sales guaranteeing at least near capacity for the next several months into the next year. She was a certified Broadway star.

Incredible as this may seem, this couple managed to plan their wedding, scheduled for November 23, just three days after David's 22nd birthday. They were originally contemplating the Log Cabin for their reception, but Genevieve's mom and dad convinced them to use their eighteenth century farmhouse and barn, and pray for good weather. Just in case, they rented a rainproof tarp, which covered the continuous path from house to barn where the reception would be held. The guest list topped 200, which put a strain on the small country church, and required a bus to ferry guests from church to the reception, as parking at the farm would accommodate only half that many cars.

Genevieve awoke for the last time in her childhood bedroom as Genevieve Carter. She looked out her window toward the large pond filled with bass, and looked beyond the grassy knoll to the rolling hills and to other farms and houses in the distance.

She said a quiet prayer to herself. "Dear God, please help me be a good—no, a marvelous wife—to David, who I love with all my heart and soul. Amen."

Just then, she heard a cough and a yawn, as Jo Ann Garber, her maid of honor, slowly awakened.

"Hi, sleepy head," Genevieve kidded. "It's about time you woke up. I have been awake for hours and need some tending to."

"Awake for hours?" Jo Ann yawned. "Why, are you that nervous already?" She yawned again.

"Sure I am. One doesn't get married that often," Genevieve responded, keeping up the act.

"Well it's only 7:50. You can take a fast walk around the farm, or get on the elliptical. That may preoccupy your mind a while," Jo Ann said, yawning again.

Genevieve laughed. "Maybe I had better let you go back to sleep, or we'll have to prop you up at the altar."

"Just lead me to the coffee. I'll wake up after two cups and stiffen up after three," said Jo Ann, still groggy. She sat up, swinging her legs over the side of the bed. Genevieve sat next to her, and they held hands, then hugged. "Genevieve, today, besides being the most beautiful, you will be the luckiest woman in Longport, Suffolk County, New York State, and maybe the whole of the United States of America." Genevieve gave her a radiant smile, a kiss, and realized Jo Ann helped put it all in perspective. Bring it on. She was ready.

Ten miles away, the historic Longport Inn, still the largest hotel in town, had awakened abuzz with relatives and friends of the Carter and Kelsey families, as well as more than a few notables from the theatre and the sporting world, all eagerly anticipating this glamorous wedding taking place in historic and humble surroundings. Guests came from as far away as Europe to celebrate this union of two marvelous people. While everyone awoke to an overcast morning, the sun quickly started to burn through the haze. A 60 degree day was probable.

David lay awake in his bed. It was like a dream, this year especially. It seemed everything, like the song, was going his way. He didn't realize it, but he, like Genevieve, was compelled to pray and thank God for all his blessings. "Dear Lord, please help me to be worthy of my lovely Genevieve. Help me to be the husband she expects me to be, and give us a long and fruitful life. Amen." He stretched his athletic body and began a series of pushups, both one and two handed, then jumping jacks. Finally, he jumped into the shower, anxious to meet and greet and have breakfast with cousins and friends he hadn't seen for years. He wondered why it took weddings and funerals to renew acquaintances and friendships. Then it dawned upon him that he hadn't been very accessible this last year. College, baseball, and Genevieve, in that order, monopolized his time. From now, on it will be Genevieve in the winter and baseball spring, summer and fall, with Genevieve, his wife, as the centerpiece, so to speak. He stepped out of the shower to dry off when he heard several loud raps on the door, and the voice of his best man Stan Mars. "Hey, Dave, wake up. It is breakfast time and everyone wants to see you."

David wrapped himself in towel and, shaking his head with his hair still full of water, unlocked the door. "Morning, Stan. You're up and dressed early—what's the hurry, bud?"

"Well, there are at least 30 people waiting to eat. They wanted me to find you so we can eat together."

"O.K. I'll be down in a few. I'll shave and just throw on jeans and a t-shirt."

"O.K. I'll have them fill up on coffee and tea."

Kathy and Ken were busy rustling up a big breakfast for the ladies of the wedding. Ken left Longport Inn before David awoke to help Kathy cook and do some last minute stuff. Betty Reber and Colleen Everson, the bridesmaids, came down the winding stairs of the 1735 farmhouse rubbing the sleep from their eyes. Ken came into the dining room with a coffee pot and hot water for tea. "Here you are ladies. I'll get some juice for you. Kathy will be getting some breakfast goodies in here in a minute or two."

"Thanks, Mr. Carter. This looks great," answered Betty.

"I'll say. I need this coffee," Colleen yawned.

Kathy brought in some fresh from the oven muffins and biscuits with jam and butter. "Hi girls—how do you like your eggs?"

"Scrambled," Colleen answered.

"Over easy for me," Betty chimed in after a large sip of tea.

"Ditto for me, Mom," Genevieve answered her mom as she walked in.

"Well, there she is! Our beautiful bride," Dad said, smiling.

"Huh. I must look a mess," Genevieve muttered.

"Not to us," Kathy said.

"We should take her picture now for the history books as a before picture. Then we can put it with the wedding picture as the after image," Jo Ann, always the joker, teased as she finally got it together and came down to join them filling a mug with coffee. After taking her first sip of coffee, she sighed deeply.

"Very funny," Genevieve responded sardonically, issuing a yawn of her own. Kathy and Ken joined them at the table.

"I just can't believe that today is here already," Genevieve said, shaking her head. "It will be the best production I'll ever be a part of, because I'm not acting. I don't have to remember my lines. I'll just go with the flow and take it all in." She paused for a moment, then tackled a corn muffin.

Jo Ann couldn't resist another joke. "Pardon me, Genevieve, but you will have to remember to say 'I do.' I'll be close enough to nudge you if you forget that punch line."

They all laughed. Ken almost choked on his muffin.

David finally made it to the main dining room. He felt like he was still dreaming. His mind and body felt uncoordinated, sort of like he was in slow motion.

When he came through the door, about 60 people stood up and clapped. It was like he just hit a grand slam or some equivalent. His mom and dad were there, as well as Stan Mars and Wally Proska and George Greenly, best man and ushers, as well as aunts, uncles, cousins, Ron Barrister, the Broadway Producer and his wife, his assistant Dana Biggs and her husband, Mr. and Mrs. Truitt, Mr. and Mrs. Carter's friends, Genevieve's drama coaches from State U., his State U. baseball coaches, Mrs. Lovett and Mr. Arrington and their spouses, and several State U. professors with their spouses. It was certainly overwhelming.

He just held up his hands, "Good morning, everyone. Genevieve and I thank you for being here and sharing our very special day with us. This means so much to us. Thank you, thank you."

Everyone clapped again as he started hugging and shaking hands, accepting congratulation after congratulation.

The weather was kind. It was cooler this morning, but the weather promised an afternoon of about 60 with ample sun and little wind. Everything was working in synch. Longport Lutheran Church and parking lot were filling up fast. Excess parking was available across the way in the lot of a closed restaurant purchased by the church. It certainly was handy for such splendid occasions. The wedding was scheduled for 1:30, which fit perfectly for those checking out of the Longport Inn.

Genevieve had chosen lilies and roses to adorn the altar. She would come up the aisle with yellow roses, while Jo

Ann, Colleen, and Betty would carry a combination of pink and red roses. The organist accompanied by a saxophonist and guitarist began playing a medley of show tunes, which greatly pleased the guests, who began to arrive around noon. The commuting guests began to arrive and intermingle with those staying at the Longport Inn. Among the guests were several well known Broadway and Hollywood performers, including Alan Cranston, Vera Broderick, Derek Brandon, Lucy Smith, Glenda Bishop and Bobby Nelson with their spouses or significant others. This created quite a buzz with the other guests and would add a special dimension to the wedding and the reception. For his part, David had invited, from the Marauders, General Manager and Assistant General Manager Randy Cameron and Harold Baker, several teammates, and Manager Casey Nolan from his Single A team, his State U. coach Bob Estes, and their wives and significant others. The little country church was bulging with happy, sparkling exuberant people—an extraordinary guest list.

Back at the farm, Jo Ann, Colleen, and Betty were dressed in their bridesmaids gowns and were helping Kathy with the bride. Wally and George drove from the Inn to the farmhouse to help Ken get his antique cars ready to drive back to the church carrying five beautiful ladies. The antique auto road show pulled up to the church around 12:30 and the beautiful bride and lovely ladies in waiting were taken to the rear of the church to be certain that there would be no chance meeting with the groom. At about 12:40, the groom was delivered to another entrance. The little church was packed and abuzz with chatter and music, waiting for this glamorous wedding to commence. The newspaper and wire service photographers who had been granted permission to attend were allowed to set up for prenuptial photographs. Genevieve and David were emphatic that no photographs would be allowed of the actual wedding service.

At around 1:00, Glenda Bishop and Bobby Nelson left their seats and moved to the front of the church. The three musicians were poised, with the organist moving over to the piano. At this point the guests were truly thrilled as they were treated, by the pair of famous performers, to lovely duets including "Love is a Many Splendid Thing," "Let Me Call You Sweetheart," "You're the Light of my Life," and other well-loved tunes.

At this point in the service, David and Stan walked out toward the altar. The musician moved back to the organ and started "Here comes the bride." Genevieve and her dad started the slow walk up the aisle with the maid of honor, bridesmaids and bridegrooms following. Ken kissed Genevieve's cheek, looked into his daughter's beautiful eyes, and whispered, "I pass you over to your love. Go with God, Sweetheart." She kissed him back.

"Thank you, Dad. I love you."

David took her hand as their eyes were lost in each other's. Reverend Albert Ressman opened the wedding manual. "Dearly Beloved. We are gathered here today . . ."

A union to end all unions was about to begin.

# Chapter 19

# A NEW YORK SURPRISE

Victoria carefully reviewed her notes as she flew into New York. This trip to meet her Russian and Chinese counterparts at the United Nations had come about after their heads of state decided to peacefully mediate the solution to the increasing belligerency of Kantou and Baharain, who recently formed an alliance, threatening adjacent countries of lesser strength. It wasn't a slam-dunk, but she gradually earned the respect of her counterparts, who were amazed to be strategizing with a woman. The three leaders had been constantly in touch on this issue, being charged with developing a proposal for their leaders to review.

She left her airplane seat to give instructions to her chief of staff, Don Ellridge, and her secretary, Andrea Russett. Then she closed her eyes for a brief nap, thinking of the meetings she was facing and the night she would spend in New York, which she was especially looking forward to. She and her escorts had Broadway tickets to see one of her favorite actresses—Genevieve Carter-Kelsey. She was thinking of pulling rank, so to speak, to meet her.

The rest of the flight was smooth. They reached the hotel in plenty of time to freshen up and have dinner at the Amsterdam, which had been highly recommended to Don. Her phone rang just after five.

"Hi, Madame Secretary, it's Don"

"Yes Don."

"When would you like to leave for dinner," he asked.

"How's five sound? I trust you can get the guys in motion by then. Andrea and I will be ready. We are famished. I understand the Amsterdam has an extraordinary menu and private dining rooms avoiding the possibility of autograph seekers. Supposedly many performers dine there. I don't think that I am that recognizable and I would think the patrons at the Amsterdam would be very polite in any event," she added.

"They may be very polite but it's possible they could delay our arrival to the theatre. Also, let me add that you have recently been on television enough to make you very recognizable."

"O.K. I'll take your advice and opt for privacy. Let's have the guys stay with us. They needn't eat separately," she added, thinking of the three secret service agents the President ordered to accompany them.

The Maitre' de was waiting with the restaurant manager when they arrived. "I am so pleased to meet you Madame Secretary. We have your private dining room all ready for your party."

"Thank you so much," she responded. The popular restaurant was fairly crowded, and several patrons took special notice of their arrival.

"I recognize that woman from somewhere. She's very familiar. I just can't place her this minute," commented a well dressed gentleman in his fifties who was dining with his wife and a much younger and very attractive couple.

"Could be that she's some big wig. It looks like the gentlemen are her bodyguards," commented the younger gentleman.

"They sure do look like they mean business. They're so serious," commented his lovely blonde companion.

"Where do you think you know her from dear," asked Janice, Mayor Alfred Guardino's wife. He rubbed his chin again.

"I don't recall just yet, but after my second glass of el vino it will dawn on me," he laughed heartily, and they all raised their glasses, the young lady's being water, for a toast.

"You probably have her confused with someone else," Janice chided. Turning to their companions, she said, "He meets and greets so many people, he sometimes can't keep them straight."

The mayor briefly frowned, hoping he would remember and redeem himself. The young couple merely smiled, enjoying the repartee between the mayor and his wife.

Victoria, Don, Andrea, and the agents settled into their private restaurant within a restaurant and ordered their food. Victoria, Don and Andrea ordered wine. Being on duty, the agents politely refused. Sipping her glass, Victoria heard the melodious tone of her cell phone. It was President Layne who, while having his own dinner at the White House, received a call from the Russian leader concerning a world wide announcement of negative proportions by Baharain.

"I wanted to prepare you that they are disagreeing with all of us. They haven't been specific. So far they have been very vague, painting with a broad brush, if you will, commenting that they will not agree to modifying their stance on many issues. I wanted you to be prepared for your meeting. Your counterparts have or will be notified. I'll be awaiting the thoughts from your meeting and we'll go from there."

"O.K., Chief," she responded. "It's not going to be a slam dunk. I think we all knew that," she glumly added.

"Yes, we did" he answered and continued. "We will, probably as a group, take a more forceful step such as major trade restrictions, or even a blockade, as well as ask the U.N. to be involved, which may be difficult to accomplish."

"Let's hope we can find a way to have them agree to major provisions. What about Kantou?" she asked.

"Haven't heard a word from Kantou. Baharain is running the show. We all knew that."

"To bad we can't use one to influence the other," she responded.

"Listen, have a good night and enjoy the show. If you meet Genevieve Carter, please give her my regards. I am a big fan of her and her husband."

"O.K., Mr. President. Will do."

Victoria turned to Don Ellridge. "Baharain is stonewalling us. The Chief has been on the pipe with President Rastovich, who is also upset."

"Are we going through with our meeting tomorrow?" Don asked.

"Yes," she answered. "We must go forward and reach agreement on the steps the three of us need to take, as well as ask the U.N. for broader approval. We can't back down now."

"That's for sure. We need to enforce our position and make them realize the consequences," he responded.

Their waiter entered and rolled in their dinner.

"Just in time! I'm famished," exclaimed chief agent Patterson. His agents corroborated by rubbing their stomachs. Victoria, Don, and Andrea agreed.

Out in the main section of the restaurant, Mayor Guardino slapped his hand on his knee. "Holy Cow! It's the U.S. Secretary of State—what's her name," Mayor Guardino exclaimed.

"You mean Victoria Magnuson?" Janice asked.

"Yup, that's her, all right. I'm sure of it."

"Do you think we can just go and introduce ourselves?" she asked.

"Honey, I'll ask, but as the mayor and his wife, accompanied by our two fabulous friends here, it shouldn't be a problem, even though she belongs to the other party," he quipped. They all laughed.

Mayor Guardino saw the manager and called him over. "Would you please ask Secretary of State Magnuson if the mayor of New York City and his party can welcome her to our great city, and help her in any way we can?"

"Certainly," he replied.

Victoria was pleasantly surprised that the mayor and his wife were dining at precisely the same time and place.

"What a coincidence. Certainly, bring them in. We will be pleased to meet them. We won't have much time though—we need to get to the theater on time," she added.

Within minutes, the four of them came up to the table.

"It's a pleasure to meet our country's Secretary of State," the mayor exclaimed, extending his hand. He introduced his wife, then he turned to the other couple, two strikingly attractive young people.

The young woman extended her hand to Victoria. "It's a pleasure to meet you Madam Secretary. I'm Genevieve Carter-Kelsey. How do you do?"

Victoria and her party were flabbergasted. "Wow," Victoria gushed, her formal and polished demeanor completely shattered. She took a moment to recover as Genevieve stood transfixed, gently holding Victoria's hand. "What a marvelous surprise. We have tickets to see you on stage tonight." She quickly looked at her watch. "In about two hours. I can't believe I'm here with you shaking your hand right now. I've admired you from afar since you took Broadway by storm," she added in almost one breath.

"Why, thank you. That's an honor for me, because I have admired you also," Genevieve responded. They both were transfixed in time as they just held each other's hand.

Genevieve's escort added, "I'm David Kelsey and I, also, am glad to shake our secretary of state's hand."

"David Kelsey—wow! I'm a baseball fan, as well. You're the Marauders' great prospect," Don Ellridge excitedly exclaimed. Alan Patterson and the other agents were wide eyed and smiling at what they were witnessing.

"Prospect, anyway. We'll have to see about great."

"He's very modest," Genevieve jokingly poked David in the ribs. "Well, you say you have tickets already. Would it be O.K. if you sat in my guest seats? You'll be up front and center."

"That would be marvelous," Victoria gushed, surprised at her suddenly reduced stoicism.

"Great," replied Genevieve. "After the show we can catch a night cap at a special place I love."

"That would be great, as long as I can get about 8 hours sleep. I have an important meeting tomorrow at 9," Victoria sighed.

"Don't worry, Madam Secretary. My limo is at your disposal, but don't spread it around. We're from different parties, you know," said the mayor.

"I won't tell if you don't, Mr. Mayor," and they all got a chuckle over that exchange.

"Great. We'll all sit together then," Mrs. Guardino summarized the conversation.

"O.K., everyone, let's get moving so Genevieve can transform herself into a radiant beauty," and with that the mayor put one arm around Genevieve's waist, one around Janice's, and led the group to the limo as David moved in behind them holding Victoria's arm with Don and the agents following. They were all uplifted by this marvelous interaction they just experienced. Their evening at the theater might pale in comparison to what they just experienced.

# Chapter 20

# DIVINE INTERVENTION

Mr. and Mrs. David Kelsey. Genevieve and David Kelsey. Genevieve Carter-Kelsey and David Kelsey.

No matter how it was written or said, it was a union of two beautiful young people of tremendous intelligence, poise, and talent, ready to meet the world's challenges together. They believed their love was one for the ages that nothing could destroy.

Due to Genevieve's acting schedule, they had had to delay their honeymoon. Finally, several months after their wedding, they were able to celebrate their marriage. They were now returning to their fabulous careers.

"Wow, what a beautiful time we had, sweetheart," Genevieve snuggled up to David.

"We sure did, gorgeous, we sure did. You are so beautiful, I just can't find the words."

"Just kiss me, you big hunk. You're beautiful, too" and David did exactly that.

They were on the 757 returning from two weeks in exotic Trinidad and Tobago. "We have to make the most of this week before work starts again," she murmured, as they would be busy and separated soon. "If we stayed in bed and only get up for necessary things, that's O.K. by me," she said, snuggling even closer.

"No argument there," he said, squeezing her back. David was to report to the Marauders Florida camp and Genevieve had to start New York rehearsals for *The Longest Love*. She would be furnishing and living in their New York City apartment. They looked down at the blue-green Atlantic Ocean sparkling in the sun, then looked at some magazines, and dozed off for awhile. David would probably not see her again, on a regular basis, until mid April, when spring training would end and the Marauders returned to New York from their opening season road trip. The two were not looking forward to the separation, having discussed it ad nauseam, but both realized how fortunate they were to have such fabulous careers. They decided to enjoy their lives while they could, and to enjoy each other that much more as opportunities were presented.

The stewardess had to awaken them to ask about their lunch preferences; they had dozed off for longer than they realized. After making their choices, Genevieve and David held hands and resumed their snuggling and kissing, elongating the honeymoon. The stewardess reached them with their lunches, and good-naturedly interrupted. "O.K., you two. Take a break for lunch."

They both laughed and looked at each other's meals.

Genevieve had ordered turkey and a salad while David ordered tuna, a salad and apple pie.

"I'll have a couple of bites from that pie," she teased as she grabbed her fork.

"Oh no, not without some compensation," David winked.

She rubbed and squeezed his thigh and whispered in his ear. "When we get home, I'll pay double."

He shook his head. "Take all the pie you want. I can't resist you," he said. They both laughed as only honeymooners can. Taking their time eating, they took looked up at the sky, which seemed to be clouding up.

Genevieve became serious. "It's been a while since I performed. I'm a bit nervous about getting back on stage."

"Really? Genevieve Carter-Kelsey, nervous?" David feigned surprise. She gave him a firm punch in the arm and stole another piece of pie.

"It popped into my mind, also," he said, "that I may be extremely nervous when I play in my first game."

"There is a difference," she insisted. "In baseball one hit in every three at bats is excellent, but one bad act out of three in a play isn't good at all."

"Then do the second and third acts first, and the first act last, and maybe then the audience won't split until the end," he laughed, and she punched him again.

"Pardon me," asked a lady walking down the plane aisle. "You look very familiar. Where might I have seen you?"

Genevieve briefly hesitated, not wanting to begin long conversations and attracting attention. "Well, do you go to the theater?" she asked, hoping this wouldn't be an excessively long conversation.

"Yes, I do, quite often," the lady responded. Genevieve knew she was cornered, and took a deep breath, as did David, knowing their privacy had been demolished for the rest of the flight.

"I'm Genevieve Carter, now Genevieve Carter-Kelsey," she responded, glancing at David.

"Well, bless my soul. So you are!" the lady gushed. "I loved you in *The Swinging Fifties* and *Moon over Manhattan*. Are you appearing in another play?" she asked.

"Actually, soon, I'll begin rehearsals for *The Longest Love*."

"My, my, that's just marvelous. I'll be sure to get front row tickets. I can't wait," the woman gushed, her voice rising so that others could hear her. "I'm Blanche Landers, from New York, and I'll make sure I bring a bus load of friends."

"That's nice, Blanche. I like large, enthusiastic audiences," Genevieve felt obliged to answer, hoping for a conclusion. David nudged her slightly to cool it. She noticed but ignored the nudge.

Blanche continued asking questions, "What were you doing in the Islands?"

"It was our honeymoon," Genevieve answered rather sheepishly, hoping that wouldn't cause too much of an animated and loud response.

But that's exactly what happened. "Your honeymoon! Well bless you both, and congratulations. What's your name, young man?" she asked, leaning over a bit.

David took a hard swallow. "David Kelsey. It's nice to meet you."

"Well, David Kelsey, you have quite a beautiful bride here," she continued. He swallowed again, trying to be low-key. Baseball fans, while occasionally rabid, were confined to the stands, not direct in your face.

"I sure do madam, I sure do," he agreed.

By now, other passengers began to hear and notice them. A man a few rows back said to his friends flying together, "That's David Kelsey up there. He's the Marauders' answer to Ted Williams." The man walked up the plane to shake David's hand. His friends and more and more passengers became interested. Many left their seats, forming an organized line to meet both Genevieve and David. Blanche Landers was in her glory, introducing her to everyone.

The stewardesses were getting nervous because the captain had shared a report of a storm up ahead. The lead stewardess advised the captain about the line of passengers in the aisle.

Captain Aaron Cox came over the radio. "This is your Captain. Please take your seats and fasten seat belts. We are approaching a storm and expect significant turbulence. Thank you all."

A whole lot of grumbling went on, especially from those who hadn't yet gotten to shake hands with the famous couple. The "fasten seat belts" sign was a flashing reminder to those slow to react.

David joked under his breath, "Wow—saved by a storm. Divine intervention, I call it."

"God could have been a bit more subtle don't you think?" Genevieve responded, as the plane began to shake and bounce up and down. "I'm scared honey. This is rough weather," she added as lightning flashed all around them and the windows were clouded by heavy, heavy rain.

David put his arm around her. "Steady, darling. This storm should peter out soon. They know what their doing at the controls." For good measure he prayed to himself to avoid unnerving her any more than she was.

At the controls, Captain Cox and copilot Peter Goetz were having a difficult time holding their course as the big plane was being thrashed around like a toy model.

"This is Majestic Airlines Flight 400 out of Trinidad to Miami. We are experiencing a torrential storm. Our position is some 300 miles, North/Northeast of Port Au Prince, and we're having trouble keeping this baby steady. Request clearance to land somewhere closer if this continues." Cox turned to Goetz. "I sure hope they received that."

"We will know soon," Goetz responded, and prayed to himself.

The lead stewardess, Marge, peeked in. "Are we O.K., guys?"

"It's hard to keep her steady, Marge. I radioed for permission to land closer but there hasn't been any response. I'll keep trying. How are the passengers?"

"Nervous," she said emphatically.

"Try to keep them calm."

"Aye-aye, Captain, we'll try," and she left the cockpit.

Cox tried the radio again: "This is Majestic Airlines Flight 400 out of Trinidad to Miami or any airport. Do you read me? My position is—" he paused, looking down at his instruments, which weren't working. "Damn, we lost our navigation system Pete."

"We sure did, Captain," Goetz answered. "Why don't we turn around and see if we can find Trinidad again—it's our best bet for now." A loud crackling noise emanated from the radio, indicating a response, but it was completely unintelligible.

Cox turned to Goetz. "O.K., Pete, we'll turn her around slowly."

As he started the maneuver, the plane shuttered from lightning just above the left wing, and dangerously close to the cockpit. The upfront passengers were scared out of their wits. The men were generally stoic. Some women were screaming and crying. But to a person, they were all frightened to different degrees. The oxygen masks released, and everyone scrambled to affix them. Genevieve and David were straining in their seat belts to hug each other, as were many other passengers.

Another bolt of lightning, larger and fiercer than the previous, hit the right wing, forcing the plane to suddenly dip as if Cox and Goetz had left the controls unattended. One port side engine sputtered and quit, and it appeared that the left wing was badly damaged. Cox had Goetz ask Marge to come forward.

She appeared quickly. "Yes, Captain?"

"We're going to announce that the passengers must don life jackets. I wanted you and your crew to know."

She was worried, but remained visibly calm. He continued the craft's turn around back to Port Au Prince if he could manage to find it without instruments, but the lightning continued unabated, shaking the plane again.

Cox turned to Goetz. "Go out there, Pete, and help them prepare for a water landing."

"Aye, Captain." Goetz went back into the cabin of the plane to pass the word and help with life jackets, rafts, and slides. He flicked on the intercom, still working, "Folks, we're heading for a soft landing in the beautiful Caribbean. Please follow the crew's instructions. We will be O.K. There is no need to panic." He couldn't have said it more calmly, to his own amazement. He needed to remain calm for everyone's sake.

David and Genevieve noticed some of the older passengers were having some problems with their life jackets; their fumbling was a combination of age and fear. David told Genevieve to stay seated, and stood up to assist the stewardesses and Peter Goetz. Unfortunately, the oxygen level in the cabin was very low, and they had to continuously grab a mask from a vacant seat for oxygen lest they also succumb. Fortunately, this flight had many vacant seats. Finally, they passed the word to Captain Cox that all passengers had their seat belts secured, oxygen masks affixed, and life jackets on.

"Pete, I need you with me," Captain Cox ordered his copilot as he was preparing to make the descent. "Flight attendants, take your seats and buckle up," he added.

Goetz joined him as lightning flashed all about them and the plane continued to shake. "Pete, give them the landing instructions."

"Aye," Goetz said, lifting the radio to his mouth. "This is Copilot Goetz. Please follow these instructions to the letter. Fold your hands tightly across your chest and bow your heads. Make sure your seat belts are fastened and comfortably tight. Keep your feet flat on the floor. Maintain this position until I tell you otherwise. Do not, *I repeat*, do not panic. We will make it," he hesitated, saying a prayer to himself as to assure that remark. Continuing, he said, "The crew will then shortly open the starboard, that is, the right side exit over the wing and direct the starboard passengers out in that direction. Other crew will direct the port, or left side, passengers out over the portside wing. First, however, crew will remove the three rafts, inflate them and affix them to each wing. Then as many slides, also used as rafts will be added as necessary. There will be plenty of room in the rafts, so don't panic. We had low occupancy, so that means plenty of room."

Captain Cox was struggling with his failing plane as he began to reduce power, and start the long gradual glide into the roiling sea below. He gave Goetz a look to finish his instructions, and get ready to assist him at the controls, as necessary. His copilot got the message. "Do not take any luggage. You may take coats or wraps to help you protect from the sun. The plane will remain afloat long enough for all of us to board the rafts, and for the crew to load all water, other liquids, and snack foods before we need to clear the plane."

"Say a prayer that this baby stays in on piece when we hit it," Captain Cox said, taking a deep breath as he reduced the engine speed as low as he dared. This was his first open sea landing made with a conventional commercial plane loaded with people and gas.

In the cabin, David and Genevieve held each other's hand and their arm rests as tightly as they could after sharing a kiss to end all kisses. They noticed that many couples around them had had the same impulse.

"Whatever happens, David, you'll always be my only love," said Genevieve, tears springing to her eyes.

"Genevieve, wherever this takes us, I pray that God will always be sure we are never apart. I love you with all my heart." He leaned over with tears streaming down both their faces as a contact occurred with the sea they could not describe. It was truly surreal.

It was unlike anyone had experienced before. Captain Cox brought the craft down as skillfully as he could, buffeted by strong winds and heavy rain. Contact with the heavy sea was more than some of the passengers could bear. A few older passengers, including Blanche Landers and her husband, passed out and had to be revived with smelling salts. Captain Cox was very concerned with the possibility of cardiac arrests occurring in the older passengers. The entire crew had standard first aid training, but that wouldn't suffice with a serious occurrence.

There was no way to communicate with the outside world. The plane's radio had shorted out, and atmospheric conditions prevented cell phone use. The stewardesses, with help from co-pilot Goetz, David and a few other men, were making the slides operational so all passengers could exit the plane before it sank.

Captain Cox left the useless controls, and began helping passengers maneuver out to the wings and into the rafts and slides. All available nonperishable food was distributed as evenly possible to the rafts and slides. David and other able bodied men were holding the rafts and slides to the wings until everyone was secure, and all food, water, blankets and available pharmaceuticals were loaded. David felt like he was having an out of body experience. His adrenaline had taken over as he helped person after person who would not have survived without him and others able to help. Genevieve was also a source of strength to the elderly, realizing she and a few others needed to provide the strength, courage, and discipline to save them from this catastrophe.

Each life raft had several flares on board, but Captain Cox managed to crawl back into the remains of the 757 as the waves began to tear it apart, in order to locate more flares. They were the only hope they would have to signal to attract the attention of a ship or another plane. It took almost an hour to get everyone out of the plane, and everyone and everything into the life rafts. Cox and Goetz made sure there were at least two able bodied people onboard each raft for rowing. For the time being, however, the rough sea made rowing a moot issue except for moving the rafts away from the rapidly sinking plane. The rough sea made keeping the rafts close together a challenge; they used some salvaged rope attached to each as short mooring lines. It was difficult but the rowers were able to put sufficient distance between their craft and the defunct 757, now filled with water and beginning to submerge.

Genevieve briefly thought about some beautiful jewelry and a couple of favorite outfits disappearing, but soon came to her senses and said a thank you prayer to God for saving her and David and all her companions in these makeshift vessels.

By now, everyone was thoroughly soaked, and were using cups and a few vessels they salvaged to bale out these "luxury" yachts they were occupying. Finally, the sun pushed through the dark storm clouds, and the rain stopped. Though glad the rain was ended, they now had to suffer a worse fate under a glaring sun, with only blankets and garments soaked with salt water to cover up. They would soon be hoping for more rain for fresh water.

The ocean had calmed, and they could see the 757 with its wings now at a 45-degree angle. It would soon be a fish habitat. Some elderly were beginning to suffer terribly as empty water bottles were filled with the warm salt water to be used as a coolant, but acted in reverse.

The sun finally began to set on Day 1, and many hoped for a day 2 rescue. The more rational among them realized this would be very unlikely, but kept it quiet to avoid large scale panic. Cox and Goetz were preparing to systematically send flares skyward. Darkness finally fell. They had only four flashlights, and no extra batteries, severely limiting their use. The first flare was a test, and it worked, inspiring cheers from the rafts as if the fourth of July was underway. Now that the test launch was successful, the flares would only be employed when and if they heard aircraft or ships, or saw lights.

Thankful for the relative coolness of the night as compared to the scorching sun, everyone tried to find a comfortable position in their vessels. Since the number of passengers was well below capacity, the rafts and slides had enough space to avoid overcrowding, but they were still far from luxury accommodations. The arrival of darkness was a temporary blessing, but very spooky, as the moon was behind the heavy clouds and the air was still heavy and humid. David shifted his body to enable Genevieve to rest her head on his chest. Don Earlens, one of the "raft people," as they chose to call themselves, started a group introduction circle.

David wrapped his arms around Genevieve, kissed both her ears and whispered, "I love you. We'll get through this sweetheart." She snuggled closer and they prayed for protection and rescue. They tried to fall asleep, hoping the next day would be their last on this poor excuse for an ocean cruise.

Back home, David and Genevieve's parents were beside themselves with worry. They kept calling the airlines, and getting the same inconclusive answer: "We are searching for the plane. The radio communication, in the storm, was incoherent. As soon as we hear anything we will be in touch. We all pray that all passengers are O.K."

The families who had loved ones on board the flight were having a hard time to believe. They should have heard something by now. The national news anchors reiterated that David was one of the most promising baseball prospects in many years. The entertainment news focused on Genevieve, the promising young Broadway star.

The crash survivors were sitting ducks for the blazing red sun of day 2, just about to rise in the east. Many slept well during the night, mostly from sheer exhaustion from their frightening experience. The crew warned them to preserve water and stay covered as much as possible, but many went to the well, so to speak, too often, and a water shortage was imminent.

Genevieve and David tried to remain strong and encourage their raft companions (mostly elderly men and women), assuring them that help of some sort would find them. The couple truly believed that help would come, but privately, they questioned how soon it would happen, as it could be too late for many of their fellow passengers.

"This is Beaver to Blue Bird and Bobolink, come in," Lieutenant Spence, USN, radioed his squadron, now flying in a perfect V formation. "Roger, Beaver," they responded.

Lt. Spence gave the order to peel off to the east and then to the west for another 10, then change course again to cover a greater range of sea. Their objective was to assist local law enforcement and the Coast Guard should they see anything remotely suspicious, such as craft loaded with people headed for a remote Puerto Rican or Florida beach, or speeding yachts used by drug smugglers. Then they would slow down and swoop down for closer looks and notify the Coast Guard of a worthwhile trip on their part.

At this point, all civilian authorities had received alerts of missing Flight 400 out of Port Au Prince. The USS Harry S. Truman CVN 75 returning from the Middle East maintained a rotating schedule of practice flights to maintain pilot sharpness, as well as to assist the Coast Guard whenever possible.

On this day Lt. Spence, USN, revved up and put his FA18 Hornet to flight on a clear, hot day, followed by two of his command. He turned west with the sun to his rear. After a good twenty or so minutes covering much air space over the sparkling waters of the Atlantic, he radioed his squadron. "Bluebird and Bobolink, our gig is about over. Time to hit the deck," he ordered.

"Roger that, Beaver," they responded, and all three jets changed course back to the carrier. Spence began his turn to port and thought he saw something starboard, to the south/southwest. It looked strange. It was orange in color, and irregularly shaped. He got back on the radio and notified the carrier.

"This is Beaver to bridge."

"Come in, Beaver," was the reply from LtJg. Larry Morris.

"I'm checking something out. I'll report when I'm on it."

"Roger," Morris answered.

Spence pulled back on the throttle and glided the Hornet straight to his sighting. As he approached, he gently lowered his bird, moving about as slow as he could keep it airborne, and passed over what, at first, he couldn't believe. "What the—" involuntarily escaped his lips. He passed over and came around again, coming to his senses.

They covered their eyes from the sun. There it was: a US Navy jet gliding slowly over them. They tried to stand and wave and cheer, but the instability of the rafts and slides had them falling back and screaming in delight. Those that were barely able to move were helped by those who could to see the FA-18 so they might regain enough hope to live.

Lt. Spence pulled himself together, took a deep breath, and radioed the Truman. "Beaver to bridge."

"Come in, Beaver," Lt JG. Morris answered.

"You won't believe this, Larry."

"Try me, Beaver. We just heard from Fleet Command that we should be looking for survivors from a Vanguard 757 somewhere in the Atlantic."

"Well, let the world know I just found them." He read off his coordinates, and gave Morris a more detailed description of the scene. "I see six life boats with either six or eight people in each, about 40 plus overall. Do you copy?"

"I copy, Beaver. I'll send a message out to the 2nd fleet. If necessary, we can change course, and pick them up ourselves."

"With this blinding sun, whoever picks them up should be quicker than quick," Spence responded. He made one more pass, took a long look, and zoomed back to the Truman, feeling both exultation and major concern at the same time. He was happy to have discovered the survivors, but so worried as to their survival. Speed was of the essence.

You never saw such hugging and kissing going on as erupted in those lifeboats. Even those too weak to engage were smiling and clapping. Everyone was asking Cox and Goetz how long would it be for their rescue.

Captain Cox answered the group: "All I can tell you is that it depends on how close the nearest ship is. That fighter came, no doubt, from a carrier that is probably hundreds of miles away. The pilot is probably on the radio right now with an all points bulletin with our position and our plight. It's early yet, so let's all pray we'll be located and rescued before dark." It was indeed early, only 7:15 a.m., but the blazing sun was already a factor taking its toll again as it rose above the ocean. Both men and women had shirts and blouses off, dousing the clothes in the cool ocean water, and hanging them over their heads. The sting of salt water in their eyes was somewhat prevented by keeping their eyes closed. The shade protection from the sun was absolutely necessary.

Genevieve turned to David. "How long do you think we can stand this honey?" she asked in desperation.

"We need to do what it takes, sweetheart. We need to cover ourselves like we're already doing, and just wait it out. They'll be here for us. I just know it." David took her in both his arms, closed his eyes, and prayed for both them and their unfortunate companions.

Their four parched lips made light but reassuring contact. They looked at the other six occupants of their craft. Each one was in a sluggish and morose state. Don and Carla Earlens were holding tightly to each other, not moving. David carefully crawled across the raft to them, and touched their shoulders. They didn't move. He looked at the other two elderly couples who periodically shifted positions and wetted their bodies with the salt water. He took a deep breath and looked back at Genevieve who had her head back and partially covered with her blouse. He looked and touched both Don and Carla again. He wasn't imagining things. Their skin was cold, and he couldn't feel any breath from their nostrils. He decided to check their pulses, first removing Don's hand from Carla's back. He did not feel a pulse. He lifted Carla's hand. He could not feel her pulse either. Tears filled his eyes; he replaced their hands as best he could, realizing they died holding each other. He said a prayer to himself that their souls were together forever.

Genevieve lifted her blouse to douse it again, and saw David slowly crawling toward her. "I didn't know you left my side, sweetheart. What is it?" she asked when she saw more involuntary tears streaming down his face.

He took a deep breath "The Earlens are gone. Probably during the night," he said as he enfolded her in his arms. She, too, began to cry.

"We should tell Captain Cox," she sobbed. He looked out and saw the captain's raft about 25 feet from them tethered with their raft and the other five. David decided that trying to row closer to the captain's raft would use up strength he might need later, as well as unnerve the other passengers.

"I'll do it later. Best we don't risk panic. We all have enough problems," David explained, hugging his wife tightly. They decided to pray the Lord's Prayer quietly together, remembering the Earlens.

As the day unfolded, Captain Cox and Copilot Goetz took turns encouraging the survivors, helping keep their spirits up, as well as reminding them to conserve water while awaiting rescue.

Just before landing, Lt. Spence was ordered to come to the bridge immediately after touchdown. Captain Edward Davidson, the Skipper, was filled in by Lt. J.G. Morris, and they had notified Fleet Command. Fleet Command had, in turn, contacted the U.S. Coast Guard out of Florida and Puerto Rico, as well as the Federal Communications Commission who sent out an all points bulletin to the civilian authorities and Majestic Airlines as to the fate of Flight 400.

The news broke just after 7:30 a.m. The Carters heard it first, and immediately called the Kelseys. They were all talking together on extension phones, with Kathy and Helen half crying and laughing with joy that they finally heard their children were alive and located.

Ken and Fred decided to call their respective Naval Reserve Stations to see if they could update them on the Navy's involvement. The officers in charge were amazed to be talking to the fathers of Genevieve and David, were already aware of the developing situation, but could shed no light on the progress. They suggested that the news media would have broadcast news faster than they would learn of the rescue, given the high profile passengers involved.

Captain Davidson, Lt. Spence, and Lt J.G. Morris were on the bridge when they heard, "Davidson, you son of a gun, thank that Lieutenant Spence for me for finding those poor people."

Davidson responded, "Thank him yourself, Karl. He's right here."

"Young man, you're a hero. There's no designated medal for what you did but I *will* think of something. Kudos to you, and God Bless." The voice belonged to Admiral Karl Leonard, Commander of the Navy's 2nd fleet out of Norfolk.

"Thank you, sir. I was just lucky. I saw something far off, and had to investigate. If I hadn't turned my bird in that direction, I wouldn't have seen them."

"Call it divine intervention, young man. I believe God chose you, so just accept it," he ordered, rather like a father, and certainly like an Admiral. Lt. Spence realized the Admiral was right. He took a deep breath and wiped a tear from his eye.

Captain Davidson put his arm around Dylan's shoulder and took the mike. "Karl, is there a rescue operation—"

Admiral Leonard anticipated his words, and interrupted: "As we speak, I have ordered DD 137, The Thomas, to sail full speed ahead to the coordinates Lt. Spence provided. I have just received word that they are moving through the Anegada Passage. They should be there well before dark. There's a chopper on board already loaded with water and food that can be lowered to them well before the ship reaches them. We have also notified the airlines and civilian officials. I suggest you periodically fly to them, so they know we're on it."

"Right on, Karl. Lt. Spence will complete his mission," said Davidson, returning his response.

Spence rushed off the bridge to order "Bluebird" and "Bobolink" to suit up again, and follow him at quarter hour intervals until the Thomas or its helicopter could reach the rafts. As his FA18 left the flight deck he realized, as Admiral Leonard exclaimed, this had been a divine intervention and he had been chosen to carry it out.

The sun, as the morning progressed, was relentless. Two more of the elderly passed away, and several others were certain to. David, Genevieve, Captain Cox, Copilot Goetz, and some of the younger men and women were trying to give mouth-to-mouth resuscitation. All available water was limited to the elderly, although a few felt it was a waste at this point and some arguing ensued until Captain Cox, as weak as he was, stood up in his raft. Physically supported by Goetz, Cox demanded that his orders be followed, chastising the few dissidents. Goetz and David echoed the Captain, and the grumbling stopped.

A familiar sound came down from the sky. The jet they had seen earlier was returning slowly out of the east. Those who could stand and wave did, falling in the shifting raft and rising again, waving clothes and blankets while they were able.

"They're still checking on us," said David. "That's a good thing. Hopefully they will manage to get someone to help us really soon."

"I sure hope so," Genevieve said, fervently.

Captain Goetz, two rafts away, waved a towel, and shouted, "Hooray for the U.S. Navy! Hurry and rescue us."

Lt. Spence took a deep breath into his radio: "Spence to the Truman, come in."

"Go ahead, Spence," Captain Davidson responded.

"Sir, it looks a little worse. Some of the people in the rafts aren't moving at all. We need to step things up, sir," he firmly added.

"Roger that, Lieutenant. The Thomas, DD 137, has been alerted and will be sending emergency provisions by copter right away."

"Thank God for that, sir," Spence responded as he maintained contact with the rafts.

The Thomas, DD137, received the message from Fleet Command. Lt Avery on the bridge relayed the message to Cdr. Douglas, the Skipper, who immediately ordered him to change course and move full speed ahead for the rescue operation and to send the bird full of lifesaving water and food ahead. He also ordered that Chief Hospital Corpsman Spiker be aboard.

"Aye sir," Avery responded and the rescue mission was on its way.

The noise was unmistakable. It was the sound of a helicopter. As hoarse as they were, their chorus of cheers was resounding. Then they saw it as it appeared to come right out of the sun. Lt. McKenna maneuvered the bird right above the middle of the rafts, and had Chuck Johnson BM3 and Al Cerrone SN2 slowly lower a box at a time full of bottled water and food to where they could be reached and pulled into the rafts. The supplies became the lifeblood to some forty plus people.

In less than a minute, CHHC Spiker followed down in a rope ladder with a backpack full of medical supplies and a head full of medical knowledge. Lt. Spence made another pass in his plane, and smiled with glee as he saw the copter hovering over the rafts.

"Spence to the Truman."

"Go ahead, Lieutenant," Captain Davis responded.

"Sir, the copter is here and they are providing water, food, and supplies."

"That's great," came the response from the Captain. '"Come on back, Dylan. You carried out your mission well. The tin can Navy will take over now," he laughed.

"Aye, sir. I am on my way back," Spence responded.

Once David and Genevieve were on the Thomas and had rested a while, they asked the C.O., Cdr. Douglas, "Is it possible for us to talk to the Navy pilot who found us drifting? If it wasn't for him, many of us would not be here now."

"Certainly, I'll have you patched through to the Truman," he responded, happy to oblige.

Genevieve and David followed him to the bridge, where he put in a call to Fleet Command, who connected them. "Harry S. Truman come in."

Ensign Bonnell on the Truman answered.

"Truman, this is Commander Douglas, skipper of DD 137, the Thomas. I have an unofficial, but very special request, of you," and he turned to David and Genevieve who smiled at his comment.

Before he could continue, Ensign Bonnell asked, "Sir, have you been able to rescue those poor people who landed in the pond?"

"Yes, and I have two very special passengers on my bridge right now. They wish to personally thank the pilot that discovered them."

"I'll alert him and get back to you in about 20 or so," Bonnell said excitedly, but remaining militarily correct.

"Thank you, Truman, over and out."

Genevieve and David heard the exchange and thanked Captain Douglas, and they glanced out over the Thomas' bow, watching it part the sea like a knife as it raced back to Jacksonville.

They were at peace now, holding on to each other tightly but tenderly, fully comprehending the ordeal they experienced and had overcome with some very special help. After a while, they stepped out from the bridge and at the railing of the Thomas saw the sea from a whole different perspective than a few short hours before. They were just staring in a hypnotized state at the water with their arms around each other. Below deck, some of their fellow survivors were beginning to feel alive again, enjoying the ride as if it were a luxury cruise. They both thought of Carla and Don Earlens and the others who had not survived. Tears involuntarily formed in their eyes.

"O.K., Mr. and Mrs. Kelsey, we have Lt. Spence standing by on the Harry S. Truman for you," Captain Douglas said, leaning out from the bridge.

David and Genevieve both shook their heads as if they were exiting a dream, and climbed to the bridge.

David spoke first "Lt. Spence, this is David Kelsey. My wife and I thank you more than we can say. If it weren't for you, we and many others may not be alive today."

"Mr. Kelsey, I appreciate that, but all I can say is I'm just so glad I spotted the rafts. God just used me. I call it divine intervention. I'm sure glad he did, but I had no control over it."

"Well, we thank God for 'using' you. You are his instrument on earth, as it were."

"I'll always have a very special feeling about it all. I guess I had my special moment on earth," he said. Hesitating, he continued. "By the way, are you the Marauders' great prospect? That David Kelsey?"

David was briefly taken aback that he recognized the name. He 'fessed up. "I'm him."

"Wow, I'll be," came the response.

"Lieutenant, I'll tell you what. I'll see to it that you and your family have Marauders tickets for whenever you want."

"That's unnecessary. I didn't mean to—" he started, but David interrupted.

"I know you didn't. I offered. Please accept."

"You got it. Thanks a million."

"Thanks a billion to you. Dylan, is it?"

"Yes, Dylan."

"Hold on, Dylan, my wife wants to thank you, also."

"Hello, Lieutenant Spence. This is Genevieve Carter-Kelsey. I thank you also from the bottom of my heart. You have no idea. More people would have passed away today if it weren't for you. You were truly the tool of divine intervention. David and I and so many others will never forget you."

"Mrs. Carter-Kelsey, I just don't know what else to say, except I'm just so happy to have been in the air when and where I was. I do feel blessed."

Genevieve then lightened up the conversation. "By the way, I'll match David's offer. I'll see that you get tickets to any Broadway play you want. We'll keep in touch, and would like to meet you personally to hug you to death." She couldn't see it over the airwaves but Lt. Spence turned beet red. This may have been the most sentimental conversation ever between the bridges of two Navy ships. "That death part was speaking figuratively, of course" she laughed.

Dylan managed to blurt out, "Wow, my lucky day."

"No, Lt. Spence, our lucky day," they both echoed back.

"O.K., you will reach Jacksonville before me, but wait, I'll be looking for those hugs."

"By the way, you will be a hug cushion. There will be many hundreds of hugs besides ours. So get ready," said Genevieve.

"Wow," was the amazed response.

Captain Douglas got on the radio. It was Admiral Leonard advising that the Thomas rev it up, as relatives were arriving in Jacksonville by the dozens as he spoke.

## Chapter 21

# THE INTERNATIONAL INCIDENT A REUNION TO REMEMBER

It was some eighteen years since Victoria and Keith graduated from Northern Delaware University. For the last four years, she was Secretary of State. Now, Victoria was Vice President Elect, to be sworn in on January 20th. Keith was elated that he was chosen for the Secret Service contingent traveling overseas to protect her. He felt fortunate to have this opportunity, and hoped he would have a chance to say hello to his old classmate. Twenty agents filed into the briefing room to prepare for the trip. Ed Wayne, Senior Agent, addressed the group.

"This visit should be relatively safe since she'll be inside most of the time with government officials. However, as you know, we can't take anything for granted. We need to be especially cautious and diligent when she is being escorted to and fro in vehicles, and en route to different meetings and the airports, especially in Bakrish. Let me emphasize, however, that while Etolonia and Kashrakastani should be safer and again, should be, do not relax one iota. Remember your training. When we relax, crap happens."

Keith raised his hand.

"Yes, Agent Fredericks."

"Will we be keeping her in a pocket, or will it be the host security forces?"

"First of all, Keith, it is our responsibility, but in Bakrish they are insisting their security forces keep her in the pocket. We are trying to convince them that we should. We have a few days left to reach an agreement."

Keith interjected, "What if we suggest that we alternate agents so that we total at least half the protection?"

Ed Wayne thought for a moment and responded. "Keith, that's a good idea. I'll ask our chief to make that proposal. Yes, that certainly makes me more comfortable."

Keith thought of Victoria and their time at N.D.U., and he shuddered to think that she could be assassinated. Not on his watch. He couldn't let that happen.

Ed Wayne proceeded to begin a slide show of the three cities with close-ups of the routes to be used from each airport to each government building they would visit, and how they would enter. Well prior to their arrival, local forces would have security in place, protecting the entranceways to each building. Crowds would be restricted behind barricades. The Secret Service would put her in the pocket and keep her in the pocket until inside a building. The exception was Bakrish, where their security would escort her inside. This procedure would be reversed upon exiting. "We will arrive five days prior to the Vice President Elect to become very familiar with each route, and learn about alternatives should it be necessary."

Another agent, Jack Adair, asked, "Do we know how diligent each of the governments will be about adequate protection in terms of numbers and training?"

"That's a good question, Jack. We are confident with Etolonia, less so with Kashrakastani, and even less with Bakrish."

Keith was upset. "Why then are we going ahead with this visit? Victoria, rather the Vice President Elect," he corrected himself, "will be in considerable danger despite our efforts."

"Well," Ed hesitated, and pinched this throat before answering, "Ours is not to ask the reason why, but to do or die." He heard more than a few groans. "Having said that," he continued, "we are working with each government's security group to keep the final route decisions secret. We won't know what route we'll take until we meet their representatives at the airports. That, at least, will force dispersion of the bad guys. But government troops will need to quickly adjust to a last minute decision."

Another agent, Ray Burris, added, "Who knows how many of them are on our side anyhow?" and more groans were heard.

They continued the review, and began preparations to leave in a few days. Needless to say, the agents were not at all comfortable. They felt very concerned about the probability of disaster because of reliance on the questionable ability and trustworthiness of Bakrish and Kashrakastani special forces.

Keith, in particular, was extremely upset and expressed his concerns to Ed, as well as several of his peers. He turned to God in prayer for an answer, as he had many times in the past, to overcome his personal adversity. He prayed that he would receive a revelation that would relieve his anxiety.

In another meeting, this one at the Capitol Building, Victoria and the Foreign Relations Committee were reviewing the itinerary that she and the President had developed for her trip. She would be accompanied by the committee chairman, Senator Lawrence Collins, of the opposing political party. He often challenged her.

The major thrust of this trip was to share the thoughts of the new administration with U.S. allies, and those mainly opposing some important U.S. proposals and strategies. Two of the opposing countries were Bakrish and Kashrakastani, their geographical neighbor, leaning away from U.S. ideology. Each country was unique, and required a different type of diplomacy. As the Secretary of State, Victoria had made visits to this region. Now a heartbeat from the presidency, she would be received differently, and with hopefully more credibility and respect in countries that remain anti-feminine in the 21st century. A major concern was to assist these countries in curbing rampant terrorism, which prohibited any hope of even a semblance of democracy.

"The way I see it, we need to provide them with a detailed plan of how they should approach the terrorism in their backyards," Senator Collins strongly insisted.

Senators Ashley and Danners agreed. Senator Danners added, "Perhaps we can provide some alternatives so they do not feel as they had no choice or input at all."

Victoria took this all in, and felt that she needed to somehow direct the conversation. "I agree, Senators. We need to give them input. President Elect Cameron and I will first give them the opportunity to offer their suggestions, and we will build from there. Once we hear what they have to say, we can offer recommendations that we feel will strengthen their plans and approach. The President Elect and I believe that this approach will be much more palatable, and they won't feel as though we're dictating to them."

Senator Collins was still skeptical. "What if they don't have a plan?" he challenged.

"I don't believe that's very likely, Larry," responded Victoria. "They probably have a plan with a lot of holes in it, or something that doesn't cover all the bases, so to speak. They will, I'm sure want to take the lead, in their own country, to save face. It's our job, then, to be certain we get across to them the elements we feel are necessary to ensure success."

She came through with such authority and confidence that there was no verbal disagreement from the Committee, but she could detect some annoyance from Senator Ashley.

He added, "For good measure, madam Vice President Elect, have a plan to offer just in case they don't have a plan. We may come up empty, which would be a travesty."

"Senator Ashley, I hear you, and I have some ideas that the President Elect and I have brainstormed with General Bradford and staff. Let me review those with you now. These are crucial elements that we feel are necessary for any plan to achieve success." She grabbed a marker and walked to the board. "O.K., let's brainstorm. I will be having a follow up session with the General and his staff. I need to review all of our ideas with President Elect Cameron prior to my leaving in four days."

The Vice President Elect instantly assumed leadership of the committee, and even those who still harbored doubts came in line.

President Elect Ralph Cameron and Victoria would not be sworn in for six weeks, but they hit the ground running. She was still President Layne's Secretary of State, so this assignment was not an unfamiliar one. While on Air Force 2 she pondered their approach to foreign relations, which could be decidedly different. Her mind also wandered to her new role as Vice President, which normally would be quite different than being the Secretary of State. She wondered if accepting Ralph's offer was the right decision for her. Thinking ahead, eight years from now (assuming his reelection in four years), she would need to make the most important decision in her life—whether or not to run for President of the United States of America. *My God,* she thought, realizing that she could be the first woman to run for the presidency.

She took a deep breath to relax, realizing her mind was racing too far ahead. It usually did race a bit, but not in eight year increments, and certainly not in such dramatic fashion. She wondered if she would miss her time as Secretary of State, something she had discussed at length with Ralph Cameron. With her eyes closed listening to the music in her headset as they crossed the Atlantic, she recalled one conversation in particular that convinced her to say yes to his request to be his running mate.

"Victoria, I want you to use your intelligence, knowledge, and experience to the fullest. Just think," he continued, "as how two diplomats out in the world will greatly enhance our international presence, and I sincerely hope sooner rather than later begin to change some of our very pressing problems."

She remembered countering with, "But whoever you choose as your new Secretary of State may have decidedly different takes, seeing something from a different perspective. Won't that muddy the waters, or retard progress?"

He responded, "I want different opinions at times. It will allow us to think things through. That way, I'll know that my decisions are based on the very best advice of my top Lieutenants. Besides, it's my responsibility to prevent muddying up the waters, as they say." He gave her a full smile and laugh she had come to admire. That convinced her that she was here to serve as requested. She smiled to herself, and dozed off listening to the music until awakened for lunch.

Senator Collins walked over to her seat and she invited him to join her for lunch. "Well, Victoria who do you think our new president will choose as your successor?"

She quickly thought to herself that a question like that requires another question. "Well, Larry who would you like to see in my old job?"

He didn't take the bait, instead answering, "Whoever gets the job will have your big shoes to fill. Figuratively speaking of course." They both laughed. "Seriously, Victoria, you did an excellent job, considering you're from the other side. I've said that before, although we have certainly disagreed a few times."

"I'll say we've disagreed, even though I could see your viewpoint at times. That's the purpose of democracy."

He took a seat in the aisle seat, and continued. "Seriously though, Ralph Cameron is doing a wise thing keeping you involved in foreign affairs, in addition to the new Secretary of State, whoever that will be. It certainly ramps up our presence around the world."

"Why that's super of you to say, Larry. That's exactly what we're aiming for." They were interrupted by lunch and they toasted each other.

"Let's make this trip a diplomatic success," Victoria smiled. "Perhaps, tonight, we can lift a glass of delicious Kashrakastani wine."

"I'll drink to that," he agreed.

The Secret Service contingent now in Kashrakastani's capital, Gaharu, separated into three groups to reduce conspicuousness as they rotated through different routes to assess the lay of the land. Even though they took pains not to be obvious by dressing like the natives, using small unobtrusive vehicles, and deploying in an unobvious way, they were being watched. Kashrakastani was a major enigma to the United States as was Kashrakastani's leader President Mahdinejad. However, partly due to Victoria's influence and concerted efforts on the part of the President Elect, Mahdinejad was responding well to the upcoming visit, as well as communicating positively through friendly third parties in Europe and the Middle East. This diplomacy certainly diffused an otherwise tense situation. Economic sanctions had been gradually lifted, and some trade was initiated. Victoria's current visit, hopefully, would be a major step forward in further reducing tensions between Kashrakastani and the west, especially the United States.

As a result of President Layne's position change, other western democracies also began to develop positive relationships with Kashrakastani. President Elect Cameron had strongly supported the continuation of diplomacy, and dispatched Victoria in her new role to continue what she started under President Layne over a year ago.

However, President Mahdinejad had many problems of his own. The more he cooperated with or even stayed neutral with the western democracies, especially the United States, a growing opposition was gaining strength and influence with

Kashrakastani's extremists. This concerned him, and more recently, he had shifted to taking a less cooperative stand, at certain times, with the west.

In an obscure old tenement on the edge of Gaharu, Ashkari Restavi, a militant leader and long time rival to President Mahdinejad, was at his animated best with some two dozen of his closest followers. "This is our chance to fulfill our destiny. We cannot fail. We must show the people that we are in charge, we are the chosen ones, we are the future of Kashrakistani," he shouted, slamming his fist on the table. His cohorts rose and waved their wine glasses filled with, perhaps, the same Kashrakistani wine that Victoria and Senator Collins would drink later in the evening to toast President Mahdinejad at the palace.

"Hear, hear, all glory to our leader, Ashkari Restavi," they shouted repeatedly.

Restavi then swallowed the contents of his glass. His eyes were bulging with emotion, and he was sweating profusely. He continued his venomous emotional barrage. "We must silence that swine Mahdinejad forever and the American pig, that woman Magnuson, to show the world we are the voice of Kashrakastani. We must be heard, we will be heard, we will triumph and lead our people, our land, to glory."

"Long live our leader, Ashkari Restavi," they shouted again, and filled their glasses again and raised them to this self-proclaimed leader who stood before them as a larger than life demigod.

In his Gaharu hotel, Keith turned the hot water on as hot as he could stand it, and climbed into the tub. He was grateful that the hotel had such basic amenities as hot water. It wasn't always this way. It was around 1 p.m., about three hours before they would take their various routes to the airport to meet Air Force 2 and Victoria. He would set his alarm for an hour catnap before the re-deployment of his squad. This would be his first duty as a squad leader. Keith's thoughts of their time together at Northern Delaware University occupied his mind. Would she remember him? They were never especially close, but he had an affection for her that seemed to grow over the years. Neither had gotten married, but he didn't know if she was ever attached in any way. She was always pleasant to him but perhaps it was because of the wheel chair, and his difficult recovery period. He wanted to believe that she cared about him more deeply than that, but he didn't make an attempt to pursue her as, back then, he was emotionally affected by his condition.

They saw each other on and off and just wished each other perfunctory best wishes and good luck. He lay in the tub feeling the soothing effects of the hot water, and staring at the dull painted ceiling of this old hotel trying to think of a way to say hello to her, his former classmate, now the next Vice President of the United States. Would she even remember him? How close would he get to her so she would see him? What could he possibly say if he did get close enough? What if he was close and she ignored him or didn't recognize him? What if? What if? He shook his head and hoped the answers would soon appear. He had to get a grip and focus on the fact that he was a key player in the protection of the life of the Vice President Elect of the United States. That took precedence over everything else.

Victoria opened her eyes, but remained in her sleeping position, listening to the drone of the plane as it crossed into Europe, heading toward the Middle East. She calculated about three hours before landing, and silently prayed for a successful mission. Raising her seat to a sitting position, she looked forward and noticed that Senator Collins and the staff assistants all had their seats leaned back. She assumed they were sleeping. Agent Jack Adair, traveling with them, was on his laptop receiving updates from Chief Agent Ed Wayne concerning reports on an assassination attempt being planned on Victoria's life.

Adair, sent his message, "Are we thinking of aborting the visit?"

Wayne answered, "I don't believe so, but we are constantly in touch with the White House. It's the President's decision."

This was an unprecedented way of receiving a top level decision, as President Elect Cameron initiated this pre inauguration diplomatic visit, with President Layne's approval. But President Layne, still in charge, was ultimately responsible for this decision concerning, Victoria, his Secretary of State.

Agent Wayne continued with his message. "Jack, advise her of this update."

"Will do," Jack answered, and walked back to Victoria.

"How do we know this is a valid tip?" she asked.

"In these situations we usually rely on the informant. In this case our informant has been extremely reliable."

Victoria took an unusually deep breath. "I will rely on the service then. I am sure you know best."

"Actually madam Vice President, our chief is advising President Layne who will be making the decision. We should know before we land."

"Oh, I see. Should we make a wager, Agent Adair? I will spot you one hundred that he says continue with our mission," she quipped.

He was taken aback by her response and her resolve. "Actually, you may keep your one hundred madam Vice President, because I am of the same mind. If we backed down every time we learned of a threat, we wouldn't make much progress in this world, and we would have a respect rating below zero."

"Well said, Agent Adair, well said," she responded.

President Layne reached President Elect Cameron, who was halfway across the U.S., visiting military bases.

"Ralph, I needed to alert you regarding Victoria's visit to Kashrakastani. We have been informed by reliable sources that there may be an assassination attempt."

There was a brief silence on the part of Ralph Cameron. "She does have adequate protection doesn't she, Dave?" he asked with concern.

"Yes. We have more than two dozen Secret Service agents over there who have thoroughly studied and dissected the route they will take. Also, I have personally spoken to President Mahdinejad only a few minutes ago. He has agreed to assign four score well armed and trusted guards to protect her. In addition, our Secret Service will be using a diversionary tactic regarding the route they take from the airport."

"Sounds like we have it covered, but I still have concerns knowing there are many out there who do not value their life. You know how they think. They are fanatics after all," said President Elect Cameron.

"I know, Ralph, but we cannot let the bastards win. We must prevail and go ahead with our diplomatic efforts. If we back down to the many threats we receive, our stature in the world will continue to diminish."

"I hear you, Dave. Just give the order for all concerned to be extra diligent, and try to get that across to Mahdinejad also. I think he overestimates his palace guard."

"I will be sure to do that, Ralph," President Layne assured him. He took a deep breath and decided that this mission definitely had to be carried out. He picked up his phone and dialed his secretary "Rose, patch me through to Air Force Two, please."

The affirmative response traveled back across the Atlantic and reached Victoria as her plane was within two hours of landing.

"It's a go," Jack Adair notified her as soon as he heard.

Senator Collins awoke from his nap, saw them conferring, and walked up the aisle to Victoria's seat.

"What's the scoop, folks?" he casually asked.

Jack Adair deferred to Victoria.

"Larry, a friendly informant in Kashrakastani has notified us, through channels, of a possible assassination attempt by the rebel Ashkari Restavi."

He was alarmed. "Oh my God. What should we do? Are we going to abort the visit?" he asked, visibly concerned.

"President Layne and President Elect Cameron have discussed it, and they want us to proceed. We have adequate protection and have made, through the Secret Service, careful plans to protect us so we can carry out this mission."

"I pray that is the case," responded Collins.

"We will do our job Senator, you can be sure of that," Jack Adair assured him.

"I know you will, Agent Adair, but it's still more than a bit unnerving."

"I understand," Adair answered.

"O.K., we'll show them what the U.S.A. is made of," Victoria firmly stated, and pumped her fist. Adair smiled and returned to his seat for last minute instructions, and the Senator, shaking his head, not totally convinced, went back to his seat. Victoria, for all her bravado, took a very deep breath as a moment of uncertainty passed through her mind also. She felt a little guilt, but realized it was a human frailty. She wasn't a machine, after all, as some of her political opponents and cohorts alike sometimes described her.

Restavi and his followers left their slum hideout two and three at a time, dispersing to various stations assigned along the three routes that they had observed the American Secret Service study. They were able to identify the probable routes, but which of the three would be chosen was in doubt. Which deserved their concentration to maximize their firepower?

Advantage Americans.

However, there was a quarter mile approach, nearing the Presidential Palace, where all three routes would merge. Three key lieutenants were keeping him posted to maximize the chance for success of their mission. Now they were all waiting in alleys, vehicles, storefronts, and taverns, hiding their weapons and biding their time.

Keith reached for his cell phone on the second ring. It was Ed Wayne.

"Keith, I am assigning your squad the mother load," the code name for Victoria and her party.

Keith was confused about the change. "What's up Chief?"

"We have a reliable tip that Restavi has deployed his thugs all over the three routes, and they may merge and attack at or just pass the conversion point. So that will amount to all of us versus all of them, and whoever has the best firepower wins."

Keith quickly thought about that as he realized and replied, "A lot of people could die, including Victoria."

"You read that right, but we have another idea to circumvent bloodshed and avoid catastrophe," Ed Wayne responded.

"I'm all ears, chief"

"We'll go to the palace all right. To President Mahdinejad's summer palace in the mountains."

"O.K., Chief, how do we manage that?"

"We have worked it out with the President himself. President Layne and he conferred given the imminent danger."

"Sounds great, but how on earth do we get there?" Keith asked, now extremely interested.

"Your squad will as immediately as possible be picked up by President Mahdinejad's vans with armed escort, and race to the airport to meet Air Force 2 as soon or immediately after arrival. Mahdinejad will have an armed escort assigned to the vans all the way until you board Air Force 2. You will be in charge of the detail."

Before Keith could respond to this remarkable change in plans, Ed Wayne continued, "How's several days at a summer palace in the mountains sound to you?" Ed Wayne added some levity to a serious discussion.

"Sounds marvelous. But what about the rest of our detail?" Keith asked.

"Why they'll fly out of Kashrakastani commercially and be on their way to Bakrish and Etolonia. Your group and her party will follow them after her meetings at the mountain palace with President Mahdinejad."

"Sounds like a movie plot, Ed. Who dreamed it up?"

"Actually, the President's Chief of Security, Atollah Jaffari, and myself. He had to clear it with the president himself who was very pleased because it avoid a very infamous, messy, and possibly deadly situation bringing a lasting negative focus on him and his country."

"Are we sure Restavi won't switch gears in a hurry and surprise us?" Keith asked.

"I really believe there's a snowball's chance in hell for any possibility of that compared to Plan A. He shouldn't realize the switch until Air Force 2 takes off or later. Jaffari also will have his forces close off the airport to the public, and be the first line of defense, should Restavi get wise and try to attack the airport. It is a helluva of a lot better than splitting our forces and Jaffari's over three routes as we had planned."

"Sounds great, chief. We'll be able to protect all decidedly better in the mountains than down here."

"That's for sure. Besides, the president has a contingent of palace guards stationed full time at the mountain palace, so that makes it even better. I'm signing off for now. Keep in touch, Keith."

"Will do, chief. Over and out."

Keith hurriedly dressed to advise his contingent. He called Agent Don Mallon to help spread the word. His room phone rang. "Hello."

"Hello, Agent Fredericks, this is Kashrakastani's Chief of Security, Atollah Jaffari. Have you spoken to your chief Agent Wayne?"

"Yes, I have. I am aware of the new plan. Thank you for your involvement. It sounds much better than our original plan. I was concerned that our original plan, while having some merit, would result in some bloodshed. This should circumvent that."

"Yes, yes, I can guarantee that it will," Jaffari answered. "Have your agents ready in one hour in your hotel lobby. I have two vans standing by with my guards to accompany you to the airport. Advise your people."

"One question, sir. When and how will the President arrive safely to his mountain retreat."

"Why, he is already there. He arrived last evening on his private plane. Go, now, Go with Allah," and he hung up. Keith took a deep breath. He had underestimated his current hosts. He thought for a moment and realized it was a hell of a lot better than overestimating them and he rushed to call Don Mallon to split the call list with him.

Keith felt more relieved once the group settled in the unmarked vans, and were quickly on their way. He closed his eyes, and realized that he would actually be accompanying Victoria on Air Force Two. He would be in voice range, and most likely have visual contact. Would she remember him? It's been about 16 years since Northern Delaware University. What would he say to her? Hello, it's nice to see you again, or Congratulations Madame Vice President Elect? It all seemed so lame. He tried to refocus. He was, for this operation, agent in charge. They soon arrived at the airport without incident. Other unmarked vans using another route arrived with the balance of the Secret Service Contingent heading for Bakrish, the Vice President Elect's next stop. So far, so good.

His spotter notified Restavi, who was pleased that he was aware (or so he thought) of every move, but that the American and local authorities were ignorant of his. He started a chain call plan to have his hoodlums take their places at the merger of the three routes. He would keep spotters on all routes to keep track of every mile traveled. He turned to his key Lieutenants: "Soon these infidels will leave this earth and turn to dust." They all chuckled at their exalted leaders assurances.

Keith's group met an officer of Atollah Jaffari's security service who led them down through the tunnel to the incoming flight deck. Air Force 2 was about to land shortly, with all its special passengers safely on board. Keith was relieved that they would all be out of danger once this ingenious switch was completed. He took a moment to reflect. He was only a short time from coming face to face with Victoria. For a few minutes, he felt like the young college student again, in the wheelchair, with Victoria Magnuson taking the time to notice him. He shook his head and told himself to get on with it. This was no time to daydream. This was the most important assignment of his career. There was much at stake.

The vans pulled up quickly and Keith and his squad boarded Air Force 2 as soon as it taxied to the terminal, while the remaining agents boarded the a commercial flight to proceed to Bakrish. Jaffari had a score of elite palace guards at the ready should Restavi's thugs storm the airport. Then Keith spotted Jack Adair and two other Secret Service agents, Victoria herself, Senator Collins, and the staffers traveling with them. The baggage handlers quickly loaded their light luggage onto Air Force 2 while the agents quickly boarded. All the agents walked to the rear.

Victoria was on her cellphone, immersed in conversation, and didn't notice him. He assumed she might be talking to the President. He took a long, close look at her. She remained beautiful to him after sixteen years. Jack Adair and Keith hugged.

"Wow, what a plan. I thought about a fire fight getting to the palace and realized some of us would be killed—including yours truly," said Keith.

"You're right, Keith. Thank God for the change in plans. This castle in the mountains ought to be a paradise compared to the streets of Detelonia."

"I would think so. We'll see. I've become a bit jaded about Kashrakastani, as you can see."

They settled in as the agents began welcoming each other. Keith had his eyes fixed on the front of the plane, but he couldn't quite see Victoria. She had a window seat, and was engaged in conversation with Senator Collins.

"Welcome aboard, everyone. Glad to be of service," Major Tom Johnson and co-pilot Lieutenant Sam Raber welcomed everyone aboard while Air Force 2's engines revved up and began taxiing for its approximately 90 minute flight to the mountain palace airstrip.

"Sure glad to be aboard, Captain," Agent Mallon emphatically responded. The agents all thanked God for the positive turn of events.

Ashkari Restavi was getting restless. He knew something had gone askew. None of his spotters had any information; he kept calling his front people closest to the airport, none of whom had any information. Finally, he ordered one of his lieutenants, unknown to the government, to inquire in the airport as to the status of Victoria's flight, and then impatiently waited for the report. He finally got the answer he didn't want to hear.

"Master, the American pigs arrived over 30 minutes ago, and they took another plane to somewhere."

"Somewhere? Where is this somewhere?" He was livid.

"Master, they will give me no further information. The airport people say they do not know where some of the passengers are. They have no information."

Restavi got down on his knees, holding his head in his hands, literally screaming unmentionables. His people were taken aback, never having seen him in such anguish. He prayed to Allah to help him finish his mission. He tried to envision a way to do that.

Keith stared down the length of the plane, and fixed his gaze on Victoria's head. She was immersed in conversation with one of her staff. Given the length of the plane, their eyes would probably never meet unless he did something to induce that. Keith kept his focus on Victoria, who had put her head back, probably closing her eyes to rest. He had this wonderful opportunity to say hello after all these years, and his legs would not coordinate with his brain.

"What's up with you, old buddy? You seem to be a million miles away. Care to give me a clue?" Don Mallon asked, nudging him in the ribs.

Keith sighed deeply, turning to his friend. "Would you believe I was a classmate of Victoria's at Northern Delaware University. We graduated together 16 years ago and now I'm nervous, and too shy to walk down this plane, and I feel too shy to say 'hello' or 'how are you' or something like that."

Don laughed a bit. "You're a Secret Service squad leader here to protect her, and you know her besides. Why are you afraid to talk to her," he asked in an exasperated way. "Wait till I tell the guys."

By now some of the other agents were beginning to hear over the roar of the engines.

Keith took a deep breath and began to rise to the occasion.

Don put his hand on Keith's arm. "Wait, Keith, I believe she may be coming our way. Maybe she had to gather her courage to face you," he humorously added.

"I kind of doubt that," Keith muttered.

Victoria and Senator Collins and their staff people were stopping to talk to each and every agent, shaking hands and thanking them for their service and protection. She was only four people away from Keith when recognition occurred. He stared back and smiled, but she continued greeting. He held his breath as she came closer. Don was nudging him in the ribs. She stared at him again. It appeared to Keith that some recognition dawned in her eyes. He managed to get it all together and stood up holding out his hand. She took it and her still marvelous green eyes were fixated on him.

"Hello, Victoria, Madame Vice President. Keith Fredericks at your service. It's marvelous to see you again."

"Well, I'll be," she blurted. "It must be over 15 years, hasn't it?"

"Over 16, actually," he answered.

She smiled broadly. "It's so good to see you again, and to see you in perfect physical condition as a Secret Service Agent. This is great, really marvelous." He briefly became lost in her green eyes and still light brown hair as she continued, "Senator Collins, myself, and our staff are so appreciative of this marvelous subterfuge you pulled off. You saved us from grave danger."

"Thanks, but I can't take credit for that. Many people engineered that."

Don Mallon leaned over and interjected, "He's our squad leader to boot." Keith elbowed him. She smiled at their interaction.

"Keith, I'll free up some time to talk to you some more, O.K."

"That would be great. I'd really like to talk and reminisce or whatever," he responded realizing that he was still holding her hand, and that just about everyone else was staring from Senator Collins on wondering why Victoria was still holding his hand and talking to him. The roar of the plane prevented any eavesdropping except for those on either side of Keith. She proceeded to put both of her hands on his, squeezing hard. "I'll make sure we talk privately. I'm so, so glad to see you. You have no idea." She felt like hugging him, but realized that would create quite a stir.

"Great, Madam Vice President. I'll look forward to that," he said.

Victoria moved on to Don. Keith, always respected for his intelligence and devotion to duty, was now held at a considerably higher level of esteem. Personally, he felt a warm glow for the remainder of the trip. His mind reverted to Northern Delaware University and their pleasant meetings all those years ago. He and many others dozed off to the drone of the engines, all exhausted from their very active afternoon grateful for the success of their subterfuge.

"All passengers, please be seated and fasten your seatbelts," came the word from the cockpit, as the one and one half hour flight was in the approach stage. The pilots had a clear open view of the mountains. Then President Mahdinejad's mountain palace came into view.

"There it is Tommy, the palace," co-pilot, Lieutenant Raber proclaimed.

"Sure enough Sam, sure enough, and there's the runway. Thank God; it looks as long as a commercial air field. Let's go down for a closer look to determine our approach." Major Johnson slowly lowered the large plane and decided, nodding to Lieutenant Raber, to make the announcement.

"All passengers seated and fasten seatbelts. We will be landing momentarily."

They all felt the reduction in power, waiting for the touchdown. The strip was clear of obstruction, the landing strip in good shape, and long enough to handle Air Force 2. The landing gear was dropped. The wheels made contact and the craft was ably guided, slowed, and stopped at about three quarters of the runway length. Johnson and Raber looked at each other and exhaled. They were not expecting to use this much of the runway. They proceeded to to turn the plane around for the passengers to be closer to the disembarkation point. Everyone onboard felt gratitude for the successful flight. Almost everyone walked forward to thank Johnson and Raber. As they disembarked, Keith had his agents form a wrap around his subjects, continuing the Secret Service's commitment to protect, the presidents palace notwithstanding. Three vans were cruising down the runway to provide transportation to the palace. Victoria, Senator Collins and their staff climbed into one, with the agents and Major Johnson and Lt. Raber in the other two.

"What a massive piece of property," Senator Collins remarked as they passed acres of gardens, a beautiful lake, several buildings, walking trails, a very large swimming pool. Eventually they reached a long entrance bordered by attractive rows of flowers and shrubberies, approaching the President's palace. The residence was built of sculptured stone and marble, with a copper roof enhanced by large antique windows.

" "Wow," repeated Senator Collins. "What digs."

Victoria laughed. "Digs fit for a King."

"Essentially, that's what Mahdinejad is. He just modernized his title to make the world think Kashrakastani is a democracy," the Senator added.

"Quite opulent, eh Larry?" Victoria expressed in a low voice.

"Quite may not be quite the word, Victoria," he answered.

The vans taxiing the pilots and the Secret Service contingent stopped at two more normal house-like structures before the road to the palace.

"Looks like these are our quarters, men," Keith grumbled. He had expected they would also be berthed at the palace.

"Did you know we would be separated from Victoria and her party?" asked Don Mellon.

"No, actually. Given all our other problems I was focused only on getting out of Detelonia," Keith muttered.

"Understood," Don agreed.

"I think I'll bring it up with Victoria—I mean the Vice President elect." Keith added.

"Do you think President Mahdinejad will be insulted, and think we lack trust in him?" Don asked.

"It's our duty to protect her in the best way possible. I'll talk to her, and make it a point to remind her of that. Perhaps she can request it. It would be better from her than us," Keith answered.

Victoria was very tired. She felt like she wanted to sleep uninterrupted for the next 24 hours, but knew that could not be. The maid assigned to her advised that dinner would be served in four hours, and that she would be escorted to cocktails and to meet the president before that. Her quarters consisted of a huge bedroom, full bath, and a large sitting room overlooking some exquisite gardens and a pool. Part of the sitting room was a mini office with a desk, phone and computer. A large vase of fresh flowers adorned the desk. *Nice touch*, she thought. She needed to bathe, rather than a shower, which would hinder a catnap before dinner. She just flopped fully clothed on the bed, and closed her eyes, wondering if the Vice President's home in D.C. would pale in comparison. She then quickly realized that even the White House would. She forced herself to sit up, lest she inadvertently fall asleep through the four hours before dinner, and cause an international incident, of sorts.

She undressed and quickly put on a robe prior to showering, when the phone rang. She answered, wondering who it might be.

"Madame Vice President, I'm downstairs. If you don't mind I need to talk with you in private. It should take only a few minutes."

"Why sure, Keith. Can you find me?"

"Your maid has been assigned to escort me. I'll be right up."

"O.K.," she responded, somewhat puzzled, but convinced it was important. Actually she would be glad to see him. She immediately put on her dress, brushed her hair, and splashed cold water on her tired face and eyes. Forget the makeup. She would do that after her bath and nap. The maid brought Keith to her room, he knocked, and she opened the door.

"Sorry for the intrusion, Madam Vice President," his eyes left her face, falling to her bodice, which she had forgotten to fasten. He realized how beautiful she was. Her eyes followed his gaze. She discreetly pulled her sash closed while continuing to look at him directly. He quickly caught himself and asked, "I thought you should ask President Mahdinejad to allow us to use sleeping quarters here in the palace, also. We know that the chances of you or Senator Collins being harmed are low, but it is our duty and responsibility to protect you around the clock wherever you might be."

She wanted to be less formal, and ask him about the last 16 or so years, but she let him continue.

"We are, as you know, duty bound to post guards outside your door, and to remain close to you when you stroll the palace grounds with or without President Mahdinejad or his guards."

"Keith, I do appreciate that. I really do. I just think that it may be a little over the top in this case. I want to convey to the President that we trust him, that he is an ally and a friend. I'm concerned that he may be insulted if the Secret Service act like commandos in his palace over hundreds of miles from the Capitol where we came from today."

Catching himself before he called her by her first name, Keith said, "Madam Vice President, I truly respect your thoughts but I really," he hesitated, "feel I must insist. We are duty bound. I would be absolutely derelict in my duty if I didn't."

"All right, Keith, I see where you are coming from, and I certainly appreciate your devotion to duty and concern for my and Senator Collin's safety. I'll talk to the President and work something out. Do you have a phone where you are?"

"Yes" he answered.

"O.K., Call me on extension 15, and give me your number so I can get back to you."

"Will do, Madam Vice President."

She gave him a broad smile, touched his arm, and said, "Keith, I'd like to talk to you just like Vicky and Keith at N.D.U."

"So would I Vicky, so would I. But I'm here in charge of a Secret Service contingent protecting the next Vice President of the United States and I need to stay focused. Perhaps when your mission is finished we can reminisce on the plane home."

She smiled, thought briefly about kissing him on the cheek, but settled on kissing her hand, then touching his lips. He smiled and blushed. "You can count on it Keith," she smiled.

He left with a feeling of more than admiration.

She disrobed and immersed herself in the beautifully shaped porcelain tub, briefly thinking of Keith's stare, sixteen or so years ago and their days at N.D.U. Then she closed her eyes, realizing this was another time and another place. She thought about how she might get President Mahdinejad to agree for the Secret Service to post guards in his palace, on its grounds and accompany them around the clock.

Keith called back with his extension and made it a point to call her Vicky. After her bath, she dozed off peacefully with a smile after the long, tedious day.

The dining room rivaled that of the White House, with grand chandeliers and gold glowing candlesticks. The carpet was rich with varying shades of red and yellow. Flowers adorned the huge table, with gleaming china dishes in silver platters. The sterling was appropriately ornate in design, as were the oversize white fabric chairs outlined in gold leaf. Victoria and Senator Collins were certainly impressed. She hoped the food would not be very spicy, realizing that it is probable in this part of the world. She had changed into a deep blue dress, a change from her gray striped suit. Her hair was combed to the side giving her an altogether different look. Modest jewelry adorned her ear lobes, neck, and wrist. She felt more like a woman tonight than she had since traveling. She didn't consider the effects. Senator Collins was escorted in minutes later and immediately noticed her. "My, my Victoria you look lovely tonight. You should dress like this more often."

"Thank you, Larry. You are pretty sharp yourself. I thought I should change for dinner. I do, after a while, ditch the suit look."

"You're fortunate. Women can do that. If I changed it would be to a sweater, shirt and slacks. Not fit for a state dinner which this qualifies as," he said, taking a good look around at the room. "My God, would you look at this place. It probably rivals Buckingham Palace, and how many people even know of it. It's absolutely fantastic. The walls look as if they're gold leafed." He pointed to white brocade walls adorned with gold trimming.

"So do the chairs, and look at the gold goblets," she added.

They heard voices as President Mahdinejad entered the room with his Chief of Staff, Levani Salaya. He was dressed resplendently and perfectly matched for the room in white with gold braiding around his jacket collar and sleeves. His jet black hair, absent of any gray, was perfectly groomed, as were his short beard and mustache.

Approaching the two guests, he spoke. "Ahh, welcome to my table, Madame Vice President and Senator. Welcome. I am glad to have you at my palace. We were able to fool that criminal Restavi, who I will soon eliminate. His days are numbered, as you say in English. Yes, it was my Mr. Salaya," he said, gesturing to his Chief of Staff, "who suggested this arrangement, and I called your President Layne, who agreed. I trust you had a good flight. You were safe, no?"

"Yes, Mr. President, we were definitely safe," she answered with a dazzling smile, pleased that he was concerned for their safety. She turned to Mr. Salaya. "Thank you, Mr. Salaya, for that brilliant strategy." He smiled and bowed in recognition of her appreciation. She took notice that her physical charms were having an effect on President Mahdinejad. She immediately thought she should use that as an advantage to suggest the Secret Service be moved into the palace for the next two days of meetings and accompany them, at a distance on the palace grounds, which she understood to be extensive and densely wooded.

"Your palace is a remarkable building, Mr. President. I hope we can fit in a tour while we are here," Senator Collins asked.

"I shall arrange that, Senator. We can have our talks in the morning. I feel fresh or, how you say? alert after morning meal. Then we can tour and walk in my gardens. They are beautiful to behold and we can rest and enjoy." He flashed a wide smile and beckoned them to sit.

He picked up a brass bell, and the ring alerted three servants to enter the dining room with various wines and hors d' oeuvre's on rolling carts. Victoria smiled broadly. "Mr. President, this is truly marvelous, or shall I say, resplendent?"

He smiled back and, to her surprise, with his right hand gently squeezed hers. "Nothing but the best for my honored guests, and shall I add, especially the lovely Vice President elect of the United States."

"Why, thank you, Mr. President," Victoria responded, realizing that in Kashrakastani, women were not held in high esteem. She thought that his wife or wives, (as this was a polygamous society) may not have accompanied him on this special visit to the palace. Through a dinner of pheasant under glass, and marvelous accompanying salads, wines, and sinful desserts, the lighthearted banter continued for almost three hours without anything of a serious nature being discussed. Finally, Victoria felt it time to ask the question. "Mr. President, I would greatly appreciate it if you would permit our Secret Service associates to post someone at my door and Senator Collins' door as well as walk, at a distance, with us in the gardens. It is their responsibility, and mine, to assure they are given the opportunity to protect me and whomever travels with me."

Senator Collins added for support, "That is absolutely correct."

President Mahdinejad sat back, and momentarily closed and rubbed his eyes. Victoria wondered if he completely assimilated her question, or whether he was about to succumb to his considerable imbibing and fall asleep. She and the Senator stared at him, and waited for his answer.

"Madame Vice President," came the reply, "I do not believe that will be necessary. However, I, how do you say? acquaint, accept, agree to your request." He stood up and almost fell over until his chief of staff, Levani Salaya, supported him. "I bid you all a good night," were the President's parting words.

"We will have breakfast at 9, then stroll the gardens," Mr. Salaya advised. "You may instruct your Secret Service as you mentioned," and then he assisted the President to his quarters. They both bid them a good night and an aide led them back to their rooms.

Larry Collins whispered in her ear, "Good move Victoria. You asked at the right time."

She turned toward him, smiling. "Actually, I thought he was going to sleep on us. I was almost too late. We were fortunate."

"Well don't count your chickens yet, young lady. He may not remember any part of the conversation in the morning."

"Hmm, you could be right. I'll call Keith tonight and ask him to have four of his agents do shifts outside our rooms tonight and prepare to shadow us in the gardens tomorrow."

"Really don't you think that might be presumptuous—"

She interrupted him. "Larry, don't ask me why. Call it a woman's intuition or whatever. I could be crazy, but I just have a feeling we should do this."

He shook his head. "O.K., Victoria. I guess we'll all sleep better for it. The wine and cordials will also assist, I'm sure."

"Amen to that," she laughed as they reached their quarters.

Her covers were turned down, and there were chocolates on her pillow. She reminded herself that this was no ordinary hotel. Relaxation may have ended tonight, however, as serious discussions would begin in the morning. She called the extension Keith gave her, and gave instructions to Don Mallon, who answered the phone.

"Thank you, Madam Vice President. All of us will breath considerably easier; you have no idea. I'll advise Keith, unless you want me to have him call you. He took a walk with a couple of the guys."

"No, Agent Mallon, you can convey it." She took a deep breath and felt relieved to have that accomplished. She undressed, removed her makeup, set an alarm for 7:30, decided to eat one delicious chocolate, brushed her teeth, and then almost immediately entered dreamland.

When they left their apartments for breakfast, they found two sleepy Secret Service agents outside their doors. They thanked them for their protection, and followed the escort sent by the President to the south garden for breakfast.

"Well, we had, gratefully, a safe evening" Senator Collins joked. "I slept like a log myself. I don't think even gunfire would have interrupted that."

She acknowledged his joke. "It does seem silly, I suppose, to have insisted our Secret Service watch over us for these two days, but we brought them here after all, and that's their function."

"It's not silly, Victoria. As you say, it's their job, and they reminded us, which I am grateful for. They'll accompany us on our strolls today also, so go for it."

She let the subject drop as their escort led them out to a beautiful heated garden under glass, an arboretum, with several tables and cushioned lounges. The morning sun began the task of warming, as servants began setting a table. They looked out toward the mountain at a breathtaking view. "This is beautiful to behold," Victoria gushed.

"Amen to that," Larry Collins agreed.

"Aah, good morning, my American friends. I see you are happy." President Mahdinejad surprised them.

"Oh, good morning, Mr. President. We were just marveling over the view," Victoria replied.

"Yes, marveling—a good English word. Yes, it is very nice all year.

When we build this we try to, as you say, decide, which is best view. This is best view and maybe best view in the world," and he chuckled. "Come lovely lady and Senator, have a wonderful breakfast and then we shall stroll my gardens and grounds. It is large, so eat well." Another exquisite meal was provided, with choices of egg, ham, cheeses, and cereals to make his American guests feel at home. Special cakes and breads of Kashrakastani and other Middle Eastern origin were also offered, as well as choices of breakfast wines, coffee, and tea. This morning, the President limited his intake of wine to two small glasses to avoid inebriation like last evening. "Please try some Kashrakastani breakfast wine. You will find it very light and delicious," he pushed.

Victoria put her hand up. "Perhaps later. I make it a rule never to drink alcohol until noon or later."

Mahdinejad smiled at her. "I'll try one glass," Senator Collins answered, and Mahdinejad had a servant pour one for him.

Still completely in charge of his faculties, he stood up and announced, "Well, my American friends, shall we, as you say, walk it off and stroll my beautiful palace grounds and discuss some major issues." He offered his arm to Victoria, and led them into the resplendent gardens. Levani Salaya left them. He was arranging for palace guards to complement the security detail. He arranged for four guards, two in front and two in the rear, forming an envelope or wrap around of the President, and their two guests and, as it turned out, four Secret Service Agents.

Mahdinejad shook his head. "Never before have I worried about all this security. But Madame Vice President and Senator Collins, I want you both to be, as you say, comfortable."

"Thank you, Mr. President," they both responded almost simultaneously.

Keith was waiting in the gardens with agents Mallon, Adair, and Wallace. Don Mallon and himself would be in the front, and Adair and Wallace would keep up the rear. Don was impressed, "It sure looks like we got our message across, Keith."

"It does. For some reason, I wonder why the President feels here in this hideaway it's necessary to double the guard, so to speak."

"Maybe Victoria asked him to."

"You're right, Don. I guess I just have a doubting Thomas gene in me."

"Maybe you are extra cynical because it's Victoria Magnuson up ahead," Don quipped.

Keith gave him a broad smile. "I guess you can read me like a book, old buddy," and they both laughed, moving ahead of the principals with Adair and Wallace at the rear, beginning the slow walk in the most beautiful of surroundings.

"What a morning," Don marveled at the clear almost cloudless sky.

"The state TV channel predicted 70 degrees by noon, but it's only about 60 now," Keith added.

"I talked to a servant this morning and if I understood her broken English and calculated from meters to miles correctly, the walking path may total about 10 miles through gardens, woods, over streams and across a mountain gorge over a river on a rope suspension bridge," Don advised.

"Wow, I wish I had shorts and hiking boots on. To late now," Keith mused.

"Did you bring those things?" Don asked.

"Of course not. It's not in our Secret Service handbook," Keith answered humorously.

"If you brought them and told the rest of us, we would have packed accordingly and kept our mouths shut," Don quipped.

Keith laughed and added, "Just compare what may be a somewhat uncomfortable stroll over 10 miles to a deadly fire fight in Detelonia, and you'll understand why I'm lacking in sympathy."

"Amen to that," said Don, and they followed the slow pace of their four subjects.

Keith tried his walkie-talkie. "Keith to Jack or Ben. Over."

"This is Jack. Over," Jack Adair answered.

"Just checking. Are you keeping Alpha in sight?"

"That's affirmative," came the answer loud and clear.

"Roger that," Keith responded. Keith then radioed agent Roland Ayers who he put in charge to watch over their quarters as well as those of the Vice President and the Senator. All was copasetic there.

President Mahdinejad led his special guests out to the beginning of the trail, which kept the Secret Service contingent in step with them. Keith and Don took turns to look over their shoulders to make sure they kept the party in sight. Keith knew he could depend on Jack Adair and Ben Wallace to do the same as they protected the rear. The Vice President and Senator were pleased to notice their presence, as well as the presence of some palace guards a fair distance behind carrying what appeared to be automatic weapons.

"Seems like our concern for protection has been recognized several fold Victoria," Senator Collins told her in a quiet voice.

She smiled and nodded to him. The President, surprisingly, had heard him, "Yes, I wanted you to be, how you say, worry free. However, these lands are terrorist free. There is no outside civilization in these mountains. Ashkari Restavi knows nothing of this," he added.

For some reason, unknown to themselves, both Victoria and Larry Collins doubted that, but thought it better not to challenge him.

As the group walked, their conversation was pleasant. To a great degree, it focused on Kashrakastani's neighbors, Etolonia and Bakrish. Victoria started the conversation: "Mr. President, what should the United States do to have more cooperation from Etolonia and Bakrish? What can we do to convince them to be more accepting of our position?"

President Mahdinejad stroked his beard a few times as he cleared his throat, pondering his words carefully. "My dear Victoria," he began slowly. "You must first understand their position, as you say in America, and you must understand their place, their history with their people, and their relationships with their neighboring countries. Many of our old friends have no trust of America. Every new President in America is change. We have old customs and beliefs and want to keep our people happy and not change their customs and lives. Every country cannot and should not be like America, or we will not be our own country. Some of my fellow friends think America is a bully, and feel America cannot be trusted, as you say, to give what they offer to give," he said, speaking animatedly.

Victoria realized she needed to convince him otherwise, and took a long moment to carefully reply, trying to show understanding and sympathy to his position while developing a response putting the U.S. in a good light. Senator Collins looked at her out of the corner of his eye, wondering how she might respond. He wanted to jump in, but ultimately decided it was Victoria's answer to give.

She now realized this would be primarily a philosophic discussion over the next several miles. Perhaps no great conclusions or significant changes in relationships would evolve, but these exchanges could provide a strong basis for much needed future changes. The President was walking very slowly. He did not wait for her answer as he added, "America must do more, show more, how you say, concern and caring for our positions and beliefs," he gestured, almost imploring.

"I hear you, Mr. President," Victoria responded. "Can you give us some examples?"

"Ahh, examples you ask?" he responded quickly. "Yes, examples. I remember when Etolonia asked for weapons to protect from the renegades. You did not provide them. America did not answer when most needed." He looked her in the eyes, and also turned to Senator Collins.

"There were reasons, Mr. President. At the time, President Layne believed, based on our intelligence, that the renegades had the support of the major part of the population, and from former Premier Atubbi, who was ousted in a coup."

"Ah, yes, Premier Atubbi," he gestured animatedly. "He had your President Layne, shall we say, like you say in America, buffaloed."

Senator Collins smiled but maintained his composure as a member of the opposing party. Victoria was amused also, but kept her focus. President Mahdinejad continued his thought, "Premier Atubbi was a master, how you say? actor."

"What do you suggest we do to improve our intelligence or act in a more informed fashion," she asked, hoping for useful feedback she could bring back to President Elect Cameron.

Just then, the President stopped at a breathtaking overlook and walked to the railing of the bridge outstretching his arms. "Ahh, take moments. Breathe in and look at the beauty of my Kashrakistani." They both had to admit it was a marvelous view.

"Mr. President, on behalf of President Elect Cameron, I invite you to the United States, so that he and I can return the favor and show you our beautiful country also," Victoria offered, flashing a gleaming smile.

"Yes, I have heard of and seen some motion pictures of America. That would be good," he answered, and pointed to a rushing river and a waterfall off in the distance.

"It reminds me of the Colorado River," Senator Collins remarked.

"Ahh, yes, the Colorado River. Who was that I see by the Colorado River?" The president thought for a moment "Yes, John Wayne."

They could hardly keep from laughing. Senator Collins was grinning from ear to ear and responded, "Yes, John Wayne. A fine figure of a man he was."

Victoria was patiently awaiting an answer to her question as to how the United States might improve their intelligence, and the flow of information when negotiating with this part of the world. She was taking in the marvelous scenery as a tourist might, though with the ever-present mindset of America's second in command. Just then, she heard a crackling noise even above the gushing flow of the river below. She turned to President Mahdinejad and Senator Collins.

"Did either of you hear those noises back there?" she asked, pointing.

"It sounded, to me, like a branch cracking," the Senator answered.

"Ah, yes, we have many trees in the forest," the president added. But Victoria was not satisfied with that answer. She looked ahead for Keith and Don Mallon, and behind for Jack Adair and Ben Wallace, but she saw no one.

"I really think we need to move on and keep closer to our escorts," she implored.

"Lovely lady, I see no problem," the President replied. Then they all heard the crackling noise even more loudly.

"Mr. President I believe Victoria is right. We need to move on quickly and reach our forward escorts," Senator Collins added. He took the president by the arm so they could move quickly across the open bridge, where they were vulnerable.

The president didn't seem to comprehend any danger, and was clearly annoyed. Senator Collins, realizing that Victoria's premonition was likely and unfortunately correct, took charge.

"Mr. President, as a precaution, sir, I respectfully request that we quickly move ahead."

The president grumbled a bit but complied.

Victoria had already started to shout for Keith and Don. *How foolish of us not to carry a radio*, she thought.

"Victoria—run! Run across the bridge—go—go," Larry Collins shouted at her.

"But Larry—" she started, but he interrupted.

"Never mind, I said go, damn it," he insisted, and grabbed the president's arm, pulling him along in a very slow trot as Victoria, an able runner, jogged quickly over the bridge, continuing to shout for Keith and Don.

Keith and Don had gone too far ahead, not realizing their party of interest had stopped to sightsee on the bridge. Suddenly, Jack Adair's voice came blasting over the radio that they were under attack by automatic weapons, and that Ben Wallace had taken a hit in the arm. Wallace was using his shirt as a tourniquet. "As far as I can see the President's two guards are down and we're the targets now," Jack Adair said.

Keith had a decision to make—to stay with Victoria, the President, and Senator Collins, or rush to Jack and Ben's aid.

Don Mallon was shouting ahead, trying to get the attention of the palace guards that preceded them, but there was no response. He came back to Keith. "I can't raise those clowns, Keith. Looks like we're in a squeeze play here."

"Look's like you're right, old buddy—let's get back to Victoria and the Senator."

Keith got back on the radio, "Jack, we're coming back to help you out. This is Keith to all agents at the palace. Get on to the garden trail. Ask the president's chief of staff, Mr. Salaya, to have someone lead you out. Be prepared for an automatic weapon firefight."

"10-4," Agent Ayers answered.

"Keith, Keith! Can you hear me? It's Victoria," she was shouting as loud as she was able while running full speed. *Glad I'm in good physical condition*, she thought. The two agents heard her voice, and began running back to the bridge while they affixed their long barrels to their 45's. *If only they had more compelling weapons*, Keith thought.

"Victoria, keep coming," he shouted, and then he spotted Senator Collins endangering his own life as he struggled to get the elderly President Mahdinejad across the bridge where a few short minutes ago they had stood enjoying the marvelous view and waxing philosophically.

Victoria reached the other side of the bridge. "Don, take her back to the cover of the trees—I'll provide protection for the President and the Senator."

Don Mallon wrapped his arm around the Vice President, and brought her back to the forest path, out of sight. "Jack or Ben come in. What's your 20?" No answer. He had a sinking feeling. "Roland, come in," he called for the agents coming from the palace.

"This is Roland, Keith. We're cautiously entering the trail. We have our long barrels ready, as per your instruction. What's with Jack and Ben?"

Before Keith could answer they all heard, "American pigs, be prepared to meet Allah if he will have you. Long live Ashkari Restavi."

Keith realized the worst. They must have Jack and Ben's radios. He said a quick silent prayer, as did Victoria and Don and the other agents who were listening. He answered, "We'll see about that you bastards." In anger, he instinctively fired a round across the bridge toward the opening of the woods, then stopped, realizing he was wasting his shots.

Senator Collins was exhausted as he reached Keith, holding up President Mahdinejad. Keith took the president, and Larry Collins went down on one knee to catch his breath. Don briefly left Victoria under cover to help Keith with the president, and they heard the dreaded crackling sound. Victoria screamed, "Oh my God!" as Senator Collins fell face down on the path.

Keith turned and fired into the bridge, downing one terrorist, then feeling much pain in his left shoulder before he was able to reach cover and release the president to Don, who was able to avoid being shot.

Don got on the radio. "Roland, the bastards are on the bridge. We may be able to pin them down and get them in crossfire. But be careful—they have our radios and they may be planted on the path between you and the bridge."

"10-4 to that," Roland answered. After a short radio silence, Roland felt compelled to advise Don, "We found two Palace Guards with knives in their backs minus their weapons."

"Figures," Don responded.

"That will soon be you, American pigs," came the terrorist's response. The American agents didn't favor them with a reply.

Don called to Senator Collins, as did Victoria. There was no response, either verbal or physical. Don decided to crawl out to check the Senator's pulse. Keith took his and Don's extended barrel 45's and fired a burst as Don hurriedly crawled out to the Senator's body. He felt no pulse. He hurried back as Keith fired another burst with his left arm, wrapped in a shirt by Victoria, which retarded but couldn't quite stop the bleeding. When he got back to the shrubbery, Don looked at Victoria and Keith with his head down. "He's gone," he confirmed.

Victoria cried silently. Keith put his good arm around her, and said a prayer for the Senator's soul. Victoria stroked his cheek and tried to pray. President Mahdinejad, who had passed out from fear and exhaustion, began to stir. "Where are we? Why are we here in the woods?" Keith figured he was in shock or denial about what had happened.

Victoria, half talking and half sobbing, recounted to him the catastrophic events of the last fifteen or so minutes. Realization dawning on his face, he looked at Larry Collins' still body, Keith's wounded arm, and Victoria's disheveled self, and said a silent prayer to Allah.

They heard the lowest of voices in the brush, moving toward them, and hid themselves as carefully as they could. Keith and Don put silencers on their barrels, and held their fingers to their lips to be sure they weren't compromised. Keith was feeling weaker and weaker as he continued to lose blood. The silence was nerve-wracking. Don and Victoria kept reminding the President to maintain silence by keeping their fingers on their lips. It seemed he couldn't believe that his trusted elite palace guards were, in fact, traitors in bed with the terrorist Restavi. The question was how many were compromised.

In their excitement, Don and Keith almost forgot to turn off their radios, until Victoria alerted them, lest agent Ayers or another agent try to reach them. Keith and Don mouthed "thank you" to Victoria. She felt gratified that she made that vital contribution to their survival. Keith and Don stared at the woods before them, while Victoria kept watch toward the bridge, lest they be attacked from the south while intently watching the north. They caught a beginning glimpse of two in full palace guard garb, their automatic weapons at the ready. They appeared to be slightly more than 90 feet, or one baseball path away, in American terms.

Keith, with silent gestures, asked Victoria to support his shooting arm as he aimed at one. President Mahdinejad couldn't resist sneaking a peak to see one of the traitors himself. He wished he had the opportunity to see this one and his fellow traitors executed under Kashrakastani law. He hoped he would see Askari Restavi meet that fate, and decided there and then that he would kick the chair out from under Restavi himself for the noose to silence him for always. The traitors came closer. Keith nodded to Don, and these terrorists were forever denied the opportunity to achieve Restavi's dream. Don added a shot to each to be certain, and took their automatic weapons and the extra ammunition around their shoulders.

Victoria just stared. She had now experienced firsthand the taking of human life. It was necessary, she knew, but still it was terribly shocking. She reminded herself that she had, for her entire life, avoided those Hollywood movies that imitated such events. She then urged Keith and Don to switch their attention to the bridge to the south. Another traitor in palace guard garb was slowly inching toward them. Don and Keith fired simultaneously. Keith made a key decision for Don to break radio silence to communicate with their comrades when Roland radioed, "We see the bridge. Is that one dead?"

"10-4," came the reply from Don.

"We have them all then. There were two back here. There were also two good or real guards killed."

"We may have the same situation to our north. For now, Roland, please have the palace bring three stretchers and have them call for a medical helicopter if they have such a thing. Keith is wounded and has lost a lot of blood. The president will also need a stretcher, and Senator Collins was killed. As far as I am concerned we should probably throw the terrorist bodies over the bridge to the river below, but that would be pollution of the worse kind."

President Mahdinejad looked up. "We will burn them. We will burn them until there is no proof, as you say, they were ever on earth." He spoke with extraordinary fervor. Victoria nodded her agreement.

There was nothing else to say, so she grasped Keith's good hand, and had the four of them follow suit. She then offered her own thanksgiving to God and prayed, "Please, dear Lord, save Keith's life. I know you did it once. Please find it in your mercy to do it again," she cried, burying her head in his chest. Don ripped his shirt off and wrapped another tourniquet over Keith's badly wounded arm and shoulder, and put his arm around Victoria to console her. She put her arm around his neck for comfort and support while she held Keith's hand. He had no words, but felt her pain. This certainly had turned out to be a disastrous trip, after all. The only positive was saving Victoria's life, and thank God for that.

Roland Ayers and the other two agents came into view.

"Roland, I fear the worst concerning Jack and Ben. Please check it out," Don ordered, as Keith was too weak to even speak. Roland and Ed went ahead while Sal stayed with President Mahdinejad, Victoria, Don and Keith to help with the stretchers, which they saw coming via golf carts pulling open wagons. The wagons were normally used for carrying soil and plants for the gardens, but now had a much more solemn duty. After the wounded and dead were secured, they began the slow ride back to the palace. Within ten minutes, Roland radioed Don with the news Don already knew in his head but denied in his heart. Jack Adair and Ben Wallace were dead.

When they reached the palace, Mr. Salaya and several servants were waiting to help the President to his quarters, as were the Air Force pilots.

"A medical helicopter from Bakrish will be here very shortly. They have a doctor aboard with type 0 universal blood for transfusion for Agent Fredericks," Mr. Salaya quickly informed them.

Victoria looked up from Keith. "Thank you, Mr. Salaya." He nodded solemnly.

The helicopter landed on the palace lawn. Two orderlies dressed in white were running, carrying the stretcher, with a doctor holding onto the suspended blood container. They quickly and carefully loaded Keith and took off for Bakrish, which was only 20 or so minutes away by air. The doctor felt confident that the transfusion would quickly have a positive effect. He would see to it that the wounds were properly cared for. Roland Ayers accompanied Keith to assure communication with the palace.

Mr. Salaya took Victoria aside to tell her that President Mahdinejad was alert, and wanted to speak with her. She entered his quarters, a huge room. It was absolutely sparkling, and probably as large as the entire first floor of her future home, that of the Vice President. He didn't stand, as befitting a Middle Eastern ruler when greeting a woman, and in this case, due to the recent ordeal he experienced. He was absolutely flabbergasted that his mountain palace and grounds were not secure. He realized how close he had come to dying, and conveyed his personal thanks to Victoria and the valiant American Secret Service. He was deeply saddened over the death of Senator Collins and the Secret Service agents, as well as the wounding of Keith.

"I will call your president and your new president and apologize. I will also punish Atolah Jaffari, my chief of guards. He must be sure or how you say . . ." he trailed off, turning to Victoria.

She completed the sentence, "He must be sure, without a doubt, that the palace guards are honorable and true to their country and their president."

"Yes, lovely lady. Yes, that is what I will tell him."

Her first thought was, *why weren't you concerned before?* Then she realized in a Middle Eastern country, so torn within, it was easier said than done. It will probably be many years, if at all, for a democratic republic to emerge, probably beyond her administration, even if it lasted eight years.

Victoria then had to make the most difficult phone call of her life. She decided to think about what she would say while she took the hottest bath she could remember removing all the dirt and dried blood on her body. She cried again, realizing it was Larry Collins' blood, God rest his soul. Keith's blood was intermingled. *Thank you, God, for sparing him*, she prayed. She sank into a beautiful rose colored marble tub filled by a servant with delightful fragrances, reveling in their comforting effects on her body. She was tempted to stay in this tub for the rest of the day, thinking how easy it was to get used to this life, when it dawned on her that she made the arrangement with President Mahdinejad that she would inform President Layne and President Elect Cameron first, then advise him so that he could convey his condolences.

With the deepest sigh, she reached for the ivory and gold phone next to the tub and pressed the intercom button.

"May I help you, Madame Secretary?" It was Levani Salaya, who was assigned to help her in any way he might.

"Yes, thank you, Mr. Salaya. Please try and connect me with the President of the United States."

"Yes, Madame Secretary. I shall ring you when we have the connection."

"Thank you, Mr. Salaya."

She took the deepest breath she had ever taken, thinking about the news she was about to reveal to America and very quickly to the entire world. She proceeded to bury her entire body, up to her chin, in the warm and fragrant water, formulating her thoughts for the imminent and very difficult phone discussion. She had almost dozed off when she heard the phone's musical ring.

"Yes?"

"I have your party, and will connect you," Mr. Salaya answered. She held her breath waiting for the President's office to answer. "Hello—is this Secretary of State Magnuson?"

"Yes."

"I will ask you some questions to confirm your identity."

She then rattled off ten questions, which only Victoria could answer, verified by her personal file, proved it was her.

"Very good," was the response. "This is Kathy Jones in the Presidents office. He will be in meetings the rest of the day. Can I take a message?"

"Please tell Andrea Harmon that I am still in Kashrakastani, at the President's palace. We had a terrible incident with terrorists. I am safe but I do have some terrible news. I need to communicate with the president. If he's not available relatively soon, please put me in contact with President Elect Cameron. I need to communicate with either or both before this news spreads around the world. This is imperative!" she forcefully added.

The secretary was getting the message loud and clear. "Will do. Please hold, Madame Secretary."

It seemed like an eternity to Victoria, but President Layne's secretary Andrea Harmon answered. "Hello Secretary Magnuson. This is Mrs. Harmon."

"Yes, Andrea. It's crucial that I speak to the president immediately."

"He is in a meeting now. He didn't want to be disturbed. Can you tell me, and I can pass it on to him when he's available?"

"I'll tell you, but please prepare yourself. It's not good. It's necessary he know within the hour at most. This could be on the international news wires as we speak. After I fill you in, please advise President Elect Cameron to call me." She gave the phone number for the palace. "Call me anytime, even if I have to be awakened. Are you ready to hear this Andrea?"

"Yes, I'm ready."

Andrea Harmon, a consummate professional, was no stranger to important and emergency calls, but her response to Victoria's message was one of extreme sadness. "I'm terribly sorry. This is awful news. I will tell the president as soon as possible, and try to reach President Elect Cameron. Do you want the president to call Mrs. Collins?"

Victoria thought for a moment before answering. "No, I'll do it. Please call her number while we are still connected."

She took a deep breath, said yet another prayer for Larry Collins' soul and for Vicky Collins and their family, and waited for her to answer. She wished she could have been there to hug her. She and Larry were married 39 years, with four children and several grandchildren.

About 24 hours had passed since the attacks in the garden, and Keith was alert enough to have Roland Ayers call Victoria to respond to her several inquiries. The doctors advised that Keith would be stable enough to be transported back to the palace in another 24 hours. On President Layne's orders, the balance of the mission was aborted. Don Mallon made a brief visit to Keith at the Bakrish hospital.

"I'll call Jack and Ben's families," Don said, his eyes filled with tears. Keith and Roland's eyes also welled up as they hugged.

President Mahdinejad took great care to be sure the remaining Americans were treated royally. After a brief recovery, he made it his first priority to call President Layne to express his utmost sympathy for the loss of Senator Collins and the two Secret Service Agents. He also gave his guarantee of cooperation to America, and promised his intention to do his utmost to convince Bakrish and Etolonia to do the same. Victoria thought to herself that if all that were accomplished, Larry Collins, Jack Adair, and Ben Wallace would not have died in vain. More than once, President Mahdinejad expressed his sorrow directly to her: "My dear Victoria, I am truly sad. May Allah and your God be, as you say, witness to my sorrow for the giving up of the lives of the Senator and your protectors."

Victoria cancelled her visits to Bakrish and Etolonia with apologies. Both leaders were sympathetic, and wished her and her party safe passage. They also promised to call President Layne with their condolences, and President Elect

Cameron to establish future meeting dates to establish new relationships.

The trip home was bittersweet for all. The reminder that they were going home was welcome, but truly emotionally draining as they sat in the Air Force C-147. Along with the passengers, they were bringing home three coffins. Victoria and Keith sat together, trying to go back to the past rather than dwell on the extremely somber present. They reminisced about their college days and the many years between then and now. After quite a while of just staring, Victoria tightly grasped Keith's good hand, leading him aft to the three coffins, which were strapped down.

She removed her suit jacket and placed it on the floor. She assisted him as they knelt and gently touched each coffin. Keith, with his one able arm, steadied her as she recited a prayer she had written. Keith said a silent prayer of his own. After praying she gently touched each coffin. The tears flowed. Keith, watching her, found himself crying. And he did not feel ashamed.

A bit of turbulence made Captain Johnson announce that everyone must sit and fasten their seatbelts. Returning to her seat, Victoria lost her balance. Don Mallon was able to steady her as Keith wished he could do, except for his still weakened condition.

"Thanks guys, I guess I overdid it."

"It's O.K.," Don assured her.

Keith leaned over toward her. "Lean on my good side," he said, putting his right arm around her shoulder. Without even thinking about it, he reactively gave her a soft kiss on the cheek.

"Thanks, Keith. Please pray with me," she requested, taking his free hand into her two. They began reciting the Lord's Prayer together. Their companions joined in.

A while later, Victoria broke the silence. She turned to Keith. "It's truly amazing how one's mind works."

"How do you mean?" he asked.

"Well, I remember something you told me all those years ago in Northern Delaware University's cafeteria on a rainy, rainy morning. You had a dream, a dream about your future."

He sort of rubbed his chin quizzically. "Perhaps you can shed some light on that for me. I guess I have forgotten."

She took his good hand in hers and smiled. With tears forming in her eyes, she softly reminded him. "You said you wanted to serve your country, and as a Secret Service Agent you would be doing that by protecting the President."

Keith's eyes widened as a smile of recollection crossed his face.

Victoria continued, "I hope you achieved your goal by saving the life of the Vice President."

Their smiling lips joined as they embraced as gently as possible, given his disabled arm, to begin a new life together—delayed but not denied.

The long flight and the drone of the engines eventually had them all rather groggy not interested in extended conversation. They all picked at their U.S. Air Force issue food, and occasionally took sips of water or soda. A mid air refueling was of interest, which made crossing the Atlantic seem like an eternity, but they all needed time to reflect and collect their thoughts. The tribute to the fallen, to be sure, would be painful to endure. Most slept on and off with heavy hearts.

It seemed almost forever until, finally, Captain Johnson came over the speakers. "Look down—what do you see?"

Don Mallon unhooked his seatbelt, and looked out to the starboard. "Hallelujah. It's the good old U.S.A. We're home."

Roland Ayers gazed portside. "I do believe that's Cape Henlopen light and State Park by Jove."

Keith was awakened from his deep sleep by a gentle touch of his cheek. It was Victoria, trying to be as gentle as possible, given his still weakened condition.

"What's up?" he asked with a big yawn.

"Why, I do believe we're in the first state of the good old U.S.A.," she cheered, louder than she had since she campaigned as a Vice Presidential candidate. He grimaced a bit, as his ear was less than a foot away. Then he smiled and planted a big kiss on her smiling lips. She gave him a dazzling smile.

"Fasten your seat belts. We'll be crossing over Route 1 as quick as a wink, or my name isn't Tommy Johnson" and sure enough the big craft began its descent toward the Dover Air Force Base and the grim task ahead of them.

The Dover AFB Commanding Officers limousine was headed back from Newark, Delaware, the home of Northern Delaware University, about forty miles north. It drove Vanessa and Gene Magnuson, and Barbara and Richard Fredericks to Dover to be with their adult children. Victoria and Keith had discussed it, and Victoria asked the President to have all arrangements made for the funeral service. They had both called their parents from President Mahdinejad's mountain palace to fill them in on everything lest they hear exaggerated or misleading news coverage that could seriously alarm them unnecessarily. The four hadn't seen each other since they were first introduced by Keith and Victoria all those years ago at their N.D.U. commencement. They certainly had a lot to talk about and celebrate with their children's safe return to the U.S. in the service of their country.

The service at the Dover Air Force Base was almost impossible to describe. Many members of both houses of Congress, Cabinet heads, Washington D.C. staffers, many other dignitaries and, of course the families of the deceased and returning heroes, were all present to pay their respects and honor the living and the deceased. Air Force Chaplain Colonel Gerald Marberry delivered the eulogy. President Layne deferred to Victoria for the tribute to Senator Larry Collins and Secret Service Agents Adair and Wallace. In upstate New

York, seventy four year old Ryan Gibbons, now wheelchair bound, turned to his wife.

"Mabel, would you believe that wounded Secret Service agent hero Keith Fredericks was the 9 year old I rescued with his mother some 25 years ago? I'll be darned." He shook his head in disbelief, as did his wife as she squeezed his shoulder to accentuate his warm remembrance.

Victoria's address, scribbled together between naps on the plane, was brief but poignant. "I hope you don't think it irresponsible of me but I will borrow from a speech delivered by a great man almost 147 years ago. What happened in Kazrakistani several days ago was not in vain. These valiant men in the Service of the United States of America did not die in vain. It does not diminish the heartfelt grief I have for them and for their loving families. My heart goes out to all those who knew and loved these men. I will always remember how they gave their lives in the service of their country, I will pray for their souls for the rest of my life, realizing I am standing before you now only because of their valor and the valor of their compatriots. In addition, President Layne and President Elect Cameron have received assurances from all three of the mid eastern countries we were planning to visit that relationships will change for the better."

She finished by tearfully offering a prayer, asking God to take the three into his kingdom to await uniting with their families. The Dover Air Force Band played two rousing hymns and closed with "God Bless America."

Victoria, Keith, Roland, Don and the other agents walked between the families of the fallen, hugging and crying with them, as did President Layne and President Elect Cameron. The Magnusons, the Fredericks, Victoria and Keith were taken back to Washington courtesy of the two presidents. Relationships forgotten were now reborn.

# EPILOGUE

It couldn't have been a more beautiful evening in Washington, D.C. A clear and starry sky led the way for the ever-constant flow of automobiles from chauffeur-driven limousines to two seat roadsters. The cars all brought their dashingly dressed occupants to the main entrance of the John F. Kennedy Center in order to pay homage to several great Americans for their deeds and careers, some of which changed the relationships of nations and the course of world history, and others that delighted millions of people with their talents.

The long line of vehicles continued unabated for more than one and one half hours, until those with several special people finally found their way to the guest entrance. As they entered the beautiful building and came into view the hundreds rose and the U.S. Navy band began playing "God Bless America" to thunderous applause.

They were now in their 70s, with their children, grandchildren, and great grandchildren in attendance. Former President Victoria Magnuson looked down from her balcony vantage point, located and waved to her family, and tears formed in her eyes as she thought of her beloved Keith, who past away several years ago from a long illness. God rest his soul. Adjacent to Victoria's, Keith's, Genevieve's and David's families sat the families of deceased Secret Service agents Jack Adair and Ben Wallace, who were killed protecting Victoria all those years ago in Kashrakistani, as well as the family of Senator Lawrence Collins also killed in that tragedy.

Next to them were retired Navy Captain Dylan Spencer and retired Secret Service agents Roland Ayers, Don Mallon and Ed Ward, as well as the families of deceased agents Tony Calla and Troy Wilson, who were also part of the contingent in Kashrakistani.

Jason Lowry, TV host and master of ceremonies, stepped to the podium as the Navy band played the last stanza. The President and first lady entered to applause and "Hail to the Chief." They were seated in their box, and the audience settled back into their seats. "President and Mrs. Martin, honored guests and ladies and gentlemen. It is with great pleasure that tonight we honor several great Americans who will, in turn, introduce those marvelous people that intervened to save their lives so many years ago."

Victoria looked down at her notes, which by now were crumpled in her hand, describing her wonderful Keith and wondering how she would manage. She said a prayer and sat back with her eyes closed, knowing God would be with her as he was some forty years ago.